His Magic Touch

by

Debby Grahl

This is a work of fiction. Names, characters, places, and incidents are either the product of the author's imagination or are used fictitiously, and any resemblance to actual persons living or dead, business establishments, events, or locales, is entirely coincidental.

His Magic Touch

Cover Art by *Debbie Taylor*

The Wild Rose Press, Inc.
PO Box 708
Adams Basin, NY 14410-0708
Visit us at www.thewildrosepress.com

Publishing History
First Fantasy Rose Edition, 2018
Print ISBN 978-1-5092-2340-4
Digital ISBN 978-1-5092-2341-1

Published in the United States of America

Angelique Montief flicked her wrist and set the bamboo ceiling fan spinning. Kneeling on a woven mat with sweat coating her body, she lifted a small wooden brass-bound casket from the bottom of a large trunk, inserted a gold key, and opened the lid. Inside two objects lay wrapped in thick cloth. She carefully unwrapped the smaller bundle to reveal a pentagonal mirror, a gift handed down to her by her grandmother, its ancient oak frame carved with tiny pentacles. She glanced over her shoulder at her locked bedroom door, then stared into the mirror and whispered, "Show him to me."

When the glass remained blank, fear clutched at her chest. Again, she said the words, and the image of a plantation house engulfed in flames appeared. "No, please, he can't be dead." Tears blurred her vision. The fiery image changed to reveal a human form lying beneath flowering bougainvillea.

Hope rising, Angelique peered closer.

"Show me his face."

She saw his indigo blue eyes blink open.

"I'm coming, my love."

He couldn't hear her, but she hoped that in his heart he knew she would find a way to get to him.

As the smoke in the room thickened, she knew her time was running out. She rewrapped the mirror and placed it into the smaller casket among cloth bags of herbs and potion-filled vials. Relocking the lid, she hung the key on a chain around her neck, dropped a jeweled dagger into her pocket, and tucked the casket under her arm.

Dedication

To my mom, Janet Paige,
who now lives among the angels.
I miss you, Mom.

Chapter 1

New Orleans

Crimson and gold lights flashed across the silk of the exotic dancer's ruby red dress as she swayed her hips to the sultry beat. Seated at a table near the raised stage, Jared Dupre leaned back in his leather chair and grinned. His friends, Derrick and Andre, clapped and whistled as the girl danced closer, slipping the thin straps from her shoulders, exposing pink-tipped breasts. The upscale French Quarter men's club, with its paneled walls, thick carpet, and beautiful women, was a favorite spot for out-of-town businessmen, convention-goers, and, as in Jared's case, his bachelor party.

A short-skirted waitress in a sequined halter top stopped next to Jared. Bending over so he couldn't miss her impressive cleavage, she asked him if he'd like another drink. Declining, Jared glanced around the crowded room. *Where is Philippe?* You would think that since his brother planned this party, he'd show up. Jared reached into his pocket for his phone to send him another text when a cold hand touched the back of his neck. "Damn it, Philippe," Jared swore, spilling his beer. He turned, a rebuke dying on his lips when he saw the space behind him was empty.

Icy fingers brushed across his cheek. Jared's breath caught. *What the hell?* On the faintest breath of air, he heard the words, "Come now." For a moment the sensation something was seriously wrong left him incapable of movement. As freezing air surrounded him, the sense of urgency increased. He turned to see if Andre and Derrick were reacting to the cold, but they were still engrossed in the dancer. Jared leapt to his feet, tossed some bills on the table, and grabbed his jacket.

"Hey, what you doin'?" Andre asked. "We thought we'd hit the Slick Kitten next."

Jared hesitated. He couldn't just leave his own party without an explanation, but explain what? He was hearing voices? In his world of Wiccan magic, there were many inexplicable occurrences. An invisible force tugged at his arm. He had to go, and he had to go now. "Hey, I've had a good time, but you boys go ahead. I've already seen enough T and A for one night."

"What do you mean you're leaving?" Derrick asked. "Your best man isn't even here yet."

Andre snorted. "It's not even midnight and the candy ass is fading."

"Yeah, and Philippe had a lap dance set up for you." Derrick added.

Andre leaned closer to Jared. "Hey, what's wrong? You look funny. You sick?"

"I don't know what's going on, but I feel something's wrong and I have to leave."

"Want us to come with you?" Derrick asked.

Jared shook his head. "This could be nothing but my imagination. You boys stay and enjoy yourselves." He smiled. "Perhaps one of you can take my place for the lap dance." Without another word, he turned and headed for the door.

Out on the sidewalk, the February night was unusually cool. Jared turned up the collar of his leather jacket and looked up and down the street. The unease he'd experienced inside was even stronger out here. Except for one or two lit window displays, the shops on Iberville were dark, and the wrought iron balconies above them empty. The streets of the French Quarter were never this quiet.

Senses alert, he headed toward Royal Street and home. When he heard a scuffling sound behind him, he whirled, flicked his wrist, and made the streetlight flare brighter. As a scruffy gray cat streaked past, he let out the breath he was holding and the light dimmed back to normal. But as the energy around him spiked, Jared's skin prickled and he knew he wasn't alone. The air turned frigid, and the apparition appeared.

Light from the nearby lamppost lit her translucent body as if from within. Ghosts in New Orleans were about as common as gumbo, so Jared normally wouldn't be alarmed. But considering what had happened in the club, he approached her cautiously.

When he got closer, he saw the specter had a tignon intricately wrapped around her head. Earrings of shell and beads dangled from her ears and copper bracelets encircled her arms. He discerned the faint outlines of flowers on her long, faded dress. The intensity of her striking turquoise eyes made the hair on the back of his neck rise.

When the specter reached out her hand, Jared stepped back. At a young age, witches learn to be leery of those from the spirit world. "Hey, I have no problem with you. I'll go about my business, and you go about yours."

Her earrings swayed silently as the spirit shook her head and motioned for him to follow. "You mus' come. He has bad magic, and he has your brother."

Jared glanced around the eerily empty and quiet street. "What? Who has Philippe?"

The specter turned and floated away as if expecting Jared to follow.

In the past Philippe had gotten himself mixed up with dark magic, but Jared thought he'd truly learned his lesson. Philippe even talked about going back to Tulane. Jared hesitated. Could he trust this spirit? Before he could speak, the spirit turned, placed her hands on her hips, and narrowed her eyes. "Listen to me, boy. Dere's no time to explain. Your brother in bad trouble. You t'ink I got you out here for no reason? Now come wit' me."

The vehemence in her voice and the fear in her eyes sent trepidation crawling up his spine. He cocked his head. "This is for real? Philippe is actually in danger?"

"Dat what I been sayin', boy."

Without another word, Jared followed the specter as she led him through the French Quarter, past restaurants with the aromas of gumbo and spicy rice wafting from their open doors, street musicians playing Dixieland, a group of college kids carrying red go-cups, and tourists streaming in and out of the clubs on Bourbon Street. As they made their way around a cluster of laughing teenage girls catching strings of beads, a tall girl with long dark hair and an alabaster complexion spotted Jared and with blood red lips smiled at his ethereal guide.

Jared, not wanting her to bring attention to them,

shook his head and placed his finger on his lips. She nodded, but as her friends moved away, she kept looking back.

Jared rounded the corner onto St. Ann's and silently cursed. There, directly in front of him, concluding her ghost tour, stood his fiancée Kendra O'Connell. As her group wandered off, she turned, her pearl-gray wool cape swirling around her slim legs. Clad in a black sweater, tight black jeans, and knee-high leather boots with two-inch heels, she smiled and walked toward him. "Hey, is the bachelor party already over? I expected you to stay out all night."

Jared hesitated. Whatever was happening with Philippe, he didn't want her involved. But as he looked down at her pretty face, into those intelligent gray eyes, he knew that persuading her to stay out of it would take all the cunning he possessed. "No, the boys are still at the bar." Before he could finish, Kendra wrapped her arms around his neck and kissed him passionately.

When she broke their kiss, she grinned and pressed her body against him. "Perfect. That was my last tour. My mom is going to close up the office, so we can go to your room at the hotel. I imagine after watching half-naked women for most of the night, you're ready for a little fun. You could only look at *them*, but you can put your hands all over *me*." She kissed him again. "We'd go to my apartment, but my wedding dress is hanging on my closet door and I don't want you to see it."

Hours watching skimpily clad girls dance hadn't affected Jared at all, but a few kisses from Kendra set his blood racing. He clamped down on his desire and gently removed her arms from around his neck. "Kendra, listen to me. Something's come up, and I can't go with you."

She frowned. "What's wrong?"

As he tried to decide how much to tell her, the spirit floated into view.

"We got to get goin', boy. You take care of dis later."

Kendra's eyes opened wide with surprise. She looked from the spirit to Jared. "Who's your friend? And what's she talking about?"

Unable to come up with a plausible lie, Jared sighed. "All she'll tell me is that Philippe is in trouble and I have to go with her."

"What kind of trouble? And go where?" Kendra asked.

Scowling, the spirit folded her arms. "Dat none of your concern. Now you get on home and let him be."

Annoyance filled Kendra's voice. "Excuse me?" When the spirit just glowered, Kendra glowered back, then turned to Jared. "Didn't Philippe show up?"

Jared shook his head. "This spirit came into the club to get me. I thought at first Philippe might be playing a joke, but what if he's mixed up with those scumbags from Black Cross coven?"

"I'm coming with you."

"No, you're not. And you can wipe that stubborn look off your face. As I said, I have no idea what's happened, but I need to find out, and I don't want you involved." Seeing the retort forming on her lips, he gritted his teeth. "Kendra, please don't fight me on this. Go home and I'll call you as soon as I can."

She tossed her long red braid over her shoulder. "Jared, those Black Cross witches are ruthless. They've even been accused of sacrificing mortals. If they have

Philippe, you can't go in alone."

Bile rose in Jared's throat at the memory from two years ago. He'd found Philippe in a circle of chanting men as the head priest placed a terrified teenage boy, his arms and legs bound, at the base of their altar. Jared and eight other men from his own coven fought with magic and fists to rescue the boy. Philippe, glassy-eyed and belligerent, had faced Jared with defiance, refusing to leave.

Jared, older and more powerful than Philippe, did something that to this day still sickened him. He used magic to subdue his own brother. It had taken months in a special rehab center to cleanse Philippe of the drugs and undo the brainwashing of the Black Cross. Now Jared feared he'd fallen under their influence once again.

"I'm not sure it's even them. That's what I'm saying. Kendra, please let me handle this. If I see I need help, I'll call for it."

"You listen to what he say," the spirit interjected. "You stay here. Dis for him alone."

Kendra narrowed her eyes. "If you know what's going on with Philippe, why don't you just tell him?"

The spirit's striking turquoise eyes brightened and she leaned close to Kendra. "I tell him as soon as you *git*."

Kendra stared back into the spirit's eyes, then relented. "I'll stay because Jared asked me to, not because some bossy ghost did. Who are you anyway? I know all the ghosts in the Quarter, and I've never seen you before."

The spirit snorted, turned, and hovered. "You comin', boy?"

7

"Kendra, I've got to go. I'll call you as soon as I know something."

"All right, but I don't like this one bit. I'm not going to sleep until I hear from you." She gave him a quick hug. "I hope you're wrong and Philippe is just being an ass. Be careful and call me."

He bent down and kissed her. *"Je t'aime."*

She smiled. "I love you, too."

Once Kendra was well out of sight, Jared followed the spirit across Rampart heading toward Louis Armstrong Park and Congo Square. During the seventeenth and eighteenth centuries, slaves and free people of color would meet in the square on Sundays to dance and play their music. Some say there are times when you can still hear the beat of the bamboulas and the wail of the banzas.

Jared and the spirit passed under the arch and through the gate. They stopped in the middle of the square where she pointed to the ground.

"He vowed revenge, and now he's come."

Jared raised his hand. A burning torch appeared, illuminating the darkness around them. Written across the gray stone pavers, in what seemed to be dried blood, they read, "All Dupres will die." Beneath this, a black candle dripped wax onto a photograph of him and his brother.

Apprehension coiled in Jared's stomach as he carefully scanned the area around them. The twisted arms of the ancient live oaks reached out toward them. The black night beyond the dense foliage teemed with silent spirits.

"Do you know who did this?" Jared asked.

"He a witch name of Adam. He of da Montief

blood and calls hisself the Chosen One."

Despite the pulsating dark energy surrounding them and the underlying currents of his brother's terror, Jared forced himself to remain calm and asked, "When was Philippe taken, and what has this Montief done with him?"

"He got him now. He takin' him to dat dark place in the north. He'll use Philippe to get to you. He has evil magic and mus' be stopped."

"What are you talking about? What *place* in the north?"

"Angelique and the mirror hold da truth. They will guide you."

He narrowed his eyes. "My great-great-grandmother?"

The spirit nodded.

Jared compressed his lips into a thin line, then said, "Considering she's been dead for two hundred years, just how in the hell is she supposed to do that?"

"Don't you be cussin' at me, boy. You got her mirror—use it. Now get goin'. Da longer you stand here, da farther Montief get."

"Yeah, well, I'd like to know what this Montief person has against my family before I go chasing after him."

The spirit's eyes flashed and she snapped, "Your brother needs you. Now stop askin' me questions and get da mirror."

Jared frowned. "Wait a minute, why are you saying the mirror belonged to Angelique? The mirror came to me from my mother's side. She was the one with power. Angelique was on my father's, who has no magic."

"Da mirror belong to Angelique. You ask your papa, but not now; ders no time."

Both puzzled and irritated, Jared waved his hand and a small pentagonal mirror appeared in his palm, its ancient wood frame carved with tiny pentagrams. He stared into the glass. "Show me Philippe."

Nothing happened. He glanced at the spirit. She nodded, and again he said the words. An image finally appeared and Jared's pulse quickened. A dark, cloaked figure was shoving Philippe into a black van. His brother's face was battered and swollen and his eyes devoid of emotion.

"Fils de putain," Jared cursed.

Hands on hips, the spirit nodded. "Now you see, boy."

The guilt he felt for doubting Philippe made his words sharper than he intended. "Who are you, and what do you know about this?"

Her earrings danced as she shook her head. "Dere no time. Da truth is in the past. Da mirror and Angelique will help you. Now go. Dis square has always been our sacred place. We must cleanse away da evil Montief left here."

Jared headed back toward the gate. At the sound of voices, he turned to watch in fascination as one by one the spirits of chanting slaves, their filmy bodies swaying to a beat only they could hear, filled the square.

When he stepped onto the street, the mirror began to glow. A figure in the glass materialized and Jared saw a chiseled face with thick black hair and brown eyes set beneath arched brows. The man stared back at Jared and laughed, a sound straight out of a horror film.

Jared's jaw clenched. Now that he had a face to put to the name, the truth of what was actually happening became horribly real to him.

The scene in the mirror changed to show Kendra standing in her apartment smiling as she ran her hand down the silk and lace of her wedding dress. An intense love for her flowed through Jared.

In the next second, a cold sweat broke out on the back of his neck as a streak of light shot through her window and sent her beautiful dress crumpling to the floor. The image in the mirror switched back to Montief, his features now twisted in hatred.

"Give Kendra your name, and she also dies. Leave her and she may live."

Jared held back the panic that threatened to overwhelm him and growled, "What do you want?"

The man in the mirror again uttered his chilling laugh. "I am the Chosen One, here to exact retribution from the Dupres for Augustus Montief's death."

"Listen to me, asshole. I don't know what the hell you're talking about. No one in my family killed anyone. But if you hurt my brother or Kendra, you're a dead man."

A taunting sneer replaced the laughter on Montief's face.

"Come and get me, Dupre. I'll be waiting. But I warn you, my patience is running short. I suggest you don't delay. Perhaps you'd like a demonstration?"

Before Jared could respond, Phillipe's limp body appeared, slumped in the back seat of the van. A searing flash of green light hit Philippe and he screamed.

Jared's heart clenched at the pain inflicted on his

brother. The image vanished. Jared slid the mirror into a coat pocket and ran toward home. Montief couldn't be too far ahead of him. He wished he could make his car appear before him as easily as smaller objects. He increased his speed. He'd stop at the Dupre Hotel just long enough to pick up his car. The other things he'd need he could conjure.

As he ran, the sound of his brother's screams echoed in his mind. Montief's evil came through loud and clear in Jared's mirror. What about Kendra? His hands balled into fists at the thought of Montief anywhere near her. Would marrying her truly put her in danger? Could he take the chance the threat toward her wasn't real?

"*Putain de merde*," Jared cursed as he turned onto Royal Street.

Should he call her to explain he had to leave? And tell her what? Until the mirror guided him, he didn't know where he was going. And if he talked to her, she'd insist on coming with him. Since he didn't know if this Montief was really dangerous or just crazy, he didn't want Kendra anywhere near him. He'd phone her from the road. Besides, he should be able to take care of this and be back in a few hours. Breathing hard, he headed toward the hotel.

Chapter 2

In her loft apartment on Dauphine, Kendra smiled as she ran her hand over the smooth, cool silk of her wedding dress. Tiny seed pearls adorned the bodice and hand-tatted lace fell in folds to the hem. Her grandmother had married in this dress, and Kendra cherished every inch.

When Kendra was three years old, her father had died in a fishing accident. To this day the smell of his spicy cologne brought back memories of his warm green eyes and his comforting embrace. Her mother, devastated by his death, took Kendra and her younger brother, Josh, to live with their grandmother. *Grandmere* taught Kendra the art of glass-blowing and a love of New Orleans' history.

Kendra's heart still ached at her death a year ago. She thanked the Gods *Grandmere* lived long enough to see Kendra graduate with a degree in history.

Kendra stared at her wedding dress hanging on the door of the armoire and a foreboding such as she'd never known filled her heart. Instinctively she grasped the tiny gold blown-glass unicorn she always wore on a chain around her neck. As she lay dying, *Grandmere* had lifted it from her own neck and placed it around Kendra's.

"This has been handed down to glass blowers in our family for generations," *Grandmere* said. "You understand how magic can be woven into the glass as we make our enchanted figurines. Now I pass it along to you. Each owner has increased its power. Keep it close to your heart and call on its magic when you need it."

A scream lodged in Kendra's throat as a streak of lightning shot through the French doors that led out to her balcony and struck the dress. The smell of scorched fabric filled the room as the satin crackled then crumbled to the floor, pooling at her feet. Horrified, Kendra stood, heart pounding, one hand on her glass unicorn, the other raised to strike back. She scanned her open loft but saw nothing out of the ordinary.

Near her sat the brass bed and skirted vanity. The center of the room was furnished with an antique love seat, chair, and coffee table on a braided rug. Either side of a small brick fireplace, shelves held books on magic, the blown-glass figurines she loved to create, and her crystal ball. The bathroom and galley kitchen were at the far end.

With trembling fingers, Kendra lifted the dress and hung it back on the hanger. She inspected every inch of the smooth material. She sighed in relief. No damage. A slight smell of ozone hung in the air as she sat on the edge of her bed. What had just happened? She could have sworn she'd felt the presence of someone else in the room seconds before the light flashed through the door.

A sudden chill passed through her. She rubbed her hands up and down her arms. Something was definitely wrong. Kendra rummaged through her purse until she came up with her cell phone. She scrolled the list for Jared's number. When his phone rang, she glanced at the clock—twelve-fifteen. His phone kept ringing. She couldn't shake the fear he was in trouble.

She ended the call and picked up a picture of her and Jared taken at the lake the day he'd proposed. They sat cuddled together on a bench drinking champagne.

She had met Jared Dupre five years ago on her eighteenth birthday. The coven asked her to light the ceremonial candles. She noticed him standing at the edge of the circle, and when she gazed into his deep blue eyes, the currents of physical and mental energy flowing between them took her breath away. She knew who Jared was, but the six years' difference in their ages kept them in separate social circles, even among the Wiccans. But on that night she knew, without any doubt, that this strikingly handsome man, with his thick dark hair and tall muscular build, was the man she would give her heart and body to.

Anger and frustration filled her. *I should have ignored Jared and gone with him.* For years, Philippe had gotten into one mess after another, expecting Jared to bail him out. But since leaving rehab, he was doing so much better. He even showed an interest in the hotel now. If Philippe was back with the Black Cross Coven, Jared would be both furious and disappointed.

Kendra paced back and forth across the polished wood floor. She spotted her crystal ball. *I could take a little peek just to calm my fears.* Most witches had some kind of gift, and Kendra's was the ability to see through the mist in her crystal ball.

She gnawed on her bottom lip. Breaking through someone's privacy charm could be difficult, especially a powerful witch like Jared. Knowing she needed all the luck she could get, she opened a drawer and took out the case that held her special gemstones, placing one each of agate, jasper, tiger's eye, beryl, and green malachite around the crystal ball.

She laid her hands gently on either side of the smooth sphere and said, "Clear the mist so I may see the one who means the most to me. As I will, so mote it be." When the ball remained cloudy, she increased her energy flow and concentrated harder.

The mist cleared and she peered closer. "Come on, come on, show me." Jared's image appeared. He was running. Panic clawed at her chest. Was someone chasing him? Although he was capable of taking care of himself, there were areas of New Orleans that weren't safe even if you were a witch. Again, she grabbed for her phone and punched in his cell number.

"Jared, where are you?" she cried when his voice mail picked up.

She tried his private number at the hotel. It also went to voice mail. She clutched the phone. The man made her crazy. He repeatedly forgot to charge his cell or lost the damn thing. Sometimes his energy level was so high it interfered with the signal. That might be why she couldn't get through.

Kendra exhaled a long breath. *I could be blowing this all out of proportion. What I saw could be nothing more than him hurrying across a street.* Every possible scenario that could end in harm to Jared played through her mind.

She stepped out onto her balcony. The night air was cool, and a full moon glowed in the clear sky. Her apartment looked over Dauphine Street where a couple strolled arm in arm. Faint sounds of laughter and the notes of a sax drifted from the bar on the corner. The clomp-clomp of a mule-drawn carriage slowly passed. At her feet, an orange tiger cat brushed against her legs.

"Did I wake you, Clementine?" She bent down and picked the cat up. Stroking her thick fur, Kendra held her tight. "Jared might be in trouble, and I'm not sure what I should do."

Clementine nuzzled closer and yawned.

I could go to the Dupre Hotel and wait for him. She frowned. *Then what would I say when he shows up unharmed? Hi, I thought you were in trouble so I raced over here. He'd probably think I'd lost my mind.*

As she rubbed her cheek against the purring cat, her anxiety rose until she imagined Jared dead and bleeding in the street. *That's it. I don't care how late it is.* She hurried back into her room, dropped Clementine on the bed, picked up her phone, and called the hotel's front desk.

"Hello. Dupre Hotel. This is Kathleen. How may I help you?"

Damn it. Kathleen Leblanc was the last person she wanted to talk to. What was she doing working this late anyway? Kendra started to hang up, but her concern for Jared was stronger than her dislike of Kathleen. "Hello, Kathleen, this is Kendra. I'm trying to get in touch with Jared. Have you seen him?"

Silence filled the phone before Kathleen replied. "No, Kendra, I haven't, but isn't tonight the bachelor party? He's probably having one last fling before he's shackled to you."

Cursing under her breath, Kendra was about to slam down the phone when Kathleen said, "Hold on a second. I see his father. Perhaps he can help you."

Before Kendra could tell her never mind, she heard

Kathleen lay down the phone. A few minutes later, Jacques Dupre's low, cultured voice came on the line. "Hello, this is Jacques Dupre."

Kendra cleared her throat, willing herself to sound calm. Since the first time Jared had introduced her to his father, she'd felt uncomfortable around him. Although Jacques had always treated her kindly, she got the impression he thought Jared could have done better than a fisherman's daughter whose mother ran ghost tours.

"Hello, Mr. Dupre. I'm sorry for calling so late, but I was trying to get in touch with Jared. Have you seen him?"

"No, Kendra, I haven't. I've been in my office and lost all track of time. Is something wrong?"

She hesitated. Should she tell him she'd had a premonition Jared was in trouble? Considering how much Jacques disapproved of magic, he'd probably dismiss it as nonsense. "No, nothing's wrong. I'm sorry to have bothered you."

"Wait, Kendra. Jared just walked through the front door."

Relief flowed over Kendra like a warm spring rain.

"I'm sorry. I tried to get his attention, but he hurried into the elevator," Jacques continued.

"Thank you, Mr. Dupre. I'll try his cell." She disconnected but paused before punching in Jared's number. He was home and he was fine. All her panic was for nothing.

She yawned. She'd get ready for bed and wait to hear from him. Kendra brushed her teeth, washed her face, and slipped on the oversized T-shirt she liked to sleep in. Jared still hadn't called. Frowning, she got into bed. Her earlier disquiet resurfaced. She'd give him a few more minutes. If she hadn't heard from him she'd try him again. She plumped the pillows behind her head and opened the latest Heather Graham novel she was reading.

Distracted by the book, she didn't notice the fine mist forming in the corner of the room. Kendra's eyes drifted closed. She fought to stay awake, but a heavy tiredness flowed over her. The book fell from her hands, and she was asleep. A man with a handsome chiseled face, thick black hair, and intense brown eyes set beneath arched brows filled her dreams. Desire caressed her body and a smile formed on her lips.

On her bedside table, her unicorn glowed. Clementine rose, the fur on her back stiff along her spine. She crouched next to Kendra, stared into the corner and with teeth bared and ears laid back uttered a long, low *hiss*.

A whisper of laughter filled the room as the mist swirled and the image disappeared.

Chapter 3

Jared took the front steps two at a time and raced through the double stained-glass doors of the hotel. *Damn.* His father was in the lobby speaking on the phone. Did the man ever sleep? Hoping to pass unnoticed, he hurried across the black and white-checked marble floor toward the family's private elevator.

Not only had he and his father butted heads over updating the hotel, his father's refusal to attend his Wiccan wedding ceremony angered Jared so much he'd been avoiding him.

The loss of Jared's mother to cancer six years before had devastated them all. The Wiccan healers she'd insisted upon had done their best, but in the end failed to save her. His father's grief manifested itself as hatred toward his mother's people and the Wiccan way of life. Now Jared had neither the time nor the desire to explain Philippe's latest trouble to their father.

Just before the elevator doors slid closed, their eyes met. His father's hand rose as if to stop him but dropped back to his side when Jared shook his head.

In his suite of rooms, Jared grabbed the keys to his Porsche and a lightweight jacket. He placed his crystal ball into his backpack and slid a sheathed knife into his boot.

He checked his cell phone. *"Merde."* The display

read "low battery." The damn thing didn't work half the time anyway. He tossed it into his pack. *I'll charge it in the car.* He glanced at the clock—twelve forty-five. It was later than he'd thought.

He took his mirror from his pocket. "Show me Kendra." When her sleeping face filled the glass, Jared sighed with relief. Hopefully by the time she woke up he'd be back with Philippe. He picked up his backpack and, not knowing what he might face when he found his brother and Adam, added the tooled leather sheath which held his falcata with its ancient, charmed, curving blade, and went out the door.

****

Once the room was empty, a young woman emerged from the adjoining bedroom. She removed a small crystal ball from her bag and set it on Jared's desk. Placing her hands on either side of the cool orb she called, "Chosen One, can you hear me?"

Adam Montief's face appeared.

"I hear you, Kathleen. Is he gone?"

"Yes."

"Did he contact the girl?"

"No."

"Good. Soon Dupre will be dead, and Kendra will be mine for the taking." The mist in the crystal ball turned oily black as it swirled, obscuring his laughing face.

****

Hours later, as the sun's rays peeked over the horizon, Jared found himself in Tugaloo State Park near Gumlog, Georgia. How far was the bastard going? He climbed out of the Porsche and stretched cramped muscles. Morning light reflected off the surface of the lake. Exhausted, he wiped sweat from his forehead and took in his surroundings. Other than a stately great blue heron eyeing him speculatively and a family of turtles sunning themselves on a log, there wasn't another creature to be seen. His mirror had led him to this spot, but the van with Philippe was nowhere in sight.

Frowning, he blinked the sleep from his eyes and noticed a patch of reeds which looked crushed. Afraid he was about to discover his brother's lifeless body, Jared cautiously stepped forward. The only sound was the startled heron's flapping wings as it took flight.

"Son of a bitch," he swore through gritted teeth. Burned into a small cleared patch of dry ground were the words, "Not yet, Dupre." Next to this lay a silver chain with a tiny black and green snarling gargoyle, something Philippe always wore. Jared took a deep breath as relief pumped through him.

"I'll find you, motherfucker," he yelled as he kicked a rotting log. "Fuck." Pain shot through his foot and up into his knee. Jared limped back to the Porsche and jerked the door open. Wearily he slid onto the seat and gratefully laid his head back. He'd been one step behind Adam all night.

He glanced down at the pentagonal mirror lying on the seat next to him, a gift from his mother on his eighteenth birthday. She'd told him he'd been the first in many years who could work the magic in the mirror. He assumed it had been passed down through his mother's people. But if the spirit was right, it had belonged to Angelique Dupre. The mirror, with its ability to show him whatever he wished to see, had never failed him. But, somehow, Adam had the power to block the images and sense when he was being watched.

Jared knew now Adam had led him to this spot, playing him like a fool, letting him see what he wanted him to see. Well, the time for games was over. The digital clock displayed eight forty-five. How had he lost all sense of time? Kendra would be awake by now and franticly wondering why she hadn't heard from him. If he drove much farther, he'd never make it back in time. Would they have to postpone their wedding day? He'd wanted to wait and marry Kendra after his father trusted him enough to give him more responsibility in running the hotel. Now, on the brink of beginning their future together, here he sat miles from New Orleans and the woman he loved.

"Merde." He punched the steering wheel. He had no choice but to go on, but what could he tell Kendra? He was following some deranged witch who'd threatened to kill both him and Philippe and harm her as well? She'd be determined to follow and help him. No, he had to convince her he left New Orleans because Philippe was in serious trouble and he had to find him. She'd be pissed, but he'd rather deal with that than have her in danger. He could only hope she'd understand.

He shook his head. *Yeah right.* She was going to be mad as hell, and he couldn't blame her. With any luck he'd soon locate Philippe, and the wedding only delayed for a couple of days. Resigned, he took a deep breath and called Kendra. *Crackle, crackle, crackle.* Static was all he heard.

"Merde." Why did he bother with the damn thing? Cell phones were great, unless you were a witch with too much power. He had three voice mails and one text message from Kendra. He winced when he read,

"Where the hell are you?"

If his cell refused to work, he'd have to find an actual payphone. He snorted. If any still existed. Not knowing whether it would get through, he sent Kendra a reply, "Georgia. Call when I can. Cell won't work. Love you."

His gas gauge read half a tank. Eyes burning with fatigue, he ran his hands over his face. He'd used refreshing charms to stay awake, but they only worked for so long. *All I need is a few minutes of sleep to clear my head, then I'll get gas and try to call Kendra.* These were his last thoughts before he laid his head back and exhaustion overtook him.

Chapter 4

By eight o'clock in the morning, Kendra's emotions swung from panicked to pissed. She'd called Jared's cell repeatedly without success. Her imagination had careened from Jared lying dead alongside the road to Philippe getting him mixed up in some black magic ritual. Not knowing what else she should do, and not wanting to upset her mother when she didn't know what to tell her, Kendra had awakened her two friends, Deanne Charbonneau and Loren Tureaux. The three had been close since they were six years old and attended their first coven meeting together.

"I can't believe you dragged me out of bed at this hour because Jared Dupre isn't answering his phone," Deanne said with a yawn. "Wasn't the bachelor party last night? He's probably hung over and turned off his cell—like I should have done. You do know I had to work last night, don't you? And we're going to be up late tonight for the pre-wedding party." Deanne was petite with *cafe-au-lait* skin. She wore colorful clothes and wove bright glass beads into her hair.

Sunlight glimmered off the surface of the water as Kendra drove her red Mustang across the Lake Pontchartrain causeway toward Loren's cottage in Mandeville.

"Thanks for coming along," Kendra said. She saw

the dark circles under Deanne's almond-shaped eyes and added, "You look beat. Did you close up Baby Blues for your parents last night?"

Again, Deanne yawned. "It's okay, girlfriend. I've had at least four hours of sleep."

Kendra's hands tightened on the steering wheel. "Deanne, I'm seriously worried, and not just because Jared's not answering his phone. I think he might be in real trouble."

Deanne snorted. "Girl, trouble is Jared Dupre's middle name." She shook her head. "I need more coffee before I can think clearly."

"We're almost at Loren's. I'll fill you both in on what I know after we get there." Kendra pulled into the drive and parked under the yellow two-story house. The lawn sloped down beneath an ancient live oak to the lake and a wooden dock with a bright blue Sailfish tethered to it.

"I hope Loren has something more to eat than nuts and bran," Deanne grumbled as they made their way up the stairs. "What would make a person not want to eat meat? I mean what's wrong with bacon or a nice sausage patty?"

"You know Loren doesn't eat anything with a face."

"I don't eat anything with a face either. When I get it, it's cut up and packaged in Rouse's meat counter."

They stepped up onto the cottage's wide pillared front porch. Loren was standing in the open doorway. "Good morning. Right on time. I just took apple muffins out of the oven," she said in her soft southern drawl. Tall and willowy, Loren had long silver-blonde hair and soft-green eyes set in a pretty, elfin face. From a family of herbalists, she had already established her name in the coven as a gifted healer.

Kendra sniffed appreciatively. A mixture of herb scents and fragrant candles blended with the delicious aroma of baking muffins, making the house smell incredible. "I love coming here. Just walking through the door makes me feel better."

Loren smiled. "Well, thank you. But it's the day before your wedding, and you're not supposed to need cheering up. Let's sit in the kitchen and you can tell us what's wrong."

"What's wrong is named Jared Dupre," Deanne said, "and I hope you have strong coffee to go along with those muffins."

"I brewed a pot of French roast." Loren gave Kendra a quizzical look. "And some soothing chamomile tea if needed."

As they entered the bright kitchen with its red counter tops, Kendra's cell beeped indicating a text message. "It's from Jared."

"Thank the Gods," Deanne said. "Now I can go back to bed."

"Georgia," Kendra exclaimed. "What's he doing in Georgia?"

Deanne and Loren stared. Then Loren said, "That's hundreds of miles from here. Does he say why he's in Georgia?"

"No. He just says he's having trouble with his phone signal, and he loves me. I'm afraid something awful has happened, and it's all Philippe's fault."

"Philippe's involved in this?" Deanne asked, taking a seat at the table.

Kendra nodded.

"Then, girlfriend, this is not good."

Kendra's eyes narrowed. "I'll tell you one thing. If Philippe makes Jared late for the wedding, I'll hunt Philippe down, and I guarantee you when I get my hands on him, it won't be pretty."

Loren took Kendra by the arm and led her to the butcher-block table. "Sit here and I'll get us some coffee and muffins. Then you can start at the beginning."

After she'd placed the muffins on the table, put a cup of tea in front of Kendra, poured coffee for Deanne, and sat down with a cup of coffee for herself, Loren nodded. "Okay, we're listening."

Kendra took a sip of her tea, sighed as the warm brew caressed her throat, then told them about seeing Jared with the spirit who said Philippe was in trouble and demanded he follow her. She concluded with, "And that's really all I know."

Loren frowned. "Who was this spirit?"

"I have no idea. She was dressed like a nineteenth-century slave, but she wasn't at all timid. In fact, she was rather bossy. She told me it was none of my business."

"It wasn't Marie, was it?" Deanne asked. "She can be bossy as hell."

Marie Laveau, the voodoo queen, was Deanne's maternal ancestor.

Kendra helped herself to another muffin. "No. Besides, Marie usually doesn't leave the cemetery. Does she?"

Deanne shook her head and the beads tinkled. "Not unless someone's in trouble and needs her help. Like the time those thugs tried to rob me. We're not supposed to use magic on mortals, but I was pissed and about to kick some ass when Marie showed up. They couldn't see her, but she scared the crap out of them."

Loren's face took on a puzzled expression. "It's strange. Most ghosts haunt one area. They don't wander all over the city." She turned to Kendra. "When you do your ghost tours, don't you usually see the same ghosts in the same places?"

Kendra nodded. "Occasionally you'll see one out on the streets, but that's rare."

"And Jared told you this spirit actually went into one of the clubs to get him because Philippe was in trouble?"

"Oh, for the love of the Gods, Loren, yes, that's what she said, so tell us what you're thinking," Deanne said.

Loren hesitated. "I don't want to sound like an alarmist until we hear from Jared, but if this spirit was so insistent Jared go with her, maybe this time Philippe really is in deep trouble."

Deanne snorted. "Philippe Dupre is a train wreck waiting to happen. It's just too bad Jared is the one who has to keep saving his ass."

Kendra finished her muffin and wiped her hands on a napkin. "This time Jared was sure Philippe had finally straightened up and gotten his act together. He even showed some interest in the running of the hotel, and now this. If he's back to his old tricks, he could be involved with any number of scumbags. What if this time he's led Jared into something dangerous?"

"Sitting around here imagining all kinds of horrors isn't going to help." Deanne turned to Kendra. "You're the queen of the crystal ball; let's take a look."

"Jared has a strong privacy charm blocking anyone from watching him. I tried last night and could hardly get through," Kendra replied. "The three of us together might have a better chance. And if he gets mad, right now I don't really care. So let's do it."

Loren rose, crossed the kitchen to a glass front cabinet, and took down a crystal ball. "My grandmother had powerful magic. Perhaps there's enough left in here to break through Jared's charm." She set it in the middle of the table and resumed her seat. Each of them rested three fingers of their right hand on the crystal ball. The lavender mist inside swirled. As one they recited,

"Pierce the barrier and let us see
the place in which Jared might be.
If he's far, or if he's near,
Show us his face strong and clear.
As we will, so mote it be."

When the mist swirled faster and faster, but remained cloudy, Kendra gritted her teeth. "See, I told you."

"Let's give it one more shot," Loren said. "Concentrate."

"Wait a minute. There's something," Deanne said.

A shadowed figure faded in and out of the mist. "Is that Jared?" Loren asked.

Kendra peered closer. "I'm not sure. Damn it, show me." Energy pulsed through her fingers as she pressed them hard against the ball.

For a second, the mist cleared. "That's not Jared," Deanne exclaimed.

Kendra's nose was inches from the ball. "His face is partially in shadow, but you're right. It's not Jared, it's Philippe."

"Are you sure?" Loren asked.

The image disappeared into the mist and Kendra sat back. "Oh, it was Philippe all right, and there didn't seem to be a thing wrong with him. In fact, he looked as if he was asleep in the back seat of a car."

"Uh oh," Deanne murmured.

Kendra narrowed her eyes. "*Uh oh* what?"

Deanne glanced from Loren back to Kendra and jumped to her feet. "Nothing. We're out of coffee. I'll make more."

Unease coiled in Kendra's stomach and she tried to hold the panic at bay. "I know what the two of you are thinking, and it's not true. Jared isn't lying to me. He would never run out on me. There's a logical explanation for all of this. There has to be."

Loren squeezed Kendra's hand. "You're absolutely right. We shouldn't jump to conclusions. Perhaps using the crystal ball wasn't a good idea. Especially when we only got a glimpse. We honestly don't know much more than we did."

Tears trickled down Kendra's cheeks. "I do know it's the day before my wedding and my husband-to-be is hundreds of miles away. Tonight is my pre-wedding supper. When do I tell my mother to call Arnaud's and cancel? I have fifty people coming to my wedding tomorrow. When do I notify the coven there may not be a ceremony, an event I've been planning for years?" She sniffled. "And damn it, I don't know if I'm crying because I'm afraid of what he's gotten into or pissed because he left."

Loren handed her a tissue. "Dry your eyes and don't worry about any of that. Dinner tonight was for a small group of people. If you have to cancel, Arnaud's will understand. As for the coven and the guests, we have a little time before we have to start making calls."

Deanne set a cup of strong chicory coffee in front of Kendra. "Loren's right. We'll wait until we hear from Jared before we track him down and turn him into something disgusting."

Loren started to speak, cleared her throat, then hesitantly said, "Yes, well, perhaps for the moment what we need to do is try and take our minds off Jared."

Deanne's brow rose. "Like what?"

"This probably isn't the right time, but I have the lease for the store." She turned to Kendra. "Are you up to discussing this now?"

Kendra hesitated, then nodded. "Sure, a little distraction might help. But I can't guarantee I'll remember anything you say. I can't get that image of Philippe out of my mind."

"Okay, well, um, Mr. Byrd said the previous tenants are already gone, so he'll give us the keys as soon as we sign the contract."

Deanne frowned. "Part of me still thinks this is a crazy idea. What do we know about running a business? You work at a Montessori school. Kendra helps her mom with her ghost tours, and I work at my parents' bar."

"We're intelligent women. How difficult can it be? We already have our Wiccan merchandise. You make beautiful pottery, and Kendra's jewelry and blown-glass figurines are exquisite."

"And your herbal shampoos, soaps, lotions, and oils are incredible," Kendra added.

Loren's cheeks turned pink with pleasure. "Thanks.

I think we're all talented and could make this work. I also have tons of dried herbs, crystals, and hand-dipped candles. What we don't make ourselves we can purchase from Wiccan catalogs. Mr. Byrd, the owner, said he'd give us a discount on the rent if we did all the painting and fixing up ourselves. The store is in good shape. It wouldn't be hard at all to get it ready. I even have drawings of how we could decorate and lay out the shelves. The apartment above is small but could really be cute." Loren hesitated. "What's wrong? Why are you two smiling at me like that?"

Deanne glanced at Kendra. "Girl, you've got enough enthusiasm for the three of us. Bring on the lease."

Loren crossed to where a small desk sat against the wall. She opened the center drawer, removed a manila envelope, and hurried back to the table. "I had my dad read it over and he thought it sounded fine." She removed the papers from the envelope and handed them to Deanne. "You two read them and tell me what you think. Also, my mom said naming the store 'Enchantment' was a great idea."

"When could we be ready to open?" Kendra asked.

"If we start now and work our butts off, I don't see why we couldn't be ready in time for Ostara."

"By the spring equinox?" Deanne said incredulously. "Working our butts off is right."

"Like I said, the space doesn't need a lot, and we have most of our merchandise. The apartment needs furniture and some decorating, but we can get stuff from our parents."

"Which of us would get the apartment?" Deanne asked.

33

"I have this house," Loren said. "So it's up to you two to decide."

"We don't have to worry about that at the moment," Kendra said. "I'm really getting excited about this. With the occupants gone, I'd like to go through the store again. Jared and I aren't leaving on our cruise until Monday. Perhaps…" Her words trailed off as a sob caught in her throat.

"Oh, honey." Loren hurried to put her arms around Kendra's shoulders. "It's going to be fine. He'll call soon, I know he will."

Chapter 5

Groggy, Jared opened his eyes to see a crow peering at him through the windshield. Momentarily disoriented, he blinked. *What the hell?* Then memories of the night before came rushing back. The crow cawed sharply and flew away.

Jared rubbed the sleep from his eyes and squinted at the digital clock. It was nearly eleven. "Damn." By now Kendra would be out of her mind with worry. He picked up his mirror. "Show Kendra to me." When the glass revealed her tear-streaked face, Jared cursed. Knowing she couldn't hear him, still he whispered, "Baby, I'm so sorry. I love you, and I promise I'll make this up to you."

He popped the Porsche into gear. He'd find gas, food, and coffee, then he'd call her. He had to make her understand his need to go on and his certainty that if he didn't find Philippe soon, his brother would die at the hands of a crazy man with a mysterious grudge.

****

A few miles down the road, Jared sat parked at a gas station, a cup of steaming coffee in the cup holder and two donuts in a bag on the seat next to him. He picked up his cell, took a deep breath, and hit the call button.

"Kendra, baby, it's me," he said when she answered.

"Oh, thank the Goddess you're all right. Jared, I've been worried something had happened to you. What are you doing in Georgia?"

The anguish he heard in her voice tore at his heart. How could he tell her the wedding had to be postponed? The first time he'd laid eyes on her he'd known she was the one for him. Now he was about to hurt her, and there wasn't anything he could do about it. He swallowed hard before whispering, "Kendra, I'm so sorry."

"Sorry about what? Jared you're really scaring me. What's going on?"

He steeled himself for what was about to come. "Philippe has gotten himself into serious trouble, and I have to help him. Kendra, I love you and I'm so sorry, but I'm not going to make it back in time for the wedding. Please try to understand."

Kendra was silent for so long, Jared assumed he'd lost the connection. Then she spoke in a quiet voice Jared knew meant trouble. "I saw Philippe in Loren's crystal ball, and he seemed fine. So, I'll ask again, what's going on?"

Jared silently cursed. He should have cast a blocking charm on Philippe. He didn't want her to see what kind of violence Adam was capable of. "Kendra, what do you mean?"

"When we saw him, Philippe looked as if he were either sleeping or passed out in the backseat of some car."

"He wasn't asleep, he was drugged."

"Drugged? Are you telling me you might miss our wedding because Philippe is doing drugs again? I don't mean to sound unfeeling, but we've been down this road before. Tell him to get his ass in rehab, and you get on a plane and come home. We'll figure out how to get your car afterward."

Jared knew she had every right to be angry, but what was he to do? "Kendra, I'm as upset as you are, but there's more to this than I can explain. I promise we'll get married the minute I get home."

Kendra's volume rose with each word she spoke. "You're saying you won't be back for our wedding, but you won't tell me why?"

Jared knew she was right. He had to tell her about Adam, but he also had to keep her from following after him. He had no doubt Adam would prove to be a powerful adversary. If Kendra was there, Jared would be focused on keeping her safe thus giving Adam the upper hand.

"All right, listen to me. There's this deranged witch who has some kind of vendetta against my family. He's kidnapped Philippe and threatened to kill him if I don't come and get him."

"What? What are you talking about? What vendetta? Jared, who is this witch?"

"I've told you what I know. All I can do is keep following them." He hesitated. Should he tell her Adam had also threatened her life if he were to marry her? He knew Kendra well enough to know her reaction would be to thumb her nose at Adam and dare him to try and stop them from getting married. He had no idea how dangerous Adam was and wasn't about to take a chance with Kendra's life.

Jared's phone crackled. "Jared? Are you still there?" Kendra asked.

"I'm here." Before he could say more, a glow

coming from the pentagonal mirror on the dash caught his attention. A sign welcoming visitors to North Carolina shimmered in the glass. *Damn.* He hadn't slept for that long. How could they be so far ahead of him?

"Kendra, hang on."

When Adam's laughing face appeared, Jared dropped his phone in his lap and picked up the mirror. In a deadly, calm voice he said, "Show me Philippe." The image changed to reveal Philippe slouched against the back seat, his hands bound and blood trickling from his nose and mouth.

Heart pounding, Jared gritted his teeth. "You bastard, he'd better still be alive."

Adam's smug face reappeared. "For now. But you're running out of time, Dupre. Your brother continues to fight, but he's no challenge for me. Killing him, though necessary, will bring me no pleasure. It's you I want to see die."

"Then stay where you are, and we'll finish this. Or are you only tough when protected by those you control?"

Adam's eyes blazed. "I need no protection. I'm the Chosen One. My power is superior to all."

Jared snorted. "Yeah, you're powerful all right. Powerful when it comes to torturing the weak to do your will."

"In order to be superior, the submission of others is necessary. After I'm finished with you, the beautiful Kendra will learn this."

Jared's stomach clenched and his hands shook. "You stay the fuck away from Kendra. She's not a Dupre."

"At least you heeded my words and kept her out of

this. I would have hated to kill such a lovely young woman. Although I would have had her first. No, Dupre, I don't plan on harming her. I want her for my own."

"Over my dead body, you son-of-a-bitch."

"That's my plan."

Adam's insane laughter filled the car as the mirror went blank.

Deep blue energy pulsated from Jared. His adrenalin pumping, he pulled back onto the interstate and punched the gas. A beeping tone from his phone alerted him he had a text, reminding him of his interrupted call with Kendra. "Damn it." He must have lost the signal. He felt around until he came up with his cell and read, "*Call me!*"

He decided to take the coward's way out and let her calm down before calling her back.

A grin slowly spread across Adam Montief's face. Dupre was reacting exactly as he'd expected. Patience and timing were all that were required. For over two hundred years, Augustus Montief had waited for his revenge. Soon Adam would fulfill the task bestowed upon him.

He glanced at the man behind the wheel of the van. Daman Montief was both his uncle and his mentor—and the one man Adam trusted. On Adam's eighteenth birthday, Daman had shown him the scrying mirror belonging to Augustus Montief. When Adam looked into the mirror and saw Augustus' face, Daman cried with joy. No other descendant was able to see the Powerful One's image. Thus Adam was the Chosen One, and it was his duty to avenge Augustus' death.

Daman had insisted Adam accompany him to his

teaching compound on Black Island where he would learn the true arts of black magic and prepare for his task. Adam's gentle parents had emphatically opposed him leaving their Wiccan coven to follow Augustus's evil path. They'd pleaded with him not to go. Already feeling the power of the mirror, Adam had ignored them. Now, fulfilling his dark destiny was within reach.

"It will be quite a while until we arrive at the compound," Adam said. "Do you want me to drive for a bit?"

Even in the van's dim interior light, Adam saw the scowl on Daman's face. "I might be almost eighty and have one hand, but I'm still capable of driving. Besides, we'll be there in plenty of time to prepare for Dupre's arrival."

Adam nodded. "As you wish. Just let me know if you get tired." A groan from the back seat made him turn to see if his passenger was awake.

"Not much longer, Philippe, and your brother will be joining us." His lips curved with satisfaction as Philippe feebly struggled to release his hands. "I would have thought, considering the severity of your wounds, you'd have learned your minuscule power is useless against me."

"You drugged me, you bastard," Philippe slurred. "When Jared gets here, he'll kill you both."

"Ah, but that's where you're wrong. Your brother may think he's capable of destroying me, but his temper and arrogance will be his downfall."

"Arrogance." Philippe smiled around his crusted split lip. "You've got a lot of room to talk. My brother's magic is as strong as yours. After he kills you, he'll release all the others you have under your sick control."

Adam's eyes blazed as he reined in his anger. He could have easily killed Jared down in New Orleans, but Augustus had insisted Jared Dupre's demise occur on Montief land. Now, instead of eliminating one Dupre, he had to put up with this pathetic weakling while crossing half the country. He knew that to assure this fight would be on his terms, he must keep Philippe alive.

"You forget, Philippe, I'm the Chosen One. Your brother's magic is like that of a child compared to mine. And you aren't without blame. Your curiosity about our teachings made it easier to guide him into our trap."

Philippe strained against the bonds that held him. "I'll kill you myself, you motherfucker."

Adam laughed at Philippe's attempt to free himself.

"Perhaps it would hurry Dupre along if he were to watch as I sear off one of your arms." A familiar rush of excitement shot through Adam's veins at the stark terror in Philippe's eyes.

"Leave him." Daman commanded. "Dupre is coming. Injuring the boy will serve no purpose."

With reluctance, Adam turned away from Philippe and faced front.

"You must keep your head at all times," Daman said. "Philippe is of no consequence. If you lose focus, Dupre will get the upper hand, and all will be lost."

Adam gave Daman a curt nod and stared out the passenger window. He knew Daman was right, but his authoritative attitude was becoming tiresome. In the beginning, Adam had found Daman's guidance invaluable, but it was he, Adam, the Powerful One had chosen to honor the Montief curse. He must succeed in killing the man who shared his blood and whose power could match his own. Then he'd be worthy of taking Daman's place as master of the compound's coven and ready to take a wife.

Kendra's face passed through his mind and he smiled. When he'd first seen her with Jared, he'd decided to make his revenge complete by taking Kendra as his. No matter what he had to do, she would eventually be under his control. The satisfaction of knowing he'd soon conquer his enemy, and win the heart of his enemy's love, gave him such an adrenalin rush that blood-red energy visibly pulsed from his body. It was really too bad he couldn't keep Jared alive long enough to see Kendra's will broken and watch her give herself unreservedly to Adam. His smile widened. He'd make sure, before Dupre died, he knew exactly what would happen to her.

Chapter 6

"Jared," Kendra shouted into the phone. She turned to Loren and Deanne. "I think he hung up on me."

"Perhaps he just lost the signal," Loren said.

"What did he say?" Deanne asked.

"He said some deranged witch kidnapped Philippe, and he wasn't asleep, he was drugged."

Deanne rolled her eyes. "Seriously?"

"For heaven's sake, Deanne, why would he make up something so awful as a kidnapping?" Loren asked.

Kendra, the phone still next to her ear, frowned. "Wait a minute, it sounds like he's talking to someone."

"I'll bet it's Philippe," Deanne stated.

Kendra shushed her with her hand. "I'm trying to hear what he's saying. Damn, his voice is too muffled. I can't make out anything. *Jared, can you hear me?* I lost him." She gritted her teeth and hit the redial button. When she heard his voicemail, she clutched the phone and shouted, "Damn it, call me."

"Did he tell you anything else?" Loren asked.

Tears of anger filled Kendra's eyes. "He said he wouldn't make it back in time for the wedding. What am I supposed to do now?" She brushed the tears from her cheeks. "I know I heard him talking to someone. Who could it have been?"

"I don't know, but we all have to calm down and

think rationally," Loren said. "I'll fix some more chamomile tea."

As Kendra rose from her chair, spikes of pale pink energy pulsated around her, darkening to magenta as her anger built. Her heels tapped across the polished tile floor. "I want to know exactly where he is and who he has with him."

"We could try the crystal ball again," Deanne suggested.

Loren shook her head. "It would take all three of us, and Kendra's too upset to concentrate enough for us to get through."

Deanne lowered her voice. "Look at the time. We need to start calling people."

"Would you two stop talking as if I'm not here?" Kendra snapped.

"Kendra, I'm sorry, but it's getting late, and you're going to need to call your mom and the coven," Loren said as she returned the crystal ball to the cabinet.

"What do I tell everyone?" Kendra's voice broke on a sob. "My wedding won't happen because Jared's chasing after Philippe, and I don't know when he'll be back?"

Loren wrapped her arms around Kendra and held her close. "That's all you can say because that's all you know."

Loren handed her phone to Deanne. "Why don't you make yourself useful and go make some calls." When Deanne stepped into the living room, Loren eased Kendra back onto a kitchen chair. "You're trembling. Sit there and take some deep breaths."

Kendra clutched her unicorn necklace, hoping it would calm her. "I can't believe Jared's lying to me," she said, each word a tiny gasp. "I know he loves me." Before Loren could reply, Kendra was back on her feet. "I can't just sit here doing nothing." With tears streaming down her cheeks, her cell in her hand, she punched Jared's contact number. When she again heard his voicemail, she let out a string of cuss words that made Loren raise her brows.

Kendra turned a stricken face to her. "What if it was the kidnapper in the car with Jared? Maybe he's holding a gun on him and he won't let him answer his phone."

"Did Jared sound strange? I mean, could you detect anything in his voice to let you know he was in trouble?"

Kendra rubbed her temples. "I don't know. I can't think." She shook her head. "Not that I recall. Actually, at first he sounded apologetic. It wasn't until I pressed him that he told me the story about Philippe being drugged and kidnapped."

"The only thing wrong with Jared Dupre is being too chicken to answer his phone and face you," Deanne said as she reentered the room.

Loren threw up her hands in exasperation. "Deanne, we don't know what's happened, and we're not doing Kendra any good with wild speculation."

Her hands on her hips, Deanne said, "We won't do her any good pretending everything is fine."

"But assuming the worst isn't helpful either," Loren replied.

"Will you two stop?" Kendra shouted. "I'm telling you, Jared hasn't left me. He's in trouble, and I need to find out where he is and go get him."

"You're not in any condition to go anywhere,"

Loren said. "Besides, how do you plan on finding him?"

"I don't know, but I have to try. Oh, how I wish I had a mirror like Jared's." Kendra's hands shook as she punched in his number. "Damn it to hell. All I get is his frigging voicemail." She dropped the phone on the counter.

"Girl, you're going to make yourself sick," Deanne said.

Visibly shaking, Kendra balled her hands into fists and cried, "I just want Jared."

Loren took her by the arm and led her back to the table. "Deanne's right. You have to calm down. Now sit."

Frustrated by her inability to act, fearful for Jared's safety, and uneasy that Deanne's accusations might be true, Kendra laid her head on her folded arms and sobbed.

"Sit up and drink this." Loren knelt next to Kendra's chair, holding out a steaming cup. "Trust me, it will make you feel better."

Her face wet with tears, gulping in air, her temples pounding, Kendra eyed the cup dubiously. "What is it?"

"Just something to relax you," Loren said.

"It won't knock me out, will it? In case Jared calls, I don't want to be asleep."

"No. Just drink." Loren handed Kendra the cup.

Kendra swallowed the liquid and soon her eyelids grew heavy.

****

"Is she asleep?" Deanne asked.

Loren nodded. "I feel awful for lying to her, but rest is what she needs. I put mandrake root into her tea.

Help me levitate her into the guest room."

"How long will she sleep?"

"The herb affects people differently, but I think she'll be out for quite a long time." With their combined telekinesis, they settled Kendra on the bed, and Loren slipped off Kendra's low boots before covering her with a handmade quilt.

Deanne closed the curtains and quietly shut the door.

They entered the living room where sunshine poured through large windows, their filmy drapes tied back to allow the light to reflect off bowls of colorful crystals, hand dipped candles, and water color paintings of dramatic sunsets and boats on the lake.

"I assume you were able to get in touch with Kendra's mother and the coven?" Loren asked.

"Glenda wanted to come out here, and in the background I heard Kendra's brother hollering something about fracturing Jared's various body parts. I talked to my dad and he's going to inform the coven." Deanne stomped back and forth across the pale blue braided rug. "I was so afraid Jared would do this to her. I feel like breaking something myself."

Loren gnawed at her bottom lip. "I still think there's more to this than he's telling."

"Oh, for the sake of Odin, Loren, the son of a toad probably got cold feet and took off."

"Yes, because Philippe is in danger."

Deanne rolled her eyes. "Danger, my butt. Philippe is about as wild as they get. And I've heard that before he met Kendra, Jared was just as bad."

"But that was years ago." Loren shook her head. "I don't care what you say. I know he loves Kendra, and he's not going to abandon her or his life here."

"I'm not saying he's gone for good. He'll let things calm down, then he'll slink back into town. They've been together for five years, and he's just now talking marriage. I'm sure he loves her. It's making a commitment he has problems with."

Sighing, Loren flopped down in a tan and cream overstuffed chair. "What do we do when she wakes up? She's going to be mad as hell and will want to find him."

"We have to persuade her it's a bad idea. Besides, we can't go driving all over the country searching for him. Unless we can find a way to track him, we're stuck."

Loren nodded. "That's true. I'd like her to stay out here with me, for a while anyway. The fewer people she sees the better. People don't know what to say when something like this happens. They'll just fumble around and make things worse. I can show her some yoga techniques to help clear her mind. Also, some herbal baths will calm her. She just needs quiet and rest."

Deanne flapped her hands. "Whatever. Just make sure that by the time you're done, she sees Jared in a clearer light." She paused. "Hey, someone's phone is ringing." She hurried into the kitchen. "It's Kendra's. And it's him."

"Oh, no, what do we do?"

"Nothing."

"Deanne, we can't do that. What if he needs help?" Loren hurried to where Deanne stood. "Give me that phone. It's not up to us to screen Kendra's calls."

"Oh, well, he hung up. Must have gone to voicemail."

"Do you know how to retrieve her messages?"

"Nope."

"Do you know how furious she's going to be when she finds out we didn't take his call?"

Deanne shrugged. "She was sleeping. We didn't want to wake her. For the love of the Gods, Loren, don't look so upset. If he called once, he'll call back."

"You'd better hope he does."

The words had no sooner left Loren's lips when Kendra's phone rang.

"See, I told you. It's him."

Loren grabbed for the phone, but Deanne danced away. "Give it to me."

"Hello."

"Kendra?"

"No, you jerk, it's Deanne."

"Deanne, please put Kendra on."

"She's sleeping."

"Then wake her."

"I'm afraid I can't do that. Thanks to you, she's a wreck. Loren gave her something to knock her out. She'll probably sleep for hours."

Jared tried to control his temper. "Deanne, I don't have time to play games. Take Kendra's phone to her now."

"What makes you think she wants to talk to you anyway?"

Jared gritted his teeth. "I don't want to discuss this with you, so for the last time, take that phone to Kendra."

"You've got a lot of nerve calling as if you haven't hurt Kendra to the point that I'm not sure she'll ever be the same. I don't know where you are, but why don't

49

you do all of us a favor and stay there."

Before he could tell her to mind her own damned business, he heard muffled sounds, then another voice.

"Jared, it's Loren."

Thankfully someone sane. "Loren, I need to speak with Kendra."

"Where are you? Are you all right?"

Jared tried to remember the last mile marker he'd seen. Was he in North Carolina or Virginia? Hell, it didn't really matter. Adam was still in front of him.

"I'd rather not say. I just need to talk to Kendra."

"Deanne was telling you the truth. I gave her a sleeping draught. Even if I were able to wake her, she'd be too groggy to understand what you were saying. Jared, Kendra told us Philippe was in trouble and you were going after him."

"That's right."

"She's determined to come after you."

"Loren, you can't let her do that. I don't know what all Philippe has gotten himself into, but I do know it's dangerous and I don't want her involved."

"Are you alone?"

"Yes, why?"

"Before she lost the signal Kendra thought she heard you talking to someone."

Jared recalled his conversation with Adam and silently swore. Hoping Kendra hadn't heard much, and hoping he sounded convincing, he replied, "I must have been cursing the traffic."

"Jared, I'm trying to believe you, but you're not making it any easier."

"Okay, I'll tell you what I told Kendra, and by all the Gods it is the truth. Some demonic witch has kidnapped Philippe and he's threatening his life, and I'm going after him. Loren, this is killing me that I'm doing this to her, but what else am I supposed to do? Philippe's my brother. Please help her understand. Tell her I love her, and I'll call her when I can."

Chapter 7

"Well, what did he have to say?" Deanne asked.

"Not much more than we already knew. He claims Philippe is in trouble, and he has to go after him. He asked me to help Kendra understand and to tell her he loved her, and he'd call back."

"Girl, he's lying out his ass. The man got cold feet and he's using Philippe as an excuse."

"I don't think so." Loren rubbed her temples. "I honestly think there's something wrong, and for some reason he's not telling us everything."

"Come on, Loren. He's just stalling for time."

"For heaven's sake, Deanne, every man isn't like Andre. I'm sorry he broke your heart, but you have to stop comparing Jared to your ex-fiancé."

"Jared Dupre and Andre Duvall are cut from the same cloth," Deanne stated. Two years had passed since Deanne caught Andre in bed with Tarese Montaigne, a member of their coven, but to her, the heartbreak felt like yesterday. No matter how hard she tried, she couldn't forget her love for him, or forgive his betrayal. He'd been at a Mardi Gras party and claimed he'd had too much to drink, so he found an empty bedroom and lay down to sleep it off. When he came to, Tarese was naked next to him. Having to work that night at her parents' bar, Deanne had arrived late. She'd gone looking for Andre and found them together. He tried to tell her nothing had happened, but the satisfied smirk on Tarese's face told a different story.

"I was fortunate enough to discover the truth before I was dumb enough to marry him. Jared knows exactly how to play Kendra to get what he wants. You and I both know she's stupid in love with the man. All he has to do is hit her with those baby blues, and give her his devil's smile, and she'll believe anything he says."

Loren sighed. "You're right about that."

"So I suppose we'll have to tell her he called?"

"She'd never forgive us if we didn't."

Deanne flopped down on the couch and sighed. "I know you're right, but you'll have to be the one who tells her. I don't have the stomach for it."

Hours later, pale morning light suffused the room where Kendra slept. She awoke and sleepily took in her surroundings. The walls were periwinkle blue with white trim. A white wicker dresser with an oval mirror stood against the wall directly across from the bed. To her left, a pair of matching wicker chairs with colorful pillows sat in front of two casement windows. Between them was a spindle-legged table stenciled with blue and white daisies. There were bowls of colorful crystals, a vase of yellow mums, and hand-blown whimsical fairies everywhere.

Why was she in Loren's guest room? As her mind cleared, the events of the previous day came rushing back. Kendra glanced at the clock and groaned. Seven o'clock. She buried her face in the herb-scented pillow and clasped her gold unicorn. Today was supposed to be her wedding day. The day she'd stand in the circle, in front of family and friends, and tie the knot with the man she'd loved since the first time she'd gazed into his eyes.

Jared, how could you do this to me? Tears trickled down her cheeks. She angrily brushed them away. *No. No more tears.* She sat up and swung her legs off the bed. Lying around crying wouldn't accomplish anything. She'd find Jared and discover the truth.

Kendra removed her wrinkled clothes and slipped into the gown and robe Loren had laid across the foot of the bed. Her stomach growled. She needed strong coffee and food, then she'd come up with a plan.

She quietly passed Deanne asleep on the couch and headed for the kitchen where Loren was arranging cinnamon rolls on a baking sheet.

Loren looked up and smiled hesitantly. "Good morning. How do you feel?"

"Muddleheaded. What did you give me?"

"Please don't be angry. You were so upset I didn't know what else to do, so I put a little mandrake root in your tea."

Kendra poured herself a cup of coffee. "I'm not angry. I know I was a mess, so thanks for helping."

Loren slid the rolls in the oven. "These won't take long. I'll bet you're starving. We could go to the Cracked Egg after a while, and Deanne could get a real breakfast. Then if we like, we could go over to St. Philippe and take a look at the store."

Coffee mug in hand, Kendra sat down at the table in front of the bay window. She sighed. "I know you're trying to distract me so I won't think about the fact I was supposed to get married today, and I thank you. But I've decided I'm going after Jared."

Loren filled her own cup, sat down across from

Kendra, and took her hand. "I understand your need to find him, but how can you do that? We don't know where he is."

Kendra lightly squeezed her hand and gave her a weak smile. "No, but that's where Deanne comes in. I can't break through with the crystal ball, but Deanne might be able to read something in her tarot cards."

"You realize that's a long shot? Deanne can read predictions, but I'm not sure the cards will tell her where Jared is."

"I know, but it's worth a try. First, I have to call my mom and cancel a wedding. I can't believe she hasn't been calling every five minutes. She has to be frantic wondering what's going on."

"I spoke to her last night and explained the little I knew. We notified everyone the wedding has been delayed. I told her you might stay out here with me for a while. She said to tell you she loved you and for you to call when you feel like talking."

Kendra took a deep breath. "Delayed or canceled? I don't even know which."

"No matter what, we're here for you."

"I can't thank you and Deanne enough for what you did for me yesterday. I couldn't have gotten through it without the two of you."

"That's what friends are for."

Kendra glanced around the kitchen. "Where's my phone? I need to see if Jared's called."

Loren's cheeks turned as red as her countertops. Kendra leaned closer and narrowed her eyes. "What's up?"

"I think I'll check the rolls." Loren jumped up and hurried to the stove.

"Loren, what are you keeping from me? And don't tell me it's nothing. You're the worst liar I've ever known."

"Let's wait for Deanne."

"Wait for Deanne for what?" Deanne, yawning, stood in the doorway wearing Loren's yoga pants and long top. "I need strong coffee and lots of it before I can form a coherent thought." She sniffed the sweet aroma of hot cinnamon. "Are you actually cooking something gooey and fattening?"

"Contrary to your belief, Deanne, I do eat things besides nuts and berries."

"Thank the Gods." Deanne poured herself coffee. "And thank them you have something stronger than herbal tea." She pulled out the remaining chair at the table and sat down. "So what were you two talking about?" She took a long sip of her coffee.

"Jared and whatever the two of you are hiding from me. Pat her back, Loren, she's choking."

Deanne waved her hand. "I'm all right." She scowled at Loren. "That was quick. Didn't waste any time, did you."

Loren set the platter on the table. "I didn't say anything."

"She didn't have to." Kendra reached for one of the hot rolls. "I could see it in her face. So spill it. What are the two of you not telling me?"

Deanne turned to Loren. "I told you last night I wasn't going to be the one who tells her what he said."

Kendra stopped with a bite of roll halfway into her mouth. "Jared called? And you didn't wake me up?" She dropped the roll back on her plate. "What did he say? Where is he?"

"He said to tell you he loves you and he's sorry," Loren said.

"That's all?"

"He also said he'd try and call again."

Stunned, Kendra couldn't keep the anger from her voice. "Why didn't one of you wake me up? You knew I wanted to talk to him."

"Girl, you were borderline hysterical. Why do you think Loren knocked you out?"

It took everything Kendra had to keep from screaming. "Don't you two understand? I need to hear his voice. I need to know he's all right. I've imagined one horrible thing after another happening to him. I need to hear him tell me he still loves me, and we're going to be married."

"I'm so sorry. We were doing what we thought was best for you," Loren said. "I talked to Jared and asked him where he was and if he was okay. He said he was fine, but he wouldn't tell me where he was."

"If you have to be mad, be mad at me," Deanne said. "Loren wanted to try and wake you, but I told her not to."

Kendra grabbed a tissue and wiped the tears from her face. She took a deep breath. "I know you both meant well. And I know I was in bad shape yesterday, but you should have tried to wake me up." She spotted her phone on the counter and checked for messages. When there was nothing from Jared she typed *CALL ME* and sent the text. She sat back down at the table and clasped her coffee mug between her hands. "I'll wait a while. If I don't hear from him, I'll call."

"What's wrong with you?" Deanne shook her head. "The man deserted you on your wedding day. Why would you lower yourself to call *him*?"

"Look what you've done, Deanne. She's crying again." Loren stood and put her arm around Kendra.

Deanne exhaled a long sigh. "Okay, I'm sorry. I just can't stand the thought of her groveling to that man."

Kendra slammed down her empty cup. "Damn it, I'm not going to grovel. Both of you listen to me. Jared is either telling the truth and Philippe is in danger, or Deanne's right and he's left me. Either way, I'm going to find out with your help or without it."

"Of course, we'll help," Deanne said, "but we think you should be prepared if for some reason Jared doesn't come back."

Kendra wanted to pound her fists in frustration. As close as the three of them were, Loren and Deanne still didn't understand she and Jared weren't just in love, they were soul mates. No matter what her friends thought, she had to believe he loved her, and wherever he was he'd come back to her.

"Are you all right?" Loren lightly touched Kendra's arm. "We're really not trying to upset you. We just don't want to see you hurt like this again."

Kendra sighed. "I know you both mean well."

"Hey, you know what?" Deanne spoke up. "If he has a good explanation for why he disappeared, I'll actually apologize for doubting him. How's that?"

Kendra smiled. "That's a deal. And you can do something else to help."

"What?"

"Use your tarot cards to find out what's going on."

"I don't know. I usually have the person I'm reading for shuffle the cards. It might be tricky reading for someone who isn't here."

"Could the cards tell you if he's in trouble or when he might be coming back?" Kendra asked."

"Maybe." Deanne shook her head. "One thing they aren't going to tell me is where he is."

"I understand," Kendra replied. "But they might tell us something."

"I have another idea that might be more useful," Deanne continued. "What about the spirit who was with Jared? Perhaps if we found her, she could tell us where he's headed."

Kendra's face lit with excitement. "Deanne, you're brilliant. She definitely had something to do with all of this."

"Yes, but how are we going to find her?" Loren asked.

"Marie," Deanne said. "She knows every ghost in New Orleans."

"You're right." Kendra got to her feet. "Let's get dressed and go to the cemetery." She waved her hand and a clean pair of black jeans, a long gray sweater, and her low boots appeared.

Deanne arched a brow. "You're going tromping around in the cemetery in heels? Girl, one of these days you're going to break your neck wearing those."

Kendra pursed her lips. "I like heels." She grinned. "Besides, Jared said they make my ass look great."

Deanne snorted, waved her hand, and a New Orleans Saints' sweatshirt, blue jeans, and white running shoes fell into her hands. "Now this is how to dress to go visiting in a cemetery."

Chapter 8

At six in the morning, his head pounding from too much caffeine and not enough sleep, Jared crossed from New York into Connecticut. Bleary-eyed, he checked his odometer. Since leaving New Orleans, he'd driven over a thousand miles stopping only long enough for a short nap, fast food, coffee, gas, and one speeding ticket.

How far north is the bastard going? Jared drove into a gas station with a convenience store and parked. He ran his hands over his face. The refresh charms had stopped working, and his body was telling him he seriously needed sleep.

He picked up the mirror on the seat next to him. He hadn't received any taunts from Adam in quite some time. "Show me Philippe." He blinked in surprise when a sign for the Pier Point, Connecticut, ferry landing filled the glass. *What the hell?* The image changed to show him Philippe being helped by Adam and another man into what looked to be a private boat. As he watched, Adam turned, gave him a salute, grinned, and boarded the vessel.

"Fuck you," Jared growled into the mirror, as the boat pulled away from the dock. He peered closer and read "Omnipotence" in bold black across the boat's stern. The words below made the hair on the back of his neck rise. If he remembered his Latin correctly,

Dominus Laevusthe translated into something like master of the left, or sinister, hand, weird dark magic.

"*Merde*," he cursed, climbing out of his car to pump some gas.

"How far is the Pier Point ferry landing?" Jared asked the young man behind the counter.

"About an hour and a half, maybe more," he replied as he rang up Jared's dark chocolate bar, black coffee, and a canned espresso shot.

Jared glanced at a clock shaped like a beer can. Six-thirty.

"You won't make the morning ferry," the young man added as he handed Jared his change.

"Why not?"

"Because it leaves at eight o'clock." He glanced out the window at Jared's black Porsche and smiled. "Or maybe you will."

An hour and thirty-three minutes later, Jared swore a string of French as he watched the ferry pull away from the landing. "Great, now what?" The smell of the ocean greeted him as he got out of the car. A brisk wind chilled him to the bone.

He flicked his wrist and a black leather jacket and gloves appeared. This sure as hell wasn't New Orleans. As he slipped on the jacket, he scanned his surroundings. Weak sunlight pierced the morning fog swirling above the choppy gray water. He passed fishing and pleasure boats as he headed for a small clapboard building at the end of the long wooden pier.

Welcoming warmth surrounded him as he stepped through the weathered doorway of the ferry office. A pretty thirty-something woman whose name tag read "Mary Beth" smiled at him from behind the ticket

61

counter.

"The wind has a bite to it this morning, doesn't it?"

Jared nodded. "Yes, it does."

"If you'd like some, there's hot coffee over there." She pointed to a table where a pot and Styrofoam cups sat on a tray. "There's sugar, but I only have powdered creamer."

"Thanks." He helped himself to the dark brew. "When does the next ferry leave?"

"Which one? We have two."

He paused, his coffee cup half way to his lips. "Do they go to the same place?"

She shook her head. "One goes to Dog Island and the other to Black Island."

Adam had taken a private boat. Would the mirror tell him which island he'd gone to? While he was debating what he should do, she interrupted his thoughts.

"Are you going to an inn or a bed-and-breakfast? Perhaps I can help if you tell me the name."

He hesitated. How much should he reveal? If she were a friend of Adam's, he didn't want to tip his hand. "Actually, I'm supposed to meet my brother, and I lost the island information."

Her smile widened. "My eight-year-old is always losing things. Just the other day we spent hours searching for his toothbrush and finally found it in the dog's bed. Can you imagine? He was going to brush the dog's teeth with his own brush."

Jared chuckled. "I did the same thing, but I used my brother's toothbrush."

Memories of him and Philippe growing up played through his mind—their discovery of magic and all the trouble they'd gotten into. They'd enhanced the Dupre Hotel's reputation for being haunted by making frogs leap from water glasses in the dining room or making the chandelier in the lobby sway. When they'd levitated a customer's suitcase across the floor, their mother had taken a switch to them both. In their teens, their mischief-making included other Wiccan boys who, like them, couldn't resist playing pranks on their mortal classmates.

When had his brother fallen in with a crowd that wasn't just playing pranks? Why hadn't he noticed Philippe's interest in magic was going down the wrong path?

"The things boys will do," Mary Beth concluded bringing his thoughts back to the present.

"I think my brother said something about a friend having a boat called the Omnipotence. Have you heard of it?"

She nodded. "Sure, that's Adam Montief's boat. Is your brother enrolled in the academy on Black Island?"

Jared's brows rose, his instincts telling him to be cautious with his reply. "I'm not sure. I got a call from my brother telling me to meet him here."

"The academy is a private boys' school run by the Montiefs. Perhaps that's where you're supposed to go. Unfortunately, there isn't another ferry for Black Island until eleven o'clock."

Jared tried to control his impatience, but his irritation must have shown.

"You see it takes at least thirty-five minutes to reach the island," she continued. "Then they have to unload the supplies and make the return trip. If you had gotten here a few minutes sooner, you could have caught the eight o'clock ferry."

"Is there any other way to get there?" he asked.

She nodded. "By private boat." She hesitated. "If you don't mind me saying, you look as if you've been traveling for quite a while. Where ya from?"

"New Orleans." He grinned and scratched his beard stubble. "Am I that bad? I've been in a hurry to get here, and I haven't had a chance to clean up."

"Don't worry about it. You should see some of the fisherman when they come in. I've always wanted to visit the Big Easy. They say real witches live there. Is that true?"

Jared smiled. "There's magic of all kinds in New Orleans. Whether it's caused by witches,"—he shrugged—"who knows."

She leaned closer and lowered her voice. "You know people say we have witches living right on Black Island. Rumor has it strange things go on at that academy."

Jared tossed his empty cup in the trash. "Really? Like what?"

Before she replied she glanced around the room as if they might be overheard. "Weird colored lights have been seen flickering in the sky over the compound. And they say once the boys go through the gates they're never seen again." She bit her lower lip. "And sometimes screams can be heard." Mary Beth stood up straight. "But I can't believe any of that's true. The Montiefs are such nice men. I think some people have nothing better to do than talk about folks who are different."

Jared tamped down the sense of urgency washing over him. He needed to keep a cool head. He had to get to the island and he wasn't waiting until eleven o'clock to do so. Stepping closer, he gave Mary Beth his friendliest grin. "As you say, I've come a long way, and I'd rather not wait until the next ferry. Is there anyone I can hire to take me out to Black Island?"

She blinked a couple of times, smiled, and fluffed her hair. "Well, let me think. There's Rudi." She shook her head. "No, he's gone to Boston. And Brock has already taken his fishing boat out."

"I'm not choosy. Any kind of boat will do."

"If you're sure you're not particular about the boat, and you're willing to pay for the ride, I'll bet Oscar could use the extra money. If you'd like, I'll give him a call."

"Yes, please do."

"I have to warn you, Oscar is a little..." She hesitated. "Well, kind of strange."

As long as he had a boat, Jared didn't care if he was a one-eyed troll. "Strange is okay."

"Don't get me wrong, he's a great guy. People just think he's spent too much time alone on the water. He'll talk your ear off with the most outrageous stories if you let him."

"Thanks for the warning, but I'm sure we'll get along just fine."

While she made the call, Jared poured himself another cup of coffee. He'd already had so much of the damn stuff he'd probably never sleep again.

"Okay, you're in luck. Oscar said he'll be right over."

"Thanks a lot. I really appreciate your help."

"No problem. Now, I'm going to sound like your mother and ask if you've eaten lately."

He shook his head. "I had a candy bar earlier, but I'm all right."

"It's going to take Oscar at least a half hour to forty-five minutes to get his gear and get over here. At the end of the road is a diner. How about I call in and order some sandwiches for you. By the time you walk over there and eat, Oscar will be ready to go."

"I don't know." But as he said the words his stomach growled and he laughed. "Okay, it sounds as if my stomach thinks food is a good idea. Thanks. By the way, what do I do with my car while I'm on the island?"

"Leave it parked in the lot. They only allow bikes on the island, and everyone who lives out there parks here. I assume you have a cell phone?"

He patted his pockets. When was the last time he'd tried to call Kendra? The phone wouldn't work, so he'd…damn, he remembered angrily tossing it out the window somewhere in Maryland. Conjuring an electronic device could be tricky. "I must have lost it. Do you know where I could buy one?"

"Next to the diner there's a general store. They have a little of everything. Perhaps they'd have one of those throwaway cell phones. On the island, the post office and the harbormaster's house have landlines. Also, the businesses are the only places you'll find electricity. The others use oil lamps or gas-powered generators."

The consternation on his face made her laugh.

"Pretty primitive, I know. The people who live out there are no-frills nature types." She paused. "Like I said, people say they're all witches, but I think they're kind of like the Amish."

On his way back from the diner, Jared stopped off at his car to pick up his backpack. He slipped his knife into his boot. If there were witches on Black Island, and not knowing if they were friendly, or dark like Adam, he wanted to be prepared.

Exactly forty-five minutes later, Jared sat next to Oscar McBride, a weathered older man who wore his cap low over bushy brows and kept the stub of a cigar clamped between his teeth. The boat reeked of dead fish and looked as if it was held together with rust. They bounced and dipped over the waves while an icy wind blew through the open cabin windows. Jared wanted nothing more than to surround them both in a nice warm protective bubble but didn't want to scare the old man into having a heart attack. So he gritted his teeth and hoped he didn't freeze to death. He swore to himself once Philippe and he were back in New Orleans, he'd never go north again.

Seeming to read his thoughts, Oscar smiled at him from around his cigar.

"Nice brisk wind gets the blood movin', don't it?"

Jared nodded. "That it does."

"Hah, you southern boys are too used to warm weather. Makes a man soft. Why, I'd say it's at least forty degrees out here. Practically a heat wave. I've been out on the boat when it was twenty and the wind howling."

"Is that right? Well, I've been in a hurricane or two. Does that count?"

Oscar chuckled. "I guess it does. You're okay, son. Fog's liftin'." He pointed to a patch of blue sky just visible in the distance. "And there's Black Island." Again, he pointed.

Jared squinted through the mist to where a dark speck broke the flat horizon. He couldn't imagine why anyone would want to live surrounded by water and so far from civilization.

Oscar, whose face took on a serious expression, asked, "You part of that Montief devil cult?"

Surprised at the question, Jared shook his head. Then, hoping to learn more about Adam, he said, "I don't know the Montiefs or anything about a cult. My brother is on Black Island, and I'm going to see him. But I did hear people think witches live out there." He studied Oscar's face closely as he asked, "What do you think?"

Oscar shrugged. "I believe anything is possible. I can tell you most of them mind their own business and are harmless. It's those Montiefs who are pure evil. For his sake, I hope your brother isn't involved with that bunch."

Pressing him further, Jared asked, "What makes you think the Montiefs are evil and part of a cult?"

With a pained expression, Oscar stared toward Black Island. He was silent for so long Jared wasn't sure he'd heard the question. Then the old fisherman looked hard into Jared's eyes. "Son, I've been on these seas for most of my life. I've seen strange happenings that can't be explained. One thing I've seen is the devil himself in the eyes of those Montiefs. There are some who can lead folks into believing they're good decent people and hide the darkness inside. Adam and his uncle are like that. As for you, I think there's more to you than you're letting on, but I also think you're one of the good ones. Take my advice. Get your brother away from Black Island before it's too late."

Jared not only saw decades of wisdom in the faded blue eyes, but deep sorrow as well. He heightened his senses and probed deeper. Were there traces of magic?

As he pressed harder, Oscar spoke, "That's enough, son. You've told me what I needed to know, and you've seen all you're going to see."

Jared scowled. "Why, you old coot. You knew I was a witch from the start."

Oscar chuckled. "I had my suspicions. I wanted to make sure you weren't part of Montief's following."

"And you let me freeze my ass off." Jared flicked his hand and an invisible shield blocked the open windows.

Oscar's grin widened. "Hey, cold air is good for you."

"Yeah, whatever." Jared slipped the gloves from his hands. "Now tell me what I need to know to get my brother away from the Montiefs."

Oscar's grin faded. Fear and concern filled his lined face.

"Depends on how much control they already have over him. Once the brainwashing is complete—I'm sorry, son—nothing can save him."

Jared cocked his head. "I know it's none of my business, but you sound as if someone you were close to was involved with Adam."

Moisture gathered in Oscar's eyes before he could blink it back. He sighed and took a deep breath. "It was my granddaughter, Rose. A kind child who brought home every stray and injured animal she found. She'd nurse them back to health and find them new homes. It seemed Rose would follow in her grandmother's footsteps and be a gifted healer. Like me, she loved being out on the water. She used to say someday she and I would sail around the world. When she turned eighteen, she went to Black Island with friends. That's where she met those devils.

"That bastard Adam seduced her and messed up her mind. She turned against her parents and me. I never had much power, but both my son and daughter-in-law have strong magic. They did their best to get her away from him, but his control was complete.

"They were desperate to try anything. One night three years ago, they ran into a boy Rose used to date, and who was part of the compound. They made up a story I was dying and thought Rose would want to know. The boy had enough goodness left in him he told Rose. Her love for me was still somewhere inside her, and she managed to leave the compound on her own."

Tears flowed freely down his cheeks, and he didn't attempt to brush them away.

Jared placed his hand on Oscar's arm. "A couple of years ago, my brother got involved with a bad coven in New Orleans. So I understand some of what you've gone through."

Oscar nodded and continued. "Her parents got her home without Adam following. They wanted to leave the island, but there was a storm. They locked themselves in and, after hours of pleading with Rose, thought they'd broken through his spell or whatever hold he had over her. She showed signs of clarity and remorse. Exhausted, they put her to bed, placed as many safety charms around her room as they could think of, and went to sleep."

Oscar swallowed hard before he could continue. "The next day they got up, and Rose was gone. They found her body on the rocks below the compound. My son and his wife are convinced Adam broke through their charms somehow and got to Rose and took her back with him. The police concluded it was suicide. Whether she jumped or was pushed, we'll never know. As for me, I'm convinced that son-of-a-bitch had something to do with her death."

A steely determination filled Jared's eyes. He'd gotten Philippe away from the Black Cross coven, and no matter what he had to do, he'd get him away from Adam as well. "I promise you I'll do my best to destroy Adam Montief for what he did to Rose and for what he's trying to do to my family, but I'm going to need your help."

"My son, Jack, and his wife, Sylvia, run a small B&B on the island," Oscar said. "I'm sure they'd be more than happy to help you. In fact, I radioed Jack I was coming, and if I'm not mistaken I see Sylvia waiting on the dock."

Jared turned and saw an attractive tall dark-haired woman wearing a heavy corduroy coat and blue jeans.

"Hey, Pop, we didn't expect to see you out this way," Sylvia McBride said as she caught the line Oscar threw.

"Got me a young man I want you to meet." Oscar nimbly jumped from the boat and helped secure the line. "This here is Jared. He came all the way from New Orleans to find his brother."

As Jared shook Sylvia's hand, he felt her magic and saw compassion in her deep brown eyes.

"And you think he's here on Black Island?" she asked.

Jared nodded. "I know he's with Adam Montief."

Her mouth formed a thin line. "I'm sorry to hear that."

"Let's go to the house," Oscar said. "We could both use a hot cup of coffee, and Jared can explain."

"Sure thing," she replied. "Jack's cutting firewood and I have a pot of she-crab soup on the stove. It's this way, Jared, just up the hill. Do you have a bag?"

"Only this." He held up his backpack. "I'm going to need more clothes. Didn't think I'd be gone this long."

"No problem. There's a general store." She grinned. "But I have a feeling you can conjure your own."

Chapter 9

"We can walk to the cemetery from here," Kendra said parking her red Mustang in the shade by the Basin Street Station.

Deanne glanced up at the four-story former railroad building. "They did a great job restoring it, didn't they?"

Loren nodded. "It makes a wonderful welcome center for the tourists."

"Speaking of tourists, how are we going to talk to Marie with all the cemetery tours passing through?" Kendra asked.

"I thought of that." Loren said. "Perhaps we can persuade Marie to leave her tomb for a while and go to a more secluded part of the cemetery."

Deanne snorted. "Good luck. I keep telling her she has to stop pulling women's hair and making things fly around, but she says people come to see the voodoo queen, and she's going to give them a show."

"We're just going to have to do our best," Kendra said. "Come on, let's go before it gets much later."

Bordered by Basin, St. Louis, Conti, and Treme Streets, just north of the French Quarter, St. Louis Number One was opened in 1789. Over two centuries of New Orleans legend are buried there.

The girls followed the brick wall to the cemetery gate. Once inside, Loren rubbed the chill from her arms.

"I don't care if it's day or night, this place gives me the willies."

Kendra nodded. "I agree. Even though I see ghosts all the time, there's something about this cemetery that creeps me out."

They made their way along the uneven pavement, down rows of crumbling tombs and well-kept mausoleums. A man in a Victorian frock coat and striped trousers tipped his top hat to them as they passed. The Creole gentleman, Bernard de Marigny, shot craps with a few of the other residents, while Paul Morphy sat at his chess board waiting for a game.

"No wonder they call this the City of the Dead," Deanne said. "There's as much going on in here as there is on Bourbon."

"There's Marie's tomb," Loren said. "And that tour group is leaving."

The tomb was covered with scrawled brick-red 'X's and the rotting remains of a couple of chickens, left as sacrifices by believers. "What you three doing here?" Marie asked as the girls approached.

"Kendra needs your help," Deanne said.

Marie Laveau, as beautiful in death as she'd been in life, stood proudly, her yellow seven-pointed tignon covering her head. An embroidered shawl was draped across her shoulders and trailed down her long black dress.

When Marie turned toward her, Kendra felt shaken by a powerful force. Suddenly she was afraid. Marie's presence had never affected her this way before. "Marie, what is it? What do you see?"

"I see nothing that concerns you. You girls go home and leave it be."

Kendra bit her lower lip. "It's Jared, isn't it? Has Philippe put him in danger?"

Marie's mouth formed a thin line. "The boy can take care of himself. Now, you leave him alone, and let him do what he need to do."

Kendra took a step forward. "Please, I need to know he's all right."

Marie's features hardened. "He has a job to do and he's doing it. He does not need you getting' in the way. That's all I'll say." She narrowed her eyes. "You do what I tell you and stay out of it."

"But, Marie, can't you tell us anything?" Deanne asked.

"For the last time, I said all I have to say. You three get. If I think there is something you should know, I will send for you."

As they turned to go, Kendra hesitated. "Marie, do you know a female ghost who speaks with an island accent, and wears shell earrings and a flowered dress?

Marie nodded.

"If you see her, will you tell her I'd like to speak with her?"

Again, she nodded.

The girls thanked Marie and left. When they were out of sight, a filmy figure appeared next to Marie. She wore a snowy white tignon and a long, flowered dress.

"You t'ink we're going to have trouble with those t'ree?" Taneen asked.

"Kendra needs to get her mind on something besides the boy. I'm afraid she will interfere and distract him."

"Dere bad trouble ahead. He don' need her pesterin' him."

"What do you say we calm her down and get her mind on something else."

"I don't tink it will last, but we can try." Taneen smiled and the two women grasped hands.

A short while later, Kendra, Loren, and Deanne stood on St. Phillip Street studying the narrow front of the building that would become their new business. A large picture window sat to the right of the recessed entrance with an adjacent door leading to the apartment above. A wrought iron balcony stretched across in front of French doors set in the pale brick walls.

"I love it already," Kendra said. "I can't wait to start fixing it up."

Deanne gave her a quizzical look before saying, "I agree. It's great. But would you like to tell me how you've gone from frantic worry over Jared to Miss Mary Sunshine?"

Kendra frowned. "What do you mean?"

"Girl, when we stopped for coffee after leaving the cemetery you were so upset you were practically in tears. Now you're all smiles."

Kendra opened her mouth and closed it. Deanne was right. She no longer felt it was critical for her to find Jared. Was it her intuition kicking in telling her he was safe? In the past, it had never let her down. She had to believe it was right again. "I don't know. Suddenly I'm no longer afraid for Jared."

Loren gave her a quick hug. "See, I told you everything would be fine." She placed the key in the lock and flung open the door. "Ta-da," she sang as she twirled across the empty room, her gauzy skirt skimming across the cream and dark green tile floor.

Kendra smiled while Deanne rolled her eyes.

"Isn't it perfect?" Loren beamed. "We can put shelving for the soaps, lotions, shampoos, and candles along the back wall." Her silver bracelets sparkled as she pointed. "Bins for the crystals and herbs over there and a display case here in the middle for the blown-glass figurines and jewelry. Tiered stands for the pottery. And shelving next to the cash register for tarot cards, wands, cauldrons, chalices, and things like that."

"Girl, take a breath," Deanne said with a laugh. "You're making my head spin."

Loren's cheeks turned pink. "Sorry. As you can tell, I've been thinking about this for a while."

Kendra, who'd been circling the perimeter, stopped next to Loren. "I like it. What about you, Deanne?"

"The space is great, and I like Loren's layout, but I'm picturing a few additions."

"That's fine. I was just throwing out some ideas," Loren said.

"What about a mural on the ceiling depicting some Gods or Goddesses," Deanne suggested.

"Yes," Kendra agreed. "And how about separating the displays along the walls with murals of Wiccan holidays?" She turned to Loren. "You're our artist. Can it be done?"

Loren bit her lower lip in thought. "I think so. I'll do some sketches, and we'll see how they look."

"Can we go upstairs as well?" Kendra asked.

"Sure. The entrance is outside next to the store." They climbed a slightly narrow, encased stairway and stopped at a thick wood door at the top.

When she stepped into the apartment, Kendra instantly fell in love. From the stair landing, hardwood floors led across the narrow living area to double

French doors leading onto the balcony. To the right, a small snack bar with two tall stools divided the kitchen from the living room. To her left were a bedroom and adjoining bath.

She pictured the warm tones she'd paint the walls. The scenes of New Orleans she'd hang and the furniture she'd purchase. In a month the lease on her apartment was up, and she was planning on moving into Jared's rooms at the hotel. This idea hadn't thrilled her, but she thought she'd try it until they could come up with the money for a down payment on a place of their own. Now here was a place for just the two of them, a place to begin their lives.

"Like I said, we could get furniture, dishes, bedding and essentials from our folks or thrift shops." Loren's voice interrupted Kendra's mental decorating. "But I think we could make it really cute."

Kendra glanced toward Deanne trying to gauge her feelings about the apartment. Unable to wait, she asked, "Well, Deanne what do you think?"

"It's nice, but to tell you the truth, since I mostly work late at my parents' bar, it's convenient to just walk down the street to the house. This would be quite a distance from Treme. Your mother's ghost tours are here. It would make more sense for you to take the apartment."

Kendra cocked her head. "You've been talking about moving out of your parents' house and getting your own place."

Deanne nodded. "For now, living at home helps me save money. Besides, we all know you weren't excited about moving into the hotel. And if the blue-eyed devil shows back up, this would be perfect for you two."

Kendra couldn't hold back the sob that suddenly filled her throat. What if she was wrong, and he wasn't on his way back? What if there never was a marriage?

"Honestly, Deanne, look what you've done." Loren hurried to put her arm around Kendra.

"Damn, I'm sorry. It just slipped out. I didn't mean to mention the jerk."

Kendra sniffed. "It's okay, Loren. Deanne's right, he is a jerk."

Deanne threw up her hands. "Finally, she sees the light."

"Yes, well, don't get too excited," Kendra said, as she wiped her eyes. "He might be a jerk, but he's *my* jerk, and I still love him. And I still believe he's coming back."

"If that's what you believe, we believe it, too. Don't we, Deanne?"

"Sure, okay, whatever. Now, I think we should go somewhere for a drink to celebrate our new business. In case we celebrate too much, Loren can be our DD for the night."

Loren frowned. "Why am I always the designated driver?"

"Because you're responsible, level-headed, and practical."

"Oh, for heaven's sake, you make me sound like I'm a boring lump."

Deanne grinned. "You're not boring. You just know how to keep Kendra and me out of trouble."

"I take it this means you're coming back to the cottage with us?"

Deanne nodded. "I don't have to be back to work until Tuesday, so I figured I'd hang with you two again tonight."

"Great," Loren said. "The Lafitte bar is just down the street. Let's go there." She turned to where Kendra was busily inspecting the kitchen cabinets. "Is that okay with you?"

"Sure, that's fine. You know, there's more space in these cabinets than I thought. And the stove and refrigerator are in good shape."

Deanne grinned. "She's already playing house. Come on, Suzy Homemaker, let's go. I'm thirsty."

As Kendra grabbed her purse, her cell phone rang. "Oh, my God, I'll bet it's Jared." She scrambled around in her large bag. "Shit. Where is the damn thing?" She tossed items onto the counter. "Here it is. Hello?"

Her expression switched from excitement to disappointment as soon as she heard her mother's voice. To Deanne and Loren she mouthed, *not him*. "Oh, hi, Mom. Yes, I'm all right. Yes, I'm with Loren and Deanne." She swallowed hard. "No, I haven't heard from Jared since yesterday. Mom, all I know is he went after Philippe. I'm sure he'll tell me everything when he gets back. No, I don't know when that will be, but I have a feeling it will be soon. She wrapped her fingers around her gold unicorn for reassurance. "Yes, of course the wedding is still on. Why wouldn't it be? No, I don't know when. Mom, I'm sorry you're having to deal with the women of the coven calling." Kendra gritted her teeth. She understood her mother was upset, but emotionally she couldn't handle her questions right now. "Mom, I have to go. I've decided to stay with Loren for a few days. I'll call you as soon as I hear from him. I love you."

She disconnected the call. "Jared had better be on

his way home, or my mom is going to make me crazy," Kendra said with agitation. "She says the phone is constantly ringing from people wanting to know what's happening."

Deanne snorted. "I'll bet he hasn't even considered how much turmoil his running off has caused."

Kendra strode back and forth across the small kitchen. Her earlier assurance Jared was all right and heading home was beginning to fade, replaced by fear and anxiety. "Damn it, why hasn't he called or texted me back?" She rummaged around in her bag until she found a small crystal ball and set it on the counter. "You know, we could always try again and see if we can find where he is."

"I still can't believe you carry that damn ball around in that bottomless bag of yours," Deanne said. "But as long as you have it, let's use it."

"He's probably increased his privacy charm to the point it's impossible to break," Kendra said.

"The three of us broke through before. We can do it again," Loren said.

Kendra held her unicorn tighter as they placed three fingers of their right hand on the ball and together said,

"Pierce the barrier, and let us see
the place in which Jared might be.
If he's far, or if he's near,
Show us his face strong and clear.
As we will, so mote it be."

The mist in the ball parted, closed, parted, then swirled faster and faster.

"Did you see something?" Loren asked.

"I'm not sure," Deanne replied.

"I thought I saw a boat," Kendra said. "Did you see it?"

The mist swirled, parted, and swirled some more.

"I definitely saw water," Loren added.

"What's that?" Deanne pointed.

They watched as once again the mist parted.

Kendra's pulse quickened and she concentrated harder. "It could be some kind of pier or dock."

"Who's that?" Loren asked.

For a second, the image cleared to reveal a pretty, dark-haired woman smiling as she took Jared's hand, then nothing but the mist.

Except for the clip-clop of a horse-drawn carriage passing on the street below, the room was silent. Loren stepped toward Kendra. "I think you should sit down."

Kendra could feel each beat of her racing heart. Her breath came in shallow gasps as her entire body shook. Scarlet spikes of energy shot all around her. "The no-good, lying, cheating, witch bastard," she managed to say between gritted teeth as she snatched up the crystal ball.

"Loren, duck," Deanne yelled as Kendra reared back and hurled the ball over their heads. Before it could hit the wall, Deanne waved her hand and it slowly dropped to the floor. "Nice throw," Deanne said. "Too bad it wasn't the prick's head."

Kendra, trembling from head to toe, barely registered what she'd done, her brain and body numb with the pain of Jared's betrayal.

Loren placed a shield around herself to protect her from the spikes of energy as she gave Kendra a slight shake. "Kendra, do you hear me? Stop it. Look at me." Loren shook her harder.

"She's either going to hyperventilate or blow a fuse from an excessive energy charge if we don't bring her around," Deanne said. "You're the healer. Do something."

Loren flicked her wrist and a small vial appeared. She held Kendra's chin and placed the vial under her nose.

As the pungent smell filled her nostrils, Kendra instinctively pulled her head back. Coughing and taking deep breaths, she gazed at her two friends through watery eyes. "What the hell was that?"

"Ammonia," Loren replied. "I'm sorry. Not very magical, but it's all I could think of."

Kendra wiped her face with the back of her hand, took deep breaths, and focused on controlling her power. Slowly the spikes of energy decreased then faded. "Thanks, I think."

"You scared the crap out of us, Brunhilda," Deanne said. "We've never seen you like that. You looked like a fourth of July sparkler."

"Sorry. I've never felt such anger or hurt. All I wanted to do was scream and hit something."

"Well, you've got a good arm on you," Deanne stated. "I'll bet the Braves would hire you as their star pitcher."

Kendra turned to where the crystal ball lay on the floor. "Did I damage anything?"

"No, Deanne stopped it before it hit the wall," Loren said.

"Thanks." Kendra pulled out one of the bar stools and sat with her head in her hands. She tried desperately to hold back tears. "This can't be happening. How could he do this to me? I thought he loved me as much as I loved him. Was our entire time together a lie? If he didn't want to marry me, why not just tell me? Why make up the story about Philippe?"

Loren picked up the crystal ball and set it back on the counter. "You know we might be jumping to conclusions. And before you say anything, Deanne, hear me out."

Deanne nodded.

"Okay, let's think about what we saw. Jared, a boat, water, and some woman. There could be a logical explanation for all of it. This seems to me a perfect scenario for a misunderstanding. This is why people shouldn't poke around in other people's business without knowing the facts."

"I hate to agree with you and give Jared any leeway, but you're right," Deanne said. "There was nothing but a jumble of images. The water could have been anywhere and the woman some innocent stranger."

Kendra sat up straight and brushed the tears from her cheeks. "I see what you both are saying, and I agree. Until Jared tells me to my face he doesn't love me anymore, I'm not going to believe he's left me. So, let's go get us that drink. I definitely could use one."

Chapter 10

Seated at the large oak table in the McBrides' cozy kitchen, Jared relaxed for the first time since leaving New Orleans. Lit by oil lamps and heated by a wood-burning stove, the room felt both safe and welcoming.

"Jared, would you like another biscuit?" Violet asked. The McBrides' nineteen-year-old daughter was a pretty, petite girl with moss-green eyes set in a heart-shaped face and light brown hair worn in braids.

"No, thanks, I've had plenty." He turned to Sylvia. "Everything was delicious. I was hungrier than I thought."

She smiled, clearing away the plates. "I'm glad you enjoyed it."

"My dad told me you're here searching for your brother," Jack McBride said. "And you think he's with the Montiefs."

A short stocky man, Jack had a strong-featured face with dark brown hair tied at the nape.

"That's right," Jared said. "I don't know much more." He hesitated. Should he tell them what the spirit had told him? They were Wiccan so they shouldn't think him crazy for listening to a ghost. Seeing the concern in their friendly faces, he decided to tell them everything.

"So, supposedly Adam is after my family for something that happened over two hundred years ago,"

Jared concluded.

"And you haven't any idea what it might be?" Sylvia asked.

"Vengeance over some old family grudge. All I know of Angelique is that she and my thrice-great-grandfather, Jean Dupre, opened the hotel in 1802, and I always believed my Wiccan magic came from my mother's side. Now it seems Angelique also had power, which is something I'll be asking my father about."

"What if Adam is using Philippe to lure you into a trap?" Jack asked.

"I'm sure he is, but I have no choice. I have to go in. That's where you can help. I need as much information about the compound and what goes on there as you can give me."

"Sure, anything we can do," Jack said. "But I have to warn you, the grounds and house are like a fortress." He cocked his head. "How strong are your powers?"

Jared hesitated. His mother had told him his powers had come to him at an early age. Before he was five he was levitating small objects. By the time he was eight he could make items appear and disappear. Although there were some witches who could levitate themselves, Jared wasn't one of them. By twelve he was an impressive swordsman, and by sixteen he'd learned to hone his energy to razor perfection. At eighteen he'd received Angelique's mirror. "I can hold my own," Jared replied.

"Good. Because you're going to need every ounce of magic you have. I'm not kidding. Between Adam and his uncle there's more power than I've ever dealt with."

"We were clever enough to get our Rose out."

Sylvia said, clasping her husband's hand. "But not strong enough to keep her safe."

Jared glanced around the table. These were good, decent people with their sorrow etched on their faces. He placed his hand over Sylvia's.

"I told Oscar, and now I'm telling you. I'm going to do my best to make the Montiefs pay for what they did to you and what they're trying to do to my family."

Oscar nodded. "Even though I just met Jared, I got a glimpse of his power. I have no doubt he can do what he says."

"Going in after dark sounds like such a cliché, but I really think it's your best chance," Jack said. "I can draw you a diagram of the grounds, but I don't know anything about the house. I do know a little about the guards and their routines." He hesitated. "I could go with you."

Jared shook his head. "This is my brother's and my problem, but thanks."

Sylvia touched his arm. "If you don't mind me asking, when was the last time you slept?"

Jared shrugged. "I have no idea. Somewhere in Georgia, I think. After that I kept using refreshing charms."

"Then I suggest you get some rest. You're going to need to be at your best and being half asleep won't help."

"Sylvia is right," Oscar stated. "You've got plenty of time before dark."

"I can give you a draught to help you sleep if you think you need it," Sylvia added.

"Thanks, but I'm sure I won't have any problem. Suddenly I feel as if I can't keep my eyes open. I don't know how long this is going to take, and I don't know what kind of shape my brother is going to be in when I find him. So, if you have a couple of rooms available, I'd like to rent them."

"Sure. You and your brother can stay as long as you wish. Come with me and I'll get you settled in."

Jared turned to Oscar and offered his hand. "I may not be awake when you leave, so thanks for the ride out and introducing me to your family."

Oscar grasped his hand tightly. "Glad to help, but I'm staying right here. I'm not about to miss this."

Sylvia led Jared to a corner room which overlooked the ocean. An oak dresser and a chest of drawers sat opposite a sleigh bed with a hand-made quilt. He stood at the window watching as the waves lashed the rocky shore. Seagulls swooped and dove, and far out to sea he could see a freighter on the horizon. "Kendra would love this view," he thought.

He rubbed his temples. *Damn it to hell, Kendra and I should be married by now. We would have enjoyed our wedding supper, and we'd be dancing together under the stars. We waited so long for this day, and I've ruined everything. I'll make it up to her if it takes the rest of my life.*

He sat down on the feather bed and pulled his mirror from his backpack. He wanted to get in touch with Kendra before he went after Adam. He gazed into his mirror. "Show Kendra to me." An image flickered, faded, then cleared. Jared frowned and peered closer into the glass. Kendra, Loren, and Deanne sat around a table having drinks. Kendra's gray eyes were full of amusement as she laughed and tossed back her long red hair.

Well I'll be damned. He'd prepared himself to see her angry and in tears, not out enjoying herself. He watched in disbelief as Kendra lifted her glass in what seemed to be a toast. So much for her being upset.

He picked up his new cell phone. *If she's in a bar, she won't be able to hear me anyway.* He tossed both his phone and the mirror on the dresser, kicked of his boots, and lay down across the bed.

****

"He's on the island," the gruff voice from behind him said.

Adam Montief stood in the library of the stately mansion gazing out the window across a broad expanse of manicured lawn to the sea beyond. Dreading each new appearance of this odious visitor, Adam steeled himself and turned.

Facing him was an oval mirror, its wood dark with age and carved with intricate pentagrams. The glass was pitted and crisscrossed with fine lines. What never failed to unnerve Adam was how much he resembled the apparition staring back at him.

"Did you hear me? The Dupre boy is on Black Island."

"Yes, Powerful One, I heard you. I'm aware Jared is here."

"Then I can assume this will soon be over, and I will have my revenge."

"Yes. As soon as Dupre comes for his brother, I'll kill them both."

"You know I have waited centuries for this. You must not fail."

"How can I fail? I'm the Chosen One."

"Too much self-assurance can be dangerous. Stay

alert. Do not take Dupre for a weakling. He not only carries that whore Angelique's power, he has his mother's as well. That is strong magic."

Adam grimaced. "It doesn't matter whose blood or how much power he's inherited. I'm still smarter and stronger. Dupre and I may share Angelique's blood, but he doesn't share yours."

Augustus Montief's image smiled. "You are right. He does not. When do you expect he will come for his brother?"

Adam shrugged. "If he continues to react the way he has, he'll come tonight."

"Have the guards been notified not to interfere?"

"Certainly. I know what I'm doing." Adam gritted his teeth with irritation. Augustus was constantly questioning his ability to take charge. Yes, Daman was still head of the compound, but killing Dupre was *his* responsibility. How he wished he could just smash the hell out of that damn mirror and be rid of the old man. He'd learned the hard way the mirror could not be destroyed. The Powerful One was determined to monitor his every move until Jared Dupre was dead. "He'll depend on his mirror to guide him, and I'll be able to watch. He'll walk right into my trap."

Augustus frowned. "You have been able to use Angelique's mirror against him?"

"It took a while, but I broke through her protection. Do you now see I'm the stronger one?"

Still frowning, Augustus shook his head. "I would not assume his mirror will continue to be of use to you. She now knows what you have done, and she will not allow it to happen again. Are you listening to me? You need to plan for that."

"Yes, I hear you." Adam paced back and forth before the mirror. "Except for the section overlooking the cliff, the grounds are surrounded by a nine-foot brick wall. I have guards constantly patrolling the perimeter who will warn me if he tries to enter. The main gates are the only way in and out. Unless Dupre has learned how to fly, or can scale the cliffs, or become invisible, there's no way he can escape me. Do you understand?"

"Do not dare to raise your voice to me! Or use that condescending tone, you arrogant pup," Augustus roared. "You might have my power, but you still answer to me. Never forget that."

The library door opened and Daman entered, scanning the room. "I thought I heard voices."

"It's all right. I was having a discussion with the Powerful One."

Daman's eyes darted to the mirror on the wall. "Is he still here?"

"No."

"Is everything all right?"

Adam snorted. "If you consider having my intelligence and power questioned, then yes, everything is just fine."

Daman fidgeted as his eyes shifted back to the mirror.

"Will you relax? I told you he's gone. Besides, he's just a face in a mirror. Augustus has no real power."

Daman glanced down to where his right hand should be and in a low voice said, "Never let him hear you say that. The Powerful One still possesses strong magic."

"Then if he doesn't think I'm capable of taking

care of Dupre, why doesn't he do it himself?"

Daman looked perplexed. "What are you talking about? Killing the Dupres is a great honor the Powerful One has bestowed upon you. Certainly, he thinks you're capable."

Adam gave a dismissive wave. "Enough about him. What have you done with Philippe?"

"He's asleep in one of the cells. I thought it best to keep him sedated until we have a plan."

Adam could barely control his irritation. "I already have a plan. My plan is to toss Philippe out onto the lawn and wait until Dupre comes to get him, and then I kill them both. Simple and foolproof."

"Do you know where Dupre is?"

"One of my trusted spies informed me he got a ride out with that old fool Oscar McBride. So I'm guessing he's with them plotting my downfall."

Daman arched his brow. "Do you think Jack McBride will come with Dupre?"

Adam shook his head. "Dupre is a soft-hearted fool and would never take a chance of anyone else getting injured. No, he'll come alone."

"McBride may insist because of Rose."

Adam whirled, fury blazing in his eyes. The pain of Rose's betrayal still clawed at his heart. He would never forget the panic and loathing on her face when she awakened in his arms after he had rescued her from her family's house. She accused him of being some kind of monster. He would have done anything for her, and how did she repay him? By running away.

He had never experienced such rage as when she tried to use her power against him. It cut him to his core when she told him she'd rather be dead than live with him. It wasn't his fault she went over that cliff. The echoes of her screams haunted his dreams. It was all the McBrides' fault Rose turned on him. Perhaps after he killed Dupre, he'd get rid of them as well.

Daman raised his one good hand and took a step back. "Adam, calm down. I'm sorry I mentioned her name, but it's something we need to consider."

Adam concentrated on taking slow deep breaths. He needed to reserve his energy for the fight ahead. He couldn't afford to weaken himself over things he couldn't change. "Dupre will come alone. After it gets dark, place Philippe on the lawn. Make sure he is drugged enough he can't help his brother. I need Dupre to do something for me before he dies. I will use Philippe to ensure his cooperation."

Daman scowled. "This would be a lot easier if magic could be used to kill."

"Well, it can't, so I'll use the next best thing." Adam turned to where a gleaming sword hung above the fireplace. "Thanks to my skill, my trusted friend has never let me down, and I don't expect it will this time."

After Daman left, Adam restlessly prowled the large lower rooms of the stone mansion. Originally built as a refuge by a coven of witches and warlocks fleeing persecution in Salem, the property was purchased in the eighteen-seventies by Adam's ancestor, Toussaint Montief. He established The Montief Academy of the Sinister Arts, or MASA. Through the next century, the academy showed young men the true meaning of their magical power, preparing them for the day when their specialized skills would conquer all other covens.

Adam crossed the wide entry hall past a painting of

a stone circle in the misty fog and a wall where medieval weaponry hung. In the main salon, he halted and stared up at Toussaint's portrait hanging above an enormous fireplace. *Soon there will be no one standing in my way, and I will be the supreme master over all.* A malefic grin spread across his face.

Chapter 11

Jared, refreshed by sleep and a hot shower, prepared for his encounter with Adam. Wearing black jeans and a loose-fitting black shirt, he slipped his knife into his boot and buckled his sheathed falcata to his belt. For added protection, Sylvia had given him an amulet of black onyx, fire agate, and malachite that he hung around his neck. He picked up his mirror. "I'll make sure you won't be watching me anymore, you bastard." As he was about to place what he hoped was an impregnable charm on the mirror, light flickered in the glass, and the portrait of Angelique Dupre appeared.

The painting hung above the fireplace in the library of the Dupre hotel. Normally smiling, with just a hint of mischief in her dark eyes, Angelique's face now held pain and sorrow. When she spoke, her voice reflected the anguish in her eyes. "My child, I cannot express my heartfelt grief in bringing this upon you, but I have confidence you will prevail and put an end to this madness. Even though Adam is descended from my beloved Anton, Augustus' evil has captured his soul, and he must be destroyed."

Momentarily taken aback by the appearance of Angelique, a myriad of emotions flowed through Jared, thrilled to actually speak to the one person who held the answers to the past, and anger toward her for putting him in this position. "I have a number of questions.

Like why in the hell did you wait until now to appear to me?"

"I hoped this day would never come and my appearance would not be necessary."

"You do realize I left my fiancée on my wedding day, chased an insane witch across half the country, and now have to fight for my and my brother's lives? And I may have to take another's life, the thought of which happens to sicken me. It would have been helpful if you had explained this vendetta threat to me years ago. But, unfortunately, I'm a little busy right now and don't have time for a family history lesson."

"I do not blame you for being angry. If I could change the past I would, but I cannot. What I can do is reiterate that Adam is evil and as much as it sickens you, he mustn't live. I love you, and I'll give you all I have to give."

Jared snorted. "That's reassuring. How much help can I get from a dead woman? Now, if you don't mind, I have work to do."

As her image faded, Jared heard her say, "Feel the power."

A slight tingling sensation flowed through his body. His right hand began to pulsate. Jared looked for Angelique, but she was gone. *Well I'll be damned.*

He slipped the mirror into his pocket and turned to where his phone lay on the dresser. Should he call Kendra? He glanced at the clock. Eleven o'clock. She was probably asleep. It wouldn't hurt to take a quick peek, but he didn't want to use the mirror. His gaze fell on his crystal ball. That would work.

He placed both hands on the smooth glass and recited,

"Clear the mist so I might see,
The one who means the most to me.
As I will, so mote it be."

The mist swirled, darkened, then cleared to show Kendra asleep in a white wicker chair, her phone clasped in her hands which lay folded on her lap. Moonlight illuminated the glistening tears drying on her cheeks.

Guilt rushed over him. He picked up his phone, then paused. What could he say? That he was about to have the fight of his life and might not survive? She would worry more. Better to leave her wondering and pissed than involve her in something that could get her killed, or worse. Jared recalled Adam's words, *I want her for my own.* At the thought of Adam's hands on Kendra, his insides turned to ice. *I'll never let the son-of-a-bitch near her. If I'm going down, he's going with me.*

Jared stared at her sleeping face and whispered, "Baby, I'm so sorry, but I have to keep you safe. I promise to come home soon and make this all up to you." He slipped his arms into his leather jacket, then hesitated. Jared could no longer ignore the terrible reality he'd pushed to the back of his mind—the chance he wouldn't come out of this alive. He couldn't leave Kendra and his father not knowing what had happened to him. He opened the center drawer of a small desk and took out paper and pen. He quickly wrote two notes, sealed them in envelopes, and headed downstairs. As he entered the kitchen, he found the entire McBride family sitting around the table drinking coffee, anxious expressions on their faces.

"Are you ready?" Oscar asked.

Jared nodded.

"I have something for you," Sylvia said, handing him a small cloth sack.

She smiled at Jared's evident puzzlement.

"It's a *gris gris* bag to help keep you safe. There's some sow thistle to protect you from evil. I picked it at daybreak when the moon was in Capricorn. Also obsidian, dragon's blood, hyssop, and patchouli. Keep it near your heart."

Touched, he took the bag and placed it into his shirt pocket. "I'm planning on this being unnecessary, but if I don't survive, please contact my father, Jacques Dupre, and give him these." He handed her the two envelopes. "One is for him, and the other is for my fiancée Kendra O'Connell. My father's number is in my phone which is on the desk upstairs. I left New Orleans in such a hurry, I didn't tell him what was happening. I'm hoping to take care of this and go home.

"Now, if I survive, but I'm severely wounded, this may mean Adam is alive, and Kendra is still in danger. Please contact my father, not Kendra. I'm afraid if she knows what's happened, she'll come here. I'm sorry for leaving you with this burden."

Sylvia lightly touched his arm. "It's no burden. You can trust me to do as you ask."

"Not to dwell on the gruesome, but how will we know if you're hurt or dead?" Oscar asked.

Jared smiled. "Oh, I have a feeling if Adam Montief kills me, you'll know."

Jack and Oscar both rose and one by one shook Jared's hand.

"Good luck to you," Jack said. "We'll be waiting."

"We're counting on you, son." Oscar gave his hand

a squeeze. "Give him hell for our Rose," he whispered.

Jared nodded. "Yes, sir."

Violet gave him a quick hug. "Please come back."

"I'll do that."

With tears in her eyes, Sylvia hugged him tightly. "All the Gods and Goddesses be with you. Please be safe."

A lump formed in the back of Jared's throat. Sylvia, with her kind and giving nature, reminded him of his mother. He bent down and kissed her cheek. "Thanks for everything."

The moon winked in and out of the clouds as Jared made his way through the sleeping village. In the distance, he saw the compound's high brick wall. Outlined against the night sky, the mansion's towers stood sentinel.

Jared turned up the collar of his jacket and slipped his gloves on. He had no doubt he was expected but didn't intend to make his capture easy. He circled the perimeter of the wall until he found a large maple that would serve his purpose. He shimmied up the trunk and grabbed a sturdy branch he could climb out on. By the light of the moon and the faint glow from the house's windows, he was able to see into the grounds below. The stone house sat in the middle of an expanse of lawn with a scattering of maple and oak trees. He heard the surf beating against the base of the cliffs and saw the beam from a lighthouse as it flashed across the black water.

He took the mirror from his pocket. "Show me Philippe." The glass shimmered and cleared revealing a still form lying curled on the ground. Jared's heart raced. He knew it was Philippe. He growled into the mirror. "Show Adam to me." The glass dimmed, lightened, then darkened. "Show me," he commanded. The silhouette of a man appeared behind a window.

So Adam thought he'd just wait for him to approach Philippe and fall into his trap. *Not going to happen, asshole.*

He scanned what he could see of the grounds and along the wall. He saw no one. Adam must have called off his guards. *Well, good.* That made it easier for him. He worked his way around to a branch that hung over the wall. He hesitated. Could there be an alarm? That seemed a bit drastic even for Adam. This was supposed to be a school, not a prison. Jared lowered himself onto the wall and sighed in relief when the night remained silent. He placed both hands on the brick and levered himself over the side. He tried to find a toehold, but the brick was smooth. Nothing to do but hope for the best. He let go.

When his feet hit the ground, Jared stayed low. With a flick of his wrist, a protective shield surrounded him. To the mortal eye, he was invisible. To another witch, his body was a dim outline. Senses heightened, he scanned the area listening for any sound. When all remained quiet, he used the trees for cover and cautiously worked his way closer to Philippe. When he was within fifty feet, he paused, took out his mirror, and whispered, "Show me Adam."

The glass flickered, revealing nothing but the darkened windows. "*Merde.*" Jared cursed. *Where are you, you bastard?* He tried the mirror again, and still nothing showed but the house. *I'm going to take that to mean he's inside and not out here.* Jared replaced the mirror and balled his hand into a fist. When a blue light encircled his hand, he threw the energy ball directly at Philippe and smiled with satisfaction as the energy glided over Philippe's body, securely encasing him in its protection. Jared took a deep breath. If Philippe was still alive, he was as safe as Jared could make him.

He turned to the house and readied himself for the task ahead. Sweat broke out on the back of his neck. Could he actually take another's life? His eyes traveled to where his brother lay crumpled, and he nodded. To save those he loved, fucking-A, he'd kill.

Jared watched the door open and a man calmly walk out. He strolled across the lawn and stopped between Philippe and the cliff.

"Come out, Dupre, and let's finish this."

His nerves taut, Jared stayed motionless and studied his opponent. About the same height, Adam may have had some weight advantage, but it was difficult for Jared to tell due to the heavy cloak he wore.

"All right, if you want to play games." Adam sent a flash of energy toward Philippe.

Jared smiled with satisfaction as it bounced off his shield.

"Well done, Dupre. But I'm afraid your little spell isn't enough to keep me out."

Adam flung out his hand and Philippe screamed.

Jared started forward but stopped. His first instinct was to protect Philippe. He gritted his teeth and stood his ground. At least he knew his brother was still alive.

"Don't be an idiot, Dupre. There's no need for your brother to suffer. Come out and face me like a man."

Jared reared back and hurled another ball of energy directly toward Adam. As it knocked Adam off his feet, Jared raised his arm and his falcata appeared in his hand. He ran to stand between Adam and Philippe. "Come on, fucker. Fight someone who isn't weak from torture."

Adam quickly got to his feet. With a wave of his arm, lighted torches surrounded them. He raised his sword, held with both hands behind his head in a medieval stance known as the Guard of Wrath. "I want to be able to see your face when I kill you."

Jared snorted. "Look your fill, because my face will be the last one you see before I send you back to Hell. But before we begin, I want Philippe out of here."

Adam's teeth flashed. "I'm afraid that's not possible. We have some business to attend to, and I'm going to need your brother's assistance."

"I thought it was me you wanted. Leave him out of this."

Adam shook his head. "Regretfully, I can't do that. I have to insist you carry out one final task for me."

"What the hell are you talking about?"

"I told you I want Kendra for my own. You're going to call the lovely lady and tell her you don't want to marry her and you're not coming back for her. After you do so, I'll let Philippe go."

Jared laughed without humor. "You really are insane. Why would I do that?"

"To save your brother's life."

"You're never getting anywhere near Kendra."

Adam sighed. "Exactly what I expected you to say. I'll give you one more chance."

"Fuck you."

Adam swung his sword forward, pointing it behind Jared. Philippe screamed.

Knowing he couldn't take his eyes from Adam,

Jared, hoping to deflect Adam's next attack, stepped back, closer to Philippe.

"Your brotherly devotion is touching, but you're beginning to bore me. You can't win, Dupre, so give it up."

"I'm not going anywhere." When the attack came, Jared was ready. Using his falcata like a bat, he deflected the spear of energy back toward Adam, smiling with satisfaction when it knocked Adam off balance and he went down on one knee. Being little league homerun champion was paying off. "You'll not get near Philippe again, so we can play games all night, or you can let him go, and we'll finish this one-on-one."

Hatred burned in Adam's eyes. Jared's body tensed with anticipation as he waited for the coming powerful assault. When Adam spoke, his words chilled Jared to his core.

"Daman, come out. It seems I need your assistance."

Jared watched an older man step from the shadows and stand to his left and slightly behind him. He glanced from one man to the other. His hands growing damp with trepidation, he tightened his hold on his sword. He couldn't allow Adam to see his fear. "What's wrong, can't take me on your own?"

"Oh, I'll have no problem killing you. But I want this business with Kendra taken care of, and I don't want to *play games* as you put it. You will do as I say, or Daman will kill Philippe. A blade through his neck should do it."

Jared knew without a doubt Adam was telling the truth. He also knew there wasn't a way in hell he could take on both men. He didn't trust the bastard to release

Philippe once the call was made, but if there was a chance, then he'd do as Adam wanted. It would just be one more thing he'd have to explain to Kendra. If she would even speak to him when this was over. With a contemptuous glare he said, "I need a phone."

Adam nodded. "Smart choice. Daman, if you would."

Daman cautiously approached Jared and handed him a phone. Jared saw he had one hand, but, judging by the coldness in his eyes, didn't think this hindered his power. Daman stepped back and pressed the point of his sword to Philippe's throat.

"The phone is on speaker so we will hear every word you say. If you try and give Kendra a signal for help, Daman will kill your brother," Adam stated.

Jared took a deep breath and placed the call. The phone rang twice before he heard her sleepy voice.

"Hello, this is Kendra."

The sound of her voice raw with tears sliced through his heart.

"Hello, is someone there? Jared?"

"Yeah, baby, it's me."

"Oh, thank the Gods you're all right," she cried. "Jared, where are you? What's happened?"

He swallowed hard. "Kendra, I'm sorry, but..." He hesitated. The tip of Daman's sword pierced Philippe's skin. Smelling fresh blood, Jared spoke. "Kendra, I'm sorry. I'm not coming back."

"What? What are you saying? What do you mean you're not coming back? Jared, what's wrong? Where are you? Is this about Philippe? Did he get you into some kind of trouble?"

"It's not just about Philippe. I think it's best if I

104

stay away."

"Stay away?" Her voice rose. "What are you talking about? I thought you loved me."

His gut twisted into knots. Sweat coated his palm as he held the phone. "Kendra, I can't marry you."

The silence stretched on until Jared thought she must have hung up. Then he heard her intake of breath.

"Are you with that woman?"

"What?"

"I saw you in the crystal ball with some woman."

For a second, Jared stood speechless. What was she talking about. "Kendra, baby, you've got it all wrong. I'm not with another woman."

"Don't lie to me," Kendra cried. "You say the words. Tell me you no longer love me, and everything we had together means nothing to you."

Jared stared into Adam's triumphant eyes, and the rage he felt toward him set Jared's entire body trembling. He knew without any doubt he could and would kill this man.

"Did you hear me, Jared? Say the words."

He prayed someday she'd forgive him. "Kendra, I thought I loved you, but I don't."

Jared heard her breathing in tiny gasps. "Jared, I loved you with all my heart. How could you do this to me?"

Jared gripped the phone tighter. He focused his fury toward these two men who not only threatened his brother but were forcing him to break the heart of the woman he loved. He said a silent prayer to all the Gods that someday Kendra would understand and forgive him.

"Jared, you son-of-a-bitch, you can rot in Hell."

The last thing he heard was her sobs, then silence.

He'd reached the breaking point. His self-control snapped. Red-hot energy pulsating throughout his body, he dropped the phone and ground it beneath his boot. In one swift motion, he flicked his wrist, placing a shield between himself and Adam. Pivoting as hard as he could, he thrust his falcata into Daman's chest. The blast of energy Adam hurled sliced through Jared's shield knocking him to the ground. Quickly rolling, Jared was back on his feet as Adam charged. Before Jared could react, Philippe's body rose off the ground and he let out a blood-curdling scream. Jared knew magic couldn't be used to kill, but it could do real damage. At his feet, Philippe lay crumpled and silent.

Jared's features twisted in a murderous rage as he stared into Adam's demonic face. "All right, fucker, let's end this right here, right now." He stepped back, dropped his jacket to the ground, and pointed his falcata at Adam's chest. "*En garde*, you son-of-a-bitch. I'm sending you to the pits of Hell where you belong."

Adam laughed. His dark eyes took on a reddish glow. He lifted his arm and extended his own blade. "Haven't you learned yet I'm the Chosen One? I've been chosen to exact Augustus Montief's revenge, and now,"—he glanced to where Daman lay—"I'll also avenge my uncle's death. You're no match for me, Dupre. I want the satisfaction of making you beg for mercy before I destroy you. Then I'll finish off what's left of that sniveling brother of yours." His demented smile widened. "And then I'll have the lovely Kendra for my own."

Bile rose in Jared's throat at the thought of Adam anywhere near Kendra. "Come and get me. Magic can't help you now."

Adam's nostrils flared and he bared his teeth. "I don't need magic to kill weaklings like you."

As the two men faced off, thunder rocked the earth beneath their feet. A cold wind howled around them. Angry clouds skidded across the dark sky. Streaks of lightning illuminated the high cliff upon which they stood. The frigid waters of the Atlantic rose and crashed against the jagged rocks below.

Jared assumed a fencer's stance, his body turned sideways to present a narrower target, right foot forward, left hand back for balance, his blade steady and level.

Less elegant, Adam crouched and faced forward, his arms extended like a wrestler, the heavy straight medieval blade of his sword twitching, the tip always moving. The unconventional stance wasn't what Jared expected. Adam looked more like a gladiator than a fencer.

Adam's sword tip nicked Jared's arm as he jumped back, parrying downward a moment too late, but the steel blades clanged against one another. Reflexively Jared disengaged his sword and pushed forward from his left leg, a hard riposte toward the heart of his enemy. But Adam was quick and strong and brought his blade up, striking Jared's and nearly knocking it from his hand. The shock of the blow reverberated all the way up his arm, and the sword loosened in his grip. Jared leaped backward to regain his hold and his composure.

Adam came at him, thrusting and cutting left and right. All Jared could manage was to block the blows and stay on his feet. He settled his mind and took confidence from his ability to defend himself.

Momentarily winded, Adam paused. Jared flicked his blade toward him in a feint, then swung it back to the right, slicing across Adam's rib cage and catching his left arm. Blood stained his torn shirtfront and sleeve.

Adam growled, "Touché. Now you've really pissed me off." Realizing he was near the cliff edge, he charged.

It was all Jared could do to protect himself, parrying left and right against hammer blows, stepping back, afraid he might stumble, feeling the tip of Adam's sword cutting into his chest, his leg, even his left ear, but he stayed focused, always looking for an opening to counterattack.

Then there was a break in the assault, a moment, a tempo as fencers call it, a breath of time, a tiny clear space. Jared felt it and attacked again and again, thrusting his blade on point, swinging it down and then forward, cutting upward and then back down, always driving for his adversary's dark heart, evading his blade, forcing him toward the cliff.

Suddenly Adam's heavier sword caught his, forced it aside, and drove into his chest, cutting through muscle and bone. Jared stumbled backward and fell to his knees.

Triumph lit Adam's eyes as he stood over him, his sword raised above his head for the final killing blow.

"This is for Augustus Montief," Adam panted. "His revenge is complete." He leaned closer. "As you die, think of me fucking Kendra, Dupre."

Kendra's face swam before Jared's eyes, and he tried to rise. He thought he heard Philippe moan his name. Angelique's image seemed to reach out to him. A deep darkness, almost like sleep, came over his mind blotting out fear and pain, then a hard, brilliant light burned through him, and he lunged upward. The sudden powerful stroke took Adam by surprise and he flailed with his blade too late.

The falcata drove into Adam's chest, smashing through ribs. He reeled back, the cliff edge crumbling away beneath his feet, and he slipped out of sight, shock and disbelief filling his face. A piercing scream echoed off the cliff side as he fell toward the rocks and the ocean below.

"Rot in Hell," Jared whispered as he collapsed, barely conscious, his life's blood draining into the dry soil. "Kendra, I love you," he rasped.

Chapter 12

The phone fell from Kendra's numb fingers. Racking sobs shook her body as she curled into the chair. Jared couldn't have meant what he said. He must still love her.

A soft knock sounded on the door, but Kendra ignored it. When she heard it open, she tucked her head under her arm and tried to stifle her sobs. All she needed now was to hear "I told you so."

"Kendra, what is it?" Loren asked. "I could hear your crying through the wall."

Deanne stumbled into the room. "What's going on?"

Loren picked up the phone from the floor. "Kendra, did Jared call?"

Deanne hurried to Kendra's side. "Is that what happened? Tell us."

Kendra nodded.

"What did he say?" Loren asked.

"Look at her," Deanne said. "I can guess what he said."

"You were right. I've been a fool," Kendra gasped. "He told me he wasn't coming back, and he doesn't love me. He's not going to marry me. I think he's with that woman we saw in the crystal ball."

"Bastard," Deanne hissed.

Loren knelt next to Kendra's chair. "It's going to

be okay, honey. We're here, and we'll help you through this." She turned to Deanne. "Stay with her while I fix something to calm her."

"Make it strong enough to knock her out." Deanne knelt on the floor and awkwardly patted Kendra's back. "Come on. You have to stop crying or you're going to make yourself sick."

"How could he do this to me?" Kendra wailed. "I love him so much."

"I know. I know. It will be all right." Deanne brushed the hair from Kendra's face.

Loren hurried into the room carrying a teacup. "Kendra, you have to sit up and drink this." When she didn't move, Loren handed the cup to Deanne, then gently ran her hand over Kendra's shoulders, down her back, then up again, the entire time murmuring softly. Once Kendra's breathing was normal, Loren took the cup from Deanne.

"Now sit up and drink this. I promise it will make you feel better."

Kendra hiccupped, wiped the tears from her face with the back of her hand, blew her nose into the tissue Deanne handed her, then sipped the tea.

"That's right. Drink it all up," Loren said.

Kendra drained the cup and took a deep breath. "It was all a lie. He told me he would always love me. We made plans for the future. We were going to have a family and be so happy. Now it's all over. How am I going to go on without him?"

"Fucking prick." Deanne paced across the floor. "If I ever see him again, I'm going to turn him into something slimy and disgusting."

"Not if I get to him first." Kendra gulped.

"Did he tell you where he was?" Loren asked.

Kendra shook her head.

"You know if we tried hard enough we could find him," Deanne stated.

"Why?" Loren asked.

Deanne narrowed her eyes. "So we could kick the shit out of him. Trust me, boyfriend doesn't want to mess with me right now."

Kendra yawned. "I'll never stop loving him, you know," she said as her eyes closed.

"The drug has taken effect," Loren said. "Help me levitate her into the bed."

Once they had Kendra tucked in, they tip-toed out.

In the living room, Deanne opened an antique curved-front cabinet where Loren kept her wine and liquor bottles. "I need something to calm *me* down. I am so pissed, I'll never sleep."

Loren nodded and sat heavily in a Queen Anne chair. "Fix me one, too. My brain is still trying to absorb the fact he actually said those things to her."

"Well, believe it." Deanne handed her a glass of wine before sitting on the couch. "How will we get her through this? She's going to hurt over him for months."

Loren sighed. "I know. We can stand by her and give her our support. We can also keep her mind occupied with other things."

"Thank the Gods we're opening the store. That should keep her plenty busy."

Loren sipped her wine thoughtfully. "I don't know if it will be enough. During the day, yes, but when she's alone at night, then the pain will hit her."

"You're right," Deanne said pouring herself more wine. "Although, there is the apartment. She's already been talking about how she'd like to fix it up. Shopping for furniture and kitchen stuff will keep her busy."

Loren brightened. "And painting the walls and finding artwork will take time."

"That's right. One way or another, we'll get her through this. And, if I ever lay eyes on Jared Dupre again, boyfriend will wish he'd stayed away."

****

Five weeks later.

The bright yellow banner announcing Enchantment's grand opening stretched across the ornate wrought iron balcony above the entrance. In glittering silver calligraphy, the store's name scrolled across the top of the large display window. A painted sign reading "Wicca Supplies, Blown Glass, Pottery, & Hand-Crafted Jewelry" hung on the smoked-glass front door.

On St. Phillip Street, the three girls stood in front of their store.

"It's absolutely awesome," Deanne said.

"All of our hard work has certainly paid off," Kendra added.

"The window display is incredible," Loren said.

Whimsical fairies, unicorns, and winged horses were just a few of the vibrant blown-glass mythical figurines Kendra had created. Deanne's uniquely shaped pottery bowls with their bold glazes held crystals and gemstones. Hand-dipped candles and colorful bottles of lotions and perfumes were Loren's contribution to the display.

The scents of herbs and incense greeted them as they entered the front door. Between the shelves of merchandise, the walls were painted with murals depicting Wiccan holidays: Ostara, the spring equinox and the lighting of the Beltane fire; Litha, the summer solstice; Samhain, the end of summer and the final harvest; Mabon, the thanksgiving feast and the autumnal equinox; and Yule, the celebration of the winter solstice. The ceiling was midnight blue with the stars of Orion in the center surrounded by the constellations of Gemini, Taurus, Eridanus, and Lepus.

Tiered shelves held ritual bath salts and oils, handmade soaps and shampoos, and fragrant candles. Crystal balls, miniature castles, and statues of gods, goddesses, and dragons were posed on cloth-draped tables. Scattered throughout were packets of herbs, decks of tarot cards, magic wands, embroidered altar cloths, divination tools, cauldrons, and scribing mirrors. In the center, a glass case held blown glass and jewelry.

Loren smiled. "Well, we did it."

"And it's all perfect," Deanne said. "So since we've got plenty of time until we open, let's head over to Café du Monde and get coffee and beignets."

"You two go without me. I'm too nervous to eat, and coffee will make me more jittery than I already am," Kendra said.

Loren gave Kendra a quick hug. "There's nothing left to do. The tourists are going to love the merchandise and will gawk at us wondering if we're real witches. And our fellow Wiccans will think the store is fabulous. So come with us and relax for a while. We'll be back in plenty of time to change before anyone arrives."

Kendra shook her head. "Really, you two go ahead. I want to be here in case the reporter covering the opening shows up early."

Deanne threw up her hands. "Come on, Loren, let's go. It would take a bulldozer to make her leave. Kendra, do you want us to bring some beignets back for you?"

"Sure. If the day is a flop, I'll drown my sorrows in powdered sugar."

As Deanne and Loren headed for the door, Loren stopped in front of the display window. "The crystal genie bottle looks pretty sitting there."

"Since the shape is so unusual, I thought it would be a nice addition," Kendra replied. "I still wish I knew who sent it. I don't recognize the fragrance, but I love it."

Deanne pulled out the gold stopper and sniffed. "Yuck," she exclaimed. "Girl, you're telling us you like this smell?"

Kendra nodded. "Very much."

Loren took the bottle from Deanne and sniffed. Scrunching up her nose, she cleared her throat. "Well, um, the bottle is pretty, but I think we should leave the stopper on."

Kendra took the bottle from Loren. "What's the matter with you two? Whatever is in here smells incredible."

Deanne lifted one brow. "I'll bet I know where it came from. I'll bet it's from your new admirer."

Kendra felt her cheeks turning pink. "He's not my admirer. He's just a nice man I met at Minerva's and who's new in New Orleans."

"Oh, yeah, he's just a nice man who's new in town. Is that why you've had dinner with him three times?"

"He asked about good restaurants, and I've been showing him around," Kendra replied with irritation.

"And I happen to like his company. He has a great sense of humor, and he's fun to be with, but that's all. Besides, if he sent the bottle, why didn't he just give it to me in person?"

"Maybe he's a romantic and likes giving you little surprises," Loren said. "If it is him, I think it's sweet."

Deanne turned the bottle in her hand. "It looks like the bottle Jeannie lived in on that old TV show. Perhaps it was meant to be a store-opening present, and they forgot to sign the card."

Kendra shrugged. "It doesn't really matter. I love the smell, and if you two don't, I'll take it back upstairs." She glanced at the clock. "If you're planning on getting coffee and beignets, you'd better get going."

Deanne snorted. "As soon as we start talking about Mr. Mysterious, she wants us to leave. Come on Loren. We'll drill her for more information later."

After they'd left, Kendra placed the bottle back in the window and gnawed on her bottom lip. Was she enjoying her new friend's company too much? Jared was gone and not coming back. When she thought of him, her heart still ached. There were nights when she cried herself to sleep. Loren and Deanne kept telling her she had to move on with her life, and that's what she was trying to do. So, if a few dinners with a new man made her happy, why feel guilty?

Kendra frowned. But there was the problem. While she was with him, she didn't feel guilty at all. In fact, Jared didn't even enter her mind. It wasn't until she was alone in the dark that the memories and the tears came. Sighing, vowing to think about all this later, she stepped up on a stool to rearrange wind chimes of sparkling crystal moons and stars. The glass bells hanging above the door behind her tinkled. Hoping it was the reporter from the Times Picayune, Kendra stepped off the stool and froze.

Like a physical blow, the certainty of who stood just out of sight hit her. *Sweet Goddess Mother, give me strength*, she prayed. Her stomach clenched into knots and her pulse raced. She desperately hoped she was wrong, but she knew she could never mistake his presence. The spicy scent of him and his intense energy created havoc in her mind and heart.

Damn him, damn him, damn him. Why did he have to come back? She was trying to learn how to live without him, moving on with her life.

She inhaled deeply. *I have to stand firm. I won't allow him to hurt me again. I won't let him upset me or ruin this day for me. And I'm sure as hell not going to let him back into my life.* She took another deep breath and recited a calming spell. She turned to face him, feeling composed and ready, but when her eyes met Jared's, a storm of emotions whirled through her. Anger and hurt jumbled together with memories of heated passion and words of love. Not trusting her voice, she stood still, hoping to regain her self-control.

Jared Dupre gave her the smile that used to melt her heart and said, "Hey, baby, you look great."

Temporarily speechless, Kendra could only stare. *You look great. Is that all he could say?* White-hot anger burned through her. She knew she should control her temper and act as cool as him, but thoughts of the wedding that never happened filled her mind. She relived the gut-wrenching pain when he told her he didn't love her and wasn't coming back. Now here he stood in front of her, smiling, acting as if he hadn't ripped out her heart.

Instead of tamping down her anger, Kendra gave it full rein. She slowly walked toward him. "You low-down witch bastard. How dare you waltz in here as if you've been gone a couple of days, not five weeks."

She made the row of tiny bells shatter, showering him with the fragments.

"Wait a minute," Jared said shaking off the shards. "I came here to explain to you what happened."

"Yeah, well, I'm not interested in hearing anything you have to say. The time for talking is long past. Unless you want to be turned into the toad you really are and give me the satisfaction of feeding you to the gators, I suggest you get the hell out of my store."

"Kendra, damn it, calm down. You have every right to be upset. Baby, I'm sorry. Please listen to me."

The floor beneath their feet shook. Red spikes of energy pulsated around her. "Don't call me *baby*." Her hands balled into fists. "Upset. Yes, since you left me for another woman two days before our wedding, I'd say I was a *little* upset." Kendra didn't know her voice could reach such volume. Seeing Jared wince, she increased it even more.

"I foolishly believed Philippe was really in trouble. Your phone call showed me how gullible I'd been. You bastard, you didn't even have the guts to tell me to my face. You slunk out of town like the snake you are. Now you have the nerve to walk in here and expect me to welcome you with open arms. Well, Jared, Lake Ponchartrain will freeze over before I take you back."

Jared's eyes darkened. Kendra knew his temper was rising. *Good, let him get pissed. Then hopefully he'll leave.*

Instead, he waved his hand and the shattered bells were back in place. As he came toward her, she retreated. Tall and lean, sinfully handsome in black jeans and a black open-necked shirt with rolled-back cuffs, Jared Dupre was an imposing and powerful witch. Kendra stiffened her spine and stood her ground.

"I'm not kidding, Jared. I want you to leave. In case you haven't noticed, I've gone on with my life. I have a new store which opens in less than an hour, and I have neither the time nor the interest in hearing anything you have to say."

"Well that's too damn bad because I have a lot to say. So control your energy spikes and listen to me. I told you I had to leave because Philippe was in trouble. I told you I loved you and asked you to trust me and wait for me. I couldn't explain because I didn't want you involved. Now I can tell you everything."

Kendra tossed her braid over her shoulder and her eyes flashed. "I'll leave my energy spikes right where they are, thank you very much. And I have no doubt Philippe was involved in all of this. He's probably the one who introduced you to that woman. Considering his debauched idea of fun, I can just imagine what you two have been up to."

"Trust me, sweetheart. What Philippe and I have been "up to" was anything but fun." His eyes turned stormy blue as he took another step closer. "And who's this woman you keep referring to?"

Images of the woman in the crystal ball passed through Kendra's mind. "The dark-haired woman I saw you with…"

"Kendra, what the hell are you talking about? I haven't been with any woman."

"Jared, stop lying. In the crystal ball, I saw you take her hand. She smiled at you and seemed awfully glad to see you."

"I don't know what the hell you saw, but it wasn't me. I was busy trying to save my brother's life."

"Then why did you call me and tell me you didn't love me and couldn't marry me?"

"I was forced to make that call. That's what I want to explain, but it's going to take longer than a few minutes. Please, let me see you later."

"Jared, I honestly can't imagine anyone forcing you to do anything you don't want to." She shook her head. "I may have been dumb enough to believe your lies once, but not anymore. As far as meeting you later, forget it."

He stopped inches from her. His intense gaze bore into hers. Before she realized what was happening, her energy spikes had disappeared and images of a clearing in the woods filled her mind. Thousands of stars lit the sky, and a warm breeze blew across her naked body. She lay in the middle of a blanket, her arms open to welcome Jared. As he entered her for the first time, and their magic merged, a warm silver mist surrounded them, growing brighter as their passion built. The wonderment of sweet release and the love she felt for him showed clearly on her glowing face.

The images in her mind faded, bringing her back to the present. Jared, the sneaky witch, had broken through her defenses, hitting her where she was most vulnerable.

"*Damn you,*" she cried. A fire sprinkler above Jared's head burst open releasing gallons of water. She quickly waved her hands to stop the deluge, but not before she had the satisfaction of seeing his stunned expression as cold water cascaded over him.

"Now hear me and hear me well, Jared Dupre. Don't you ever take me under like that again or, trust me, next time I'll do more than get you wet."

Quicker than she thought he could move, he grabbed her arms and pulled her to him, locking her in his strong embrace. His wet clothing instantly soaked her to the skin. Kendra opened her mouth to scream, but he covered her mouth with his. As his warm lips touched hers, the air around them crackled. Feelings she had tried to bury resurfaced. Searing desire coursed through her veins as she clung to the front of his shirt and melted under his seductive kisses.

"Kendra, love, I didn't intentionally leave you." He tenderly rubbed his thumb across her cheek. "Baby, I've never stopped loving you. You have to believe me." He held her close against him.

A moan of remembered pleasure escaped her lips as he ran his hands over her hips and caressed her bottom. The small part of her brain which was still thinking rationally warned her to stop, but his embrace felt so good, and his hands were making her body crave more.

He ran hot kisses along her neck. "I'm so sorry, baby. I never meant to hurt you. You've got to forgive me."

No, a voice in her head shouted. As she tried to surface from this lustful haze, she heard a faint tinkling sound followed by a female gasp and Jared's curses. Kendra's back was to the door. She heard running feet, then Loren's voice.

"Take your hands off her."

"Move out of the way, Loren, and give me a clear shot," Deanne yelled. "I'll castrate the son-of-a-bitch."

Once in full possession of her wits, Kendra was appalled at how easily she'd dropped her defenses and allowed him to seduce her. Furious with herself, she glared into Jared's amused eyes. Narrowing her own, she pushed at his chest.

"Unless you wish to become a eunuch, I suggest you release me."

He smiled, showing even white teeth. "Not until you tell Brunhilda over there to back off. As long as you're in my arms, I'm not in danger of losing a part of me I'd rather keep."

For a moment, Kendra hesitated. The image of the three of them taking him down was rather appealing, but eventually he'd get up, and the thought of the consequences made her shudder. Taking a deep breath, she looked over her shoulder at her two friends.

"It's all right. He wasn't hurting me."

"And you were certainly liking what I was doing," he murmured in her ear.

Kendra glared at Jared, her anger rekindled. Perhaps she would follow through with Deanne's threat after all. Her fury must have shown because he let her go and took a step back.

"Okay, okay, just calm down. I'll be good."

It wasn't until then that Kendra realized there wasn't a trace of water on them or on the floor.

She narrowed her eyes and he shrugged. "You were a little preoccupied, so I cleaned things up."

Kendra turned her back on him and faced her friends whose expressions of confused disbelief were identical. Deanne was the first to speak.

"What the hell has been going on here? And what is that,"—she pointed a red-tipped finger at Jared—"slimy eel doing here? And what were you doing in his arms?"

Kendra opened her mouth to reply, but quickly closed it. How could she tell them her fervent declaration she was over him had gone up in smoke the minute his lips touched hers, how easily she'd fallen under the magic of his touch?

"Jared was just leaving," Kendra said hurrying to stand next to Deanne and Loren. "We have to change. The store opens in twenty minutes."

"Not so fast." Loren touched Kendra's arm. "You haven't answered Deanne's question. What is he doing here?"

"It doesn't matter. He's leaving."

"No." The beads in Deanne's hair danced as she shook her head. "Not good enough. You swore to us you'd never let him back in your life, and here he is. Don't you remember what he did to you?"

"Yes, I remember. That is something I will never forget. Listen to me. He is not back in my life." And hopefully if she repeated this to herself enough, it would be true. She glanced at Loren. Perhaps she could mix her up some kind of potion to give her strength against Jared's seductive power.

"I'd like to be back in your life," Jared stated.

"Well, I guess you're shit out of luck, so why don't you leave?" Deanne said. "Besides, Kendra has a new man."

Jared narrowed his eyes. "Is that right? Didn't waste time, did you? Who the hell is he?"

"None of your business," Kendra snapped. "And

what do you mean by I *didn't waste time*? You have a lot of nerve. You told me you weren't coming back. What was I supposed to do, sit around hoping you'd change your mind and want me again? You need to remember who broke it off with whom before you start questioning what I do."

Deanne smirked. "And I can tell you he's ten times the man you are, you disgusting sack of rat droppings."

Kendra gritted her teeth. "Deanne, please don't. That isn't helping."

Jared turned stormy eyes on Deanne, the timbre of his voice making it clear he was losing patience. "Even though I enjoy hearing all the colorful names you've given me, I don't really give a damn what you think of me. This is between Kendra and me, so stay the hell out of it."

Loren whirled on Jared, her eyes flashing. "This is between you and Kendra? Mister, I don't think so. It was Deanne and I who helped Kendra pick up the pieces of her broken heart, so you can just stay out of her life for good this time."

Jared glared. "There's a reason I did what I did, and I'm not about to explain it to either of you. Until Kendra listens to what I have to say, I'm not going anywhere."

"Stop it. All of you, just stop it." Kendra didn't know whether to laugh, cry, or scream. She knew her friends were just trying to protect her, but this was getting out of control. "Okay, let's all take a deep breath."

She gave each girl a hug. "I appreciate your concern for me, but right now all we need to concentrate on is opening the doors to Enchantment, which is going to happen in…" Kendra glanced at her watch. "…approximately fifteen minutes. Why don't you two go upstairs and get changed, and I'll deal with Jared."

Kendra sighed seeing the stubborn set to their chins. "This was supposed to be our special day, and I'd like to keep it that way. So, please, go change and let me handle this."

Loren turned to Deanne and shrugged. "Kendra's right. We can't let him ruin our day. Let's go."

Deanne gave Jared one last scathing glance. Before Kendra could stop her, Deanne flung up her hand and hit Jared with a blast of energy.

Stumbling back, he cursed. "*Merde.*" When he turned thunderous eyes on Deanne, Kendra shouted, "Jared, don't." Loren grabbed Deanne's arm, dragging her away.

When he turned those same eyes on Kendra, she glared back. "I think for your own safety you'd better leave."

"I'm not leaving until you agree to hear me out." He took a deep breath as if to calm himself, then lowered his voice. "Kendra, this hasn't gone the way I'd hoped. I've messed this all up. Please, I know this isn't a good time, so let me take you to dinner and tell you everything that happened."

Speechless at his audacity, she gaped. Finally finding her voice, she said, "If you're under the impression that all it will take for me to forgive you is a few hot kisses, you're sadly mistaken. The sex between us was great, but I thought we had more. You didn't just hurt me; you ripped out my heart and crushed it. I'm not about to allow that to happen again." Her voice caught on a sob. She willed herself not to cry. She couldn't let him see how vulnerable to his words and touch she really was. *Remember the pain,* she told herself. *Remain strong.*

She watched him run his fingers through his hair. How she used to love to touch the thick strands, brush it back from his forehead as he looked down at her after making love. A lump caught in her throat. He took a step forward and held out his hand.

"Kendra, will you at least give me a chance to explain? Something I can't do in two minutes."

"And what makes you think I want to hear your explanation?"

He gave her an apologetic smile. "Because you're right, and there was, and still is, too much between us for you to give up on me so easily." He stepped closer and lifted her chin. "Besides, I know you still love me as much as I love you." Then his mouth covered hers.

When she felt the lure of his kiss taking her under, she gathered her willpower and stepped away. She took a deep breath. "You arrogant ass, this is exactly why I won't have dinner with you. I can't trust you to keep your hands to yourself." *And I'm even more afraid that I can't trust myself to tell you no,* she silently admitted.

A cuckoo clock with dancing elves announced the hour. "Damn. Jared, I don't have time for this. We're about to open."

Jared bent down until their eyes were inches apart. "Whether you want to hear this or not, I love you, I've always loved you, and I will never stop loving you." He softly kissed her lips. "I'll see you later." He turned and headed out the door.

Kendra stood silent, a kaleidoscope of emotions

battling inside her. Part of her wanted nothing more than to lose herself in his arms and pretend the past weeks had never happened.

The remembered pain resurfaced along with her vow to never let him hurt her like that again. Love. Pain. In her heart she knew which emotion was stronger, and as long as Jared Dupre was near, she was in danger of another heartbreak.

Chapter 13

Once outside of Enchantment, Jared found himself in a crowd of people gathering in front of the store. A plump frazzled-looking woman carrying a camera headed right for him.

"Hi, I'm Claudia Casteel from the *Times Picayune*. Isn't this wonderful? I can't wait to see the inside. I was supposed to be here earlier to interview the owners but I got held up covering some awful fashion show in the Garden District." Claudia slid her oversized glasses back up on her nose and peered at Jared. "I saw you come out of Enchantment. Are you one of them?"

He knew what she meant, but he couldn't resist teasing her. "One of *whom*?"

She waved her hand. "One of the witches. People say there aren't such things as witches, and the Wiccans just pretend to do magic, but I believe they're real. There're too many unexplained happenings around New Orleans for it not to be true."

Jared cocked his head. "I guess it's up to everyone to make up their own mind."

Claudia smiled. "You're absolutely right. As for me, I believe in witches. And I think you're one."

Just then an excited murmur went through the crowd. When Jared turned to see what had grabbed their attention, his breath caught. Kendra, Loren, and Deanne had stepped from the store onto the sidewalk, and what a bewitching trio they made. They wore identical handkerchief-draped dresses made of black gauzy material shot through with silver thread. Thin straps of the same material held up a V-shaped bodice where a moonstone nestled. Bangles of black and silver sparkled on their wrists and black strappy stiletto heels adorned their feet. Claudia gasped. "Oh, aren't they striking? A blonde, a brunette, and a red head. I hope I'm not too late for an interview." Without a backward glance at Jared, she hurried away, her camera bouncing on her hip.

Jared slipped on dark glasses and leaned against a large live oak, focusing his attention on Kendra standing on the opposite side of the street. He'd expected her to be royally pissed and could probably count himself lucky to have only silver bells and cold water dumped on him. What he hadn't been prepared for was the hurt in her eyes. That alone had almost done him in.

He planned to be on her doorstep when the store closed, and if the Gods were with him, tonight he'd be able to convince her he still loved her. Hopefully she'd listen to his explanation and forgive him. When he'd regained consciousness, he should have called, but he didn't want to explain over the phone all that had happened and how Adam had forced him to call her. She had to be able to see the truth in his eyes. He wanted to return to her strong and whole.

His mouth formed a thin line. Who was this woman Kendra kept accusing him of being with? And who the hell was this *new guy* she was seeing?

Kendra's light laughter drifted across the street interrupting his thoughts. His mind drifted back to her eighteenth birthday and the summer solstice when the coven had asked her to light the ceremonial candles and cast the circle. She stood barefoot in a flowing dress of ice blue that showed every supple curve. When a shaft of sunlight struck her long red hair turning it to burnished gold she glowed like a young goddess. He knew, despite the six years' difference in their ages, she had to be his. Four months later, on the eve of Samhain, he laid claim to her body while she had unknowingly claimed his heart.

Taking her mind back to that night had been a chancy thing to do, but he hoped that reminding her of what they once had would soften her resistance. He knew he had a long way to go to regain her trust.

He watched Deanne and Loren go inside Enchantment while Kendra remained out front greeting customers. Deanne's and Loren's hostility was going to be another obstacle. Like it or not, he was back, and they'd have to get used to it.

His eyes narrowed as a man stopped and put his arm around Kendra, then bent to kiss her cheek. The intimate smile she gave in return made his gut clench. Guessing it was the new man in Kendra's life, Jared cursed colorfully in both French and English. *Enjoy her now, asshole, because she's always been and will always be mine.*

The man glanced his way and Jared's blood ran cold. "Son-of-a-bitch." The person staring back at him was someone he thought he'd never see again, someone he thought he'd killed. He had a moment of satisfaction seeing the surprise on Adam Montief's face when he recognized Jared standing in the shadows. Then Adam's expression changed. He held Kendra against him and gave Jared an arrogantly triumphant smile.

Jaw locked, fists clenched, Jared watched as Adam followed Kendra into Enchantment. What the hell was going on? The demented bastard was supposed to be dead. Adam was a powerful witch, but even witches couldn't come back from the dead—or fly. The last time he'd seen Adam, Jared had plunged the steel tip of his falcata into his chest and sent him over a cliff to the rocks and the ocean below.

Jared stepped into a dark building entrance where he could still see the front of Enchantment but wasn't visible himself. He pulled out his cell phone and prayed the damn thing worked. There was static on the line, but thankfully he heard Philippe's voice.

"Hey, bro', it's me," Jared said when Philippe answered. "Is everything all right?"

"Yeah, sure. Why? Are you home? Have you been able to see Kendra?"

"Yes, and things didn't go all that well, but that's not my biggest problem. Adam Montief is here, and he's with Kendra."

"No way. That monster is dead."

"Unless he had a twin we knew nothing about, which I doubt, he's alive and well. I wanted to make sure you were safe and he hadn't messed with you or the McBrides."

"Yeah, no problem, we're all fine."

Not only had the McBrides' and their coven been a huge help during his and Philippe's healing process, their influence in Philippe's life was remarkable. Violet, with her gentle ways, had read to him, and they'd talked for hours. Philippe had soon opened up, sharing with them his internal turmoil over his direction in life. When Jared had left, Philippe was even talking about painting again.

"I don't understand. How can Adam be alive?" Philippe asked.

"Hell if I know, but he is. And now he's after Kendra."

When Jack and the coven had rescued Jared and Philippe, they'd also searched the rocks for Adam's body. They hadn't found it, so they assumed he was swept out to sea.

Jared watched as a group of giggling teenagers came out of Enchantment, happy and care free. How many innocent lives had Adam destroyed? He was convinced Adam and Daman had learned all they could about Philippe before planning his destruction in order to get to Jared. Now Adam had his sights on Kendra.

"Jared, I swear to you, I've learned my lesson. No more screwing up. As I said, I love it here, and I love Violet."

"I'm glad to hear Violet is a special girl."

"I'll never be able to repay you for getting me out from under that man's control. I've done some stupid things, but getting involved with the Montiefs was beyond stupid."

"We've had this conversation, and I told you that you don't owe me anything. Besides, if you hadn't been able to summon the McBrides, we'd both be dead."

"All I did was crawl to your mirror and ask for help. I didn't even know if it would work. We both have Angelique's ghost to thank. Violet can't believe how freaked she got when Angelique materialized in their kitchen. I'm still convinced that just before Adam fell off the cliff, I saw a woman's form standing behind you."

Jared recalled the burst of energy that had shot through his body. "Something sure as hell got me onto my feet. I assume it was her."

"That reminds me. The Montief school is temporarily closed. Right after you left, we spoke with some of the boys, who were grateful to have finally gotten away from Adam. There are some still living in the compound who say they will continue with the school, but without the dark magic. We were told that after Adam went over the cliff, the boys heard a sound like someone screaming in pain coming from inside the library, but when they went to investigate, no one was there."

Jared thought about the broken, disillusioned people Adam had left in his wake. "Probably one of the students mourning their leader's death."

Philippe snorted. "You can't kill the devil."

"What I'd like to know is how Adam was able to recuperate so quickly, get back here, and win Kendra over." Jared didn't know how badly he'd hurt him, but he'd felt his falcata sink into Adam's flesh and he'd watched him fall off the cliff. His injuries had to have been severe.

Adam's sword had slashed deep cuts in Jared's body. His last thrust had entered Jared's abdomen causing internal injuries. He'd been delirious for days, and the McBrides' coven doubted he'd survive. While he'd been unconscious, Jared had dreamt of Angelique and the ghost in the flowered dress.

"Listen, Philippe, I've got to go. I want you to keep your guard up and stay alert."

Jared ended his call as Adam came out of

Enchantment. Adam glanced up and down the street, then headed away from where Jared stood. *Okay, let's see where you go.*

Jared flicked his wrist and a New Orleans Saints ball cap and matching jersey appeared in his hand. He replaced his own shirt with the new one and adjusted the hat down low on his forehead. Keeping his distance, he followed Adam through the narrow streets of the French Quarter, past sidewalk musicians, gift shops selling everything from T-shirts to Mardi Gras masks, a Cajun restaurant with patio tables where people sat eating gumbo, a small grocery advertising muffalettas, and a wine and cheese shop.

Adam neared the crowded French Market on Decatur, and Jared quickened his pace. They wove their way past endless displays of tourist souvenirs. The pungent breeze carried the smell of the Mississippi. An air horn blasted as a riverboat churned past.

When Adam took a seat in the outdoor section of the Café Du Monde, Jared scanned the crowd. He sensed the energy of other witches, but no one seemed interested in him or Adam. As he watched, a young waitress took Adam's order. To Jared's dismay, she smiled and seemed instantly smitten. He supposed Adam's rugged good looks could be attractive to women, but couldn't they see the evil lurking behind his eyes? The thought of that witch anywhere near Kendra brought the taste of bile into his throat. He swallowed it back as his hands curled into fists. He knew it would take every bit of self-control he possessed not to take Adam down, even in a public place.

He focused his energy inward until he felt calm

enough to confront his enemy. When he slid into the seat across the table, he was able to control his urge to punch the self-satisfied smirk off Adam's face.

"Well, look who finally showed up." Adam leaned back in his seat. "Surprised to see me?"

Jared shrugged. "Considering that the last time I saw you, your ass was going over a cliff, I would say so. I assume one of your fellow demons rescued you from Hell?"

Adam's expression turned hard. "And it seems you have our whore of an ancestor to thank for saving you. After telling Kendra you didn't love her anymore, I was wondering if you'd have the balls to come back. As usual, you're too late. I told you I'd have some fun with your girl, and I've done just that. In fact, I've done more than have fun, I've won the lady's heart. Tell me, Dupre, how does it feel knowing she's been with me?"

Jared folded his arms on top of the table and leaned forward, his self- control slipping. The smile he gave Adam could have turned his steaming cup of coffee to ice. Jared's words were a low growl. "Now listen, you son-of-a-hag, I don't know why you're not dead and rotting in Hell but hear me well. Kendra is mine, and she'll always be mine. So if you ever go near her again, I'll make sure you scream in agony while you die. I'll scatter your parts so far and wide they'll never be able to find them all. So I suggest you get the fuck out of New Orleans and never come back." Jared could feel Adam's mounting fury and leaned in closer. "Unless you'd like to finish this right now. If so, I'd be happy to oblige."

The table vibrated with the suppressed power that shot between the two men. Coffee spilled from Adam's cup and splashed onto the floor. Powdered sugar rose in a pale cloud. The waitress, wide-eyed, slowly backed away.

Now it was Adam's turn to lean in. "I'm not dead because you're a fucking poor excuse for a witch who doesn't have enough power to do the job right. Your family has always been cowardly and weak like that pathetic brother of yours. So I'll not only take great satisfaction in killing you, I'll see to it Philippe watches you die." Adam's smile was pure malice. "As far as Kendra, you fucked that up as well. So while you'll be the one lying in a grave, Kendra will be lying beneath me in my bed, moaning her pleasure."

Both men were halfway to their feet when Jared felt a strong hand clamp down on his shoulder.

"Don't either of you boys make a move," a harsh rumbling voice said.

Ready to strike, Jared stared into the black beefy face of Woodrow Charbonneau, Deanne's father and a man he'd known since childhood. Woodrow kept the pressure of his hand on Jared as he smiled. "Nice to see you back, son. Now whatever problem you're having with this gentleman, I suggest you take it out of here. The hostile energy from you two is so palpable you're attracting attention, and not just from your own kind."

Jared's rage was still flowing hot. If it hadn't been for Woodrow's timely intervention, he knew either he or Adam would be lying dismembered in the middle of the cafe. He took a few calming breaths and stared into Adam's burning eyes. "It's okay, Woodrow. He was just leaving."

Adam's eyes shifted from Jared to Woodrow before he sneered. "This isn't over, Dupre. Next time we meet, you won't have your protector to save your ass." He gave them both a contemptuous glare and turned to leave.

Before he took a step, Jared spoke. "Remember, if you want to live, you'll heed my warning and keep your filthy hands off Kendra."

Adam snorted derisively. "I don't think it's up to you who Kendra allows to touch her. According to her, you gave up that right when you left her. You lost her trust. I now have it. So perhaps it's you who should keep your filthy hands off." Without another word, Adam strolled from the restaurant.

"You look like you could use something stronger than coffee," Woodrow said, patting Jared's shoulder. "Let's go get us a shot and a beer, and you can tell me what the hell is going on."

A short time later they sat in Finnegan's bar sipping glasses of ice-cold stout. Jared filled Woodrow in on what had happened.

"So you're telling me this Adam tried to kill you over some family feud you know nothing about?" Woodrow asked.

Jared nodded. "He drugged and almost killed Philippe. He didn't do such a bad job on me either. I had some deep cuts on my arms and legs, the worst injury being a sword wound through my abdomen. Thankfully, the coven had some strong competent healers, but it was still a slow recovery. I understand both Philippe and myself were out of it for a few days."

"And Adam?"

Jared hesitated, then sighed. "I stabbed the bastard and sent him over a cliff. Until this morning, I thought he was dead. Now he's trying to use Kendra to get to me."

"Do Kendra's parents know she could be in danger?"

"I don't see how. An hour ago, I didn't know myself. Besides, if they've met Adam, I'm sure he has them convinced he's a perfectly nice guy. Considering the way they probably feel toward me, I'm sure they wouldn't listen to anything I have to say, or believe me if they did."

Woodrow studied Jared with sympathetic eyes. "Unfortunately, I'd say you're right. A number of folks were real upset. Son, we had no idea what you and Philippe were going through. I'm sure once everyone hears the truth, you'll have all the support you need."

Jared scowled and drained his beer glass. "Yeah, but in the meantime the list of people pissed at me is growing. And your daughter is at the top of that list."

Woodrow cocked his head. "You've seen Deanne?"

Jared nodded. "This morning at the store. Trust me, it wasn't a fond homecoming. She and Loren have appointed themselves Kendra's personal bodyguards, and their main objective is to keep me as far away from her as possible."

Woodrow sighed. "Those three girls are as close as sisters. Did you know that after you left, Kendra hid out at Loren's cottage until they opened the store? She did nothing but guide tours and make those blown glass figurines. She didn't want to see anyone except her mother, her brother, Deanne, and Loren. The rest of the coven tried to help, but she sent us away. When the girls came to the restaurant and told Serene and me of their plans to open the store, we were concerned about them taking on such a responsibility, but we were thrilled Kendra was showing an interest in something."

"Woodrow, if I had it to do all over again, I'd definitely handle the situation differently, but I can't turn back time. I did what I thought I needed to do to save my brother and Kendra from a monster."

Woodrow patted Jared's shoulder. "I know, son. Now that Adam's in New Orleans, we can help you. Even if there are those who aren't pleased with you, they still care about you and Kendra."

Jared hesitated. He'd like to be able to tell Woodrow he could handle this on his own, but considering Kendra's current state of mind, he didn't know if she'd ever forgive him or allow him back into her life. So for the time being, Woodrow and the others in the coven were trustworthy people he could count on.

"Thanks. Since Kendra is barely speaking to me, I'm happy to accept your help."

"Good. What do you want us to do?"

"Kendra doesn't know who Adam is or how dangerous he is. Tonight I plan on putting a security charm around her store." Jared frowned. "She needs protection at home as well, but I just realized I don't even know where she's living."

"That's simple—in the apartment above the store," Woodrow replied.

"I also want to block Adam's ability to spy on her, so I'll put a charm around Kendra as well. If you and the others could keep an eye on her when she's out, that would be a big help."

"No problem. I'll spread the word. And what will you do?"

"Oh, I have two simple tasks—convincing Kendra

I love her, and it was necessary for me to leave; and convincing her that her new boyfriend is a demented killer."

Woodrow smiled. "Good luck, son. I wouldn't want to be in your shoes for all of Midas' gold."

Chapter 14

"I'm happily exhausted." Loren kicked off her heels, sat in a high-backed chair, and accepted a chilled glass of wine from Kendra.

"I'm too exhausted to be excited," Deanne said, flopping down on the couch next to a disgruntled Clementine. "I think everyone in New Orleans came through the store."

"Wasn't it wonderful?" Kendra clapped her hands and twirled around on the braided rug that stretched across her living room. "It's a good thing we have extra stock. We about sold out of everything."

It was six o'clock and the three of them were in Kendra's apartment above Enchantment. She opened the French doors letting in the soft sound of an acoustic guitar from the street below. The last rays of the sun reflected off caramel-colored walls illuminating white-framed paintings of nineteenth-century New Orleans. Fringed lamps sat on antique end tables beside the mismatched sofa and overstuffed chairs. Colorful woven rugs were scattered across the worn hardwood floor. Opposite the French doors, narrow bookcases on either side of the gas fireplace held her library on magic, glass blowing, and the romance novels she couldn't live without. Small tables held bowls of crystals and the whimsical glass figures she created.

"How can you have so much energy?" Deanne

asked. "We've been on our feet for hours."

Kendra laughed. "I'm on a success high. We kicked butt, and Claudia Casteel from the *Picayune* is going to give us a great review."

Loren sipped her wine. "She's fascinated with magic. She kept asking me if I was a witch and could I perform a séance for her."

"What did you tell her?" Kendra asked.

"I told her if she wanted to see ghosts, she should take one of your mother's cemetery tours."

"Good answer," Kendra said. "Mom could take her to St. Louis Number One to meet Marie Laveau."

Deanne sat up so quickly she almost spilled her wine. "*That's* who Marie was talking about. Has to be."

Loren and Kendra looked questioningly at each other, then back at Deanne who waved her hand in impatience. "A week ago, I was in the cemetery visiting Marie, and she was pretty upset. She said there was a new force of dark magic in New Orleans and for the three of us to be careful."

"And you're just now getting around to sharing this tidbit?" Loren asked.

"We've been so busy it slipped my mind. Besides, you know Marie can be over protective. It has to be Jared she was talking about. And it's Kendra who's in danger."

Loren and Deanne's eyes were now on Kendra, who frowned back. "Deanne, Marie couldn't have been talking about Jared. He's a low-life scum-of-the-earth jerk, but he's not evil."

"You don't know what he's been doing or who he's been involved with while he's been gone," Loren said.

"And it's just too much of a coincidence Marie tells me that and he shows up a few days later," Deanne added.

Kendra gnawed her bottom lip. It was true she didn't know what Jared had been up to, but becoming a dark witch was hard to believe. On the other hand, *that woman* could have seduced him into some weird cult. She sighed. They never took Marie's warnings lightly. Marie had been watching over the three of them since childhood, and more than once her premonitions had kept them out of trouble.

"We'll have to cast a protective spell around you. I'll make you up a *gris gris* bag of my best herbs," Loren was saying as Kendra returned from her musings. "But the best protection is for you to stay away from Jared." She cocked her head. "Okay, spill it. I can tell by the expression on your face there's something you're not telling us."

Kendra braced herself for their reaction. "Jared wanted to take me to dinner tonight and explain why he left and where he'd been."

Deanne set her glass down on the trunk Kendra used as a coffee table. "And you told him what?"

"I told him no. But I have a feeling he's going to show up here anyway."

"That's easy enough to take care of," Loren said. "We won't answer the door."

Kendra sighed. "I know how stubborn he is. He won't give up until I hear him out. I should just go to dinner with him and get it over with."

"What?" Loren and Deanne cried as one.

"Are you crazy?" Deanne rose to her feet, her dress swirling around her knees. "Girl, how could you

143

stomach being in the same room with that man?" She placed her hands on her hips. "Besides, I thought we were going to go out and celebrate our success. Instead you're talking about dumping your best friends to go out with the man who not only broke your heart but might be some crazed demon as well."

Kendra sighed. "First, I don't think Jared is a crazed demon." She held up her hand forestalling Deanne. "Wait a minute and let me finish. But I'll be sure to be on my guard. As far as dumping my friends, didn't we decide we'd wait and see if we were a success or failure before we celebrated?"

Loren laughed. "She's got us there."

"And," Kendra continued, "we told Deanne's parents we'd pick a day when they could set aside room in the restaurant for a party."

Deanne scowled. "Okay, so we can wait, but that doesn't mean you have to go out with Jared. What about Thaddeus? He's a great guy. Are you just going to ignore him because the asshole is back?"

"No, I'm not going to ignore Thaddeus. I still plan on seeing him. Jared being here has nothing to do with that relationship."

"Deanne, I'm afraid you're wasting your breath," Loren stated. "She's determined to see Jared, and nothing we say is going to stop her." She turned to Kendra. "Can you at least explain to us why you're considering this?"

"Because I need closure. I don't want to spend the rest of my life wondering why he left me." Her eyes filled with tears. "Can't you understand that?"

They each put an arm around Kendra.

"We just don't want him to hurt you again," Loren

said. "Promise us you'll have dinner with him, hear what he has to say, and come straight home."

"That's right," Deanne agreed. "Do not let him sweet-talk you, especially into bed."

Kendra shook her head. "That's the last thing you have to worry about."

Deanne's brows rose questioningly. "Is that right? Things seemed pretty hot and heavy when we caught you in his arms earlier. Girl, you melt like ice in July when he looks at you with his baby blues."

Loren nodded. "I'm afraid Deanne's right. You've never had any self-control around that man. Perhaps we should go with you tonight just to be sure you don't do something you'll regret."

Kendra sighed with exasperation. "Okay, say I agree with everything you're saying, but things have changed between Jared and me. I'm not the naive love-struck girl I once was. I'm perfectly capable of having dinner with Jared and not ending up in his bed."

Loren squeezed Kendra's hand. "Tell us the truth. Do you still love him?"

Kendra turned away from Loren's intense gaze. Coming from a family of healers, Loren could easily perceive emotions. "I don't honestly know." Her voice was barely above a whisper. "He hurt me more than I ever imagined, and I never want to experience that again. I also don't know if I could ever trust him." She frowned. "He actually acted surprised when I asked him about that woman we saw in the crystal ball."

"How did he explain what he said to you on the phone?" Loren asked.

"He said he was forced to make the call and didn't mean what he said."

145

"Forced by whom?" Deanne asked.

Loren bit her lower lip. "Perhaps he's telling the truth."

"That's just great," Deanne said with exasperation. "Encourage her to trust him and watch all the work we've done to help her get over him go right out the window the second he walks through the door. I just know she's going to let him charm her right back into his arms."

Kendra tried to conceal her annoyance. "I didn't say I was going to take him back. I'm just not sure how I feel about him." Seeing Jared, and her reaction to his kiss, had shaken her more than she wanted to admit to her friends. She'd truly thought she'd begun to heal and could go on with her life, and Thaddeus might be a part of that life. But now her wounds had reopened, filling her with pain and memories of her love for Jared as well.

Loren squeezed Kendra's hand. "We understand you need to see him for closure, but please be strong and do not let him talk you into doing something you'll regret."

"That's right," Deanne added. "Are you sure you don't want us to follow you? We could be in disguise, and if he tries to seduce you we can turn him into a troll."

Kendra grinned. "Thanks, but I don't think it will be necessary. If he tries to seduce me, I'm perfectly capable of turning him into a troll myself. Besides, I don't know for sure if he'll show up."

"Oh, he'll show all right," Deanne said. "And I still think by agreeing to go to dinner you're making it too easy for him."

Kendra paused. "Well, there might be a way to make him suffer."

"We're listening," Deanne said.

"When the arrogant ass brings me home, he'll think I can't resist him, and I'll ask him to come upstairs, but I'll just nicely thank him for dinner and close my door in his face."

"Yes, I love it." Loren clapped her hands. "You also need to use some of my passion perfume. It's been known to make men howl at the moon. Oh, and I have body lotion down in the store."

"I'm not sure about this," Deanne said. "I'm afraid leading Jared Dupre on is asking for major trouble."

"Deanne, will you please trust me? I can handle Jared. Now in case he does come, I have to find something to wear."

Deanne smiled. "All right. If you're determined to do this, you need something low cut and short-skirted."

"I have that little black halter dress I got on Royal Street."

"Perfect," Deanne said. "And those strappy stilettos."

"What about her hair?" Loren asked. "Should she wear it up?"

Deanne shook her head. "Leave it down, but not loose. She needs to gather it up in a clip so the curls flow down her back. There's nothing sexier than long hair on bare skin."

"Okay, I'll go change." Kendra frowned. "And hopefully I'm right and he's coming, and I won't be all dressed up with nowhere to go."

"We could be so lucky," Deanne murmured.

Kendra headed toward her bedroom, then stopped.

In disbelief she turned to face her friends. Her cell phone had begun to cheerfully play "When the Saints Go Marching In" while there was a persistent buzzing of her downstairs bell.

"Damn," she exclaimed and hurried to grab her phone. "Oh, damn," she said as she read the caller ID. "It's Thaddeus. What do I do?" *Buzz, buzz, buzz.* "And that's probably Jared."

"Answer the phone," Loren said getting to her feet. "I'll stall Jared before he lets himself in."

"I'm going to sit right here and enjoy the show," Deanne said, pouring herself another glass of wine.

Kendra, phone in hand, left the room. "Hello," she said after shutting the bedroom door.

"Hey, Kendra, it's Thaddeus. I hope I'm not calling at a bad time."

Kendra stifled a laugh at the absurdity of it all. "No, it's fine. Deanne, Loren, and I were just relaxing."

"So, how did it go? Was your opening a success?"

"Yes, thanks. We practically sold out."

"Great. I was calling to see if I could take you to dinner to celebrate."

She silently groaned. This was turning into a farce. She heard the door to the apartment open and Jared's voice. To keep from making this more complicated than it already was, she chose the easiest way out. "Thaddeus, I appreciate the offer, but it's been a long day and I'm awfully tired. Would you mind if we do it another time?"

"No problem. You get some sleep, and I'll see you later."

"Thanks." As she hung up, the crystal genie bottle she'd retrieved from the display window caught her eye. If Thaddeus had sent it to her, it was a wonderful thoughtful gift. But why not acknowledge he'd done so? She'd have to come right out and ask him the next time she saw him. Kendra removed the stopper and inhaled deeply. She didn't care if Loren or Deanne liked the fragrance, she did. Just then she heard Deanne's raised voice, "You hurt her again, and you'll have to answer to me and, trust me, boyfriend, it will get real ugly."

Sighing, Kendra rubbed her temples and silently prayed, *Mother Goddess, give me strength. Help me not let my guard down.*

A short time later, changed, with fresh makeup on and her hair a riot of curls down her back, Kendra murmured a quick spell for courage, clasped her gold unicorn, and stepped into the living room. *Okay, this is it. You will remain distant and aloof. You will not let him seduce you with sweet words and promises.* But she couldn't stop her heart from doing a little flip when he turned and smiled. His hair, a little long in the back, was windblown across his forehead. The open-necked shirt was deep burgundy, his leather jacket, jeans, and low boots all black.

As his eyes slid over her, the pure lust filling their blue depths was exactly the reaction she'd hoped for.

"You look…"

Kendra lifted an arched brow. "Yes?"

He hesitated. "Incredible."

She smiled. "Do I?"

"You're trying to drive me crazy, right?"

Her smile widened. "Is it working?"

"Oh, yeah, baby, it's working."

"Good."

For a few seconds, they just stood staring at one another, until the pull of his sexual energy sent Kendra's thoughts in a direction she didn't intend to go.

"I have something for you." He reached into his jacket pocket and removed a small paper bag from Laura's Candies. "I assume you still like chocolate."

Kendra inwardly groaned. *Chocolates from my favorite sweet shop. He always knew my weaknesses.* She cleared her throat. "Thank you. You shouldn't have." She noticed they were alone. "Where are Deanne and Loren?"

"They couldn't stomach being in the same room with me, so they left."

She cocked her head. "What are you doing here anyway? I thought I said I wouldn't go out with you."

"I told you I'd see you later." His lips twitched. "Besides, by the way you're dressed, it seems you were expecting me."

Kendra gritted her teeth. "What if I told you I was going out with my new friend?" *Good,* she thought, *that wiped the cockiness off his face.*

Jared leaned against the kitchen counter and folded his arms. "Then I'd tell you, you'd be going out with a demented killer."

Kendra rolled her eyes. "Really, Jared, that's a bit much."

He straightened and his face hardened. "Kendra, I'm not kidding. Adam Montief is an evil bastard who hurts people."

Kendra knitted her brows. "Who's Adam Montief?"

Confusion filled Jared's eyes. "You said he was your new boyfriend."

150

"My new friend's name is Thaddeus Marsh."

Jared hesitated. "Was your new boyfriend the man who was with you outside of Enchantment earlier?"

"Yes, that's right."

Jared's mouth formed a thin line. "Then he's lying to you. His real name is Adam Montief."

For a few seconds, Kendra stared at Jared. "Obviously, you have Thaddeus confused with this Adam person."

"There's no confusion. He's the same man, and he's a monster."

"How can you say that about someone you've never met?"

"Oh, trust me, we've met. It's because of him I missed our wedding and Philippe and I almost died."

An icy chill formed in Kendra's stomach. She opened and closed her mouth before she could ask, "What do you mean you almost died?"

He walked to the French doors which overlooked the street. "It's a complicated story, but the short version is that Adam Montief is the witch who kidnapped Philippe and threatened to kill him if I didn't break it off with you. Apparently one of my ancestors killed one of his over two hundred years ago, and now he wants revenge. I followed him to his compound on an island off the coast of Connecticut. We fought, and the last time I saw him he was going over a cliff into the Atlantic."

Incredulous, Kendra shook her head. "I don't know who this Adam person is, but if what you're telling me is true, he can't be Thaddeus, because he's alive."

"I know it sounds crazy. And I didn't explain it very well. The thing you need to know is that Adam

Montief and Thaddeus are the same person."

"But you just told me you watched him die. How could they be the same?"

"I don't know the answer to that, but I intend to find out."

She crossed the living room toward him. "Do you realize how outrageous this story sounds?"

"Yes, but it's the truth."

"Jared, you and I both know people don't come back from the dead. So how could Adam be the person I know?"

"He's the man I saw you with outside Enchantment. Adam Montief is one of the most powerful, and evil, witches I have ever encountered, so he may have somehow saved himself and healed quickly."

She threw up her hands in exasperation. "It couldn't be him. Thaddeus is a kind, sensitive person who wouldn't hurt anyone."

"Listen to me. *Kind* and *sensitive* are the last words to describe Adam. He likes to have people under his control, especially women." He stepped closer and raised her chin until he could look directly into her eyes. "And I'm afraid he's already working on you. Why else would you doubt me?"

His touch sent a jumble of conflicting emotions racing through her. There had been a time when she would never have doubted him, but that was before he destroyed her trust. Did she truly know the man standing in front of her? Mother of the Gods, how had her life become such a mess? She batted his hand away and stepped back. "First, no man, including you, has me under their control. And if this is all true, why didn't you call and let me know what had happened? If you care as much as you say, why didn't you trust me enough to include me?"

"I didn't include you, because I wanted you out of harm's way. I had enough on my hands without having to worry about you being in danger too. I didn't call you because for most of the time I was delirious and unconscious. When I was lucid again, I thought about calling, but after all those awful things I said to you on the phone, I wanted to talk to you in person."

"And the woman? Where does she fit in?"

Jared gritted his teeth. "For the love of Odin, who is this woman you keep talking about?"

Kendra reached for the open bottle of wine on the counter and poured herself a glass. She took a long sip before turning to Jared. "Deanne, Loren, and I tried to find you in the crystal ball. The image kept fading in and out, but I clearly saw you take the hand of a tall dark-haired woman."

For a moment he just stared, then let out a long breath. "It must have been Sylvia McBride."

"Who's she?"

"She and her husband are a great couple who helped me out. In fact, your wonderful boyfriend was instrumental in their daughter's death."

"What?"

"That's right. Their daughter's body was found at the bottom of a cliff, and he made it seem like suicide. All because she wanted to leave him."

Her emotions whirling, she needed to walk and clear her head. She grabbed a shawl and swung her black straw bag onto her shoulder. "I'm dressed up, hungry, and I'm going to dinner," she said, heading for the stairs.

"Running from me isn't going to change the truth," he called, following her down, slamming the apartment door behind him.

At the end of her patience, her hand on the knob to the street door, Kendra turned. "Jared, I want you to go away."

"Well, that's too damn bad because I'm not leaving." He reached for her and held her close. "Don't you see, he's already turning you against me."

Tears formed in her eyes and she blinked them away. "No one turned me against you. I thought I knew you, Jared, but the person I knew wouldn't have left me and ripped my heart out."

The anger in his eyes softened. "Baby, please believe me, I would have never done that to you if I hadn't had a good reason."

Before she could reply, his mouth covered hers. She feebly pushed at his chest fighting her body's instant reaction, but as his skillful lips teased and caressed, she knew her resistance was slipping away. She let out a soft sigh and wrapped her arms around his neck and for the moment lost herself in his kiss. This was the man she knew. The one person who could bring her body to life, fill her with love, and satisfy her completely.

He ran his hand down her back and across her bottom. "We need to get off these stairs," he murmured against her mouth.

"Hmm, what?"

He nibbled her neck. "Let's go upstairs where I can please you properly."

A tiny voice in the back of her mind told her to

stop, but when his hand stroked her breast, she ignored it. When his thumb circled her nipple, she moaned and the voice got louder. When his hand cupped her between her legs, the voice became a persistent roar. Breathing in shallow gasps, she stepped from his embrace. "Jared, no. Sex isn't the answer to our problems. It will only make things worse."

He grinned. "When did sex ever make anything worse?"

"I'm serious." She rubbed her temples. "I've got an incredible headache. I'm going back upstairs and go to bed."

"Come here." He pressed his fingers on either side of her face and gently massaged while murmuring softly.

The tension instantly drained away. "Thanks."

He kissed her palm. "You're welcome. I didn't mean for tonight to go so badly. Let me take you to dinner. We can start over."

Emotionally drained, she hesitated.

"You have to eat, don't you? And you don't want to waste that killer dress, do you?"

She let out a long breath. "All right, but just dinner. Despite your reappearance and your outrageous accusations, I had a fantastic grand opening so you can take me to Antoine's." Without a backward glance, she stepped onto the sidewalk and headed toward Royal Street.

"Well, I'm glad my return didn't totally ruin your day."

She glanced over her shoulder. "Jared, I'm serious. I want to have a nice meal and talk of general things. We can save our discussion of why you chose the most special day of my life to leave me, humiliate me, and break my heart, for another time."

Jared winced. "Nice shot." He fell into step next to her.

"You can't deny that's what happened."

He shook his head. "No, I can't. But if you'd listen to me instead of being so damn pig- headed, you'd understand I'm telling the truth."

The sidewalk became crowded forcing Jared to follow behind her. Kendra knew he was staring at her butt, so she made sure to swing her hips just enough to make her dress sway tantalizingly.

"Are you sure you can walk all the way to the restaurant in those shoes?"

"Oh, I can do all kinds of things in these shoes."

"I'll bet you can," he murmured.

Chapter 15

One of New Orleans' oldest restaurants, Antoine's is noted for its fourteen dining rooms and one of the finest wine cellars in the city. Their cuisine and special attention to service are legendary. Kendra and Jared were led to a corner table in the main dining room. The mirrored walls reflected candlelit tables laid with white linen cloths, fine china, and crystal.

"What do you feel like having?" Jared asked.

A slow smile spread across Kendra's face. "Why, the most expensive items on the menu." Her brows rose. "I assume you can afford it."

Jared scanned the wine list. "You can have anything your little heart desires, just ask."

"Good. You can order the wine. I'll begin with the *chair de crabes ravigote* for an appetizer. Then I'll have the *salade de coeur de palmier*. For my main course, how about the New York *bifstek au vin rouge et a la sauce au poivre* with their famous *pommes de terre soufflé*."

Jared grinned. "Hungry, are you?"

"Ravenous. I guess it's all the excitement of the day."

Jared leaned in close and whispered, "I used to be able to satisfy your ravenous appetites, remember?"

The low sexy sound of his voice sent a chill of delight tingling through her body. She quickly suppressed it. "See how far I've come? You've been replaced by food."

Jared snorted. "*Touché*, sweetheart."

After placing their orders, they sat in a charged silence gazing into each other's eyes. Kendra frantically tried to banish visions of him leaning over her, his eyes dark with passion, his voice raw with need, his skillful hands bringing her body to life.

"Let's go."

She blinked. "What?"

"I think we should leave before we disgrace ourselves. We want each other, so why fight it? The Dupre is right around the corner. I'll pay for the drinks and we'll go."

Kendra shook her head and pulled her hand from his. "As I said before, sex isn't going to make the hurt go away or solve our problems."

He gave her an impish grin. "No, but it's a start."

She rolled her eyes. "Perhaps we should switch to a safer subject."

Looking disgruntled, he leaned back. "Okay, what do you want to talk about?"

A number of questions formed in her mind, but the answers all had the potential to upset their precarious truce, so she chose an innocuous topic. "How are things at the hotel? From the scowl on your face, I take it that isn't a good subject either."

"You got that right."

"So tell me."

Jared shrugged. "It's the same old story. My father is convinced I'm out to destroy his hotel."

"I've never understood why he would think that. You love the Dupre."

"I do. It's a great old place." Jared grinned. "With a lot of pleasurable memories."

Kendra felt her cheeks turning pink. Her first year at Tulane, before she was able to get her apartment, she and Jared had spent many afternoons in his bed at the hotel. She'd skip class, Jared would duck out on work, and they would sneak hand-in-hand up the back stairs.

"Yes, well."

"What I don't love is working with my father," Jared continued. "He won't listen when I tell him we need to keep up-to-date. He thinks I want to degrade the Dupre's integrity and charm when all I want to do is add a few amenities to make it more appealing and business friendly."

"You're the one with the MBA."

Jared laughed sardonically. "Do you really think that matters? He has to have things his way and expects his children to agree with him and do as he says. The only saving grace is he's talking about opening another hotel in Baton Rouge. If he does, hopefully he'll run that one and leave me alone here."

Kendra couldn't hide her chagrin. "You're planning on staying in New Orleans?"

Jared nodded. "This is my home. Where else would I go?"

Kendra took a sip of wine, hoping it would steady her nerves. *Somewhere far from temptation,* she thought. Aloud she said, "Why not Baton Rouge? You're single and can live anywhere you wish."

"Well, I choose to live here in New Orleans. Do you have a problem with that?"

She ignored the irritation in his voice and shrugged. "It's none of my business where you live."

Jared glared. "Damn it, Kendra, it is your business. I'm back to stay."

Kendra's traitorous heart did a little flip when he took her hand in his.

"I love you and I want you to spend the rest of your life with me." When she slowly withdrew her hand, Jared noticed she no longer wore her engagement ring. He scowled. "Where's your ring?"

Still absorbing his words, *I love you*, Kendra blinked. "What?"

Jared pointed. "Your ring."

Kendra glanced down at her bare finger. They were at the lake when he asked her to marry him. He'd surprised her with a gourmet picnic. On a blanket in a secluded spot, he fed her rich chocolate mousse while they sipped champagne out of a single flute. So they couldn't be seen, he placed a protective bubble around them, and they made love. Naked, satiated with his lovemaking, Kendra lay in his arms. He produced the little velvet box, and smiling down at her, he'd asked her to be his wife.

A couple of weeks ago, she made herself take the ring off. What she wasn't telling anyone was she slept with it under her pillow. *Stay strong,* she told herself taking a deep breath, willing the tears in the back of her eyes not to fall. "Jared, it's too soon. Let's just enjoy our dinner and leave it at that."

He opened his mouth to speak, hesitated, and nodded.

Kendra was relieved the waiter took that opportunity to bring their food. They ate in silence until Jared said, "So tell me, what's new with your mom?"

Thankful for the change in topic, Kendra smiled.

"Actually, my mom is doing great with Spectral New Orleans. Besides the walking tours, she's added two horse-drawn carriages. The ghosts love my mom so they put on a great show for the tourists." She paused. "We've also begun doing a haunted hotel tour. Your father agreed to allow the tour to stop at the Dupre."

Jared shook his head. "You're kidding? How did you talk him into that?"

"I didn't. My mom did. But I'm usually the one doing the tour."

"Considering his opinion on everything supernatural, that's incredible. I don't suppose she put a spell on him?"

Kendra laughed. "I don't think so."

"Actually, your timing couldn't be better. We have a new addition to our family of resident ghosts."

"Really, who's that?"

"Angelique Dupre."

Kendra cocked her head. "The woman in the portrait in the library?"

"That's her."

"Interesting. I wonder why she's appearing now."

"She has something to do with why Adam wants revenge."

Kendra let out an exasperated sigh. "Jared, please."

He shrugged. "You asked."

"Yeah, well, let's change the subject."

"Okay, let's see, how about Josh? How is he doing at Tulane?"

"He still wants to be a marine biologist, and his grades are good. When he can he takes out my dad's fishing boat. Mom has kept it in good shape for him."

"Your brother has always been at home on the

water."

Kendra smiled. "Isn't that the truth."

"So tell me about Enchantment's opening day."

"If every day is like today, opening Enchantment was the best decision we've ever made. How perfect is it when the three of us can make money by selling the things we love to create?"

He frowned. "It takes a while for a new business to get out of the red and into the black. Supporting three people is pretty risky. Did you have a business plan?"

Kendra grinned. "Spoken like a true business major. Yes, we consulted a financial advisor. For the time being, we're going to continue with our present jobs and take turns working in the store."

"Who's going to take care of your books?"

"Me. And stop scowling. I can add and subtract."

"There's more to accounting than adding and subtracting, and if I remember correctly, your checkbook was always a mess."

"Yes, well, I've been doing better with that. Oh, good, here's my *gateau chocolat d'Yvonne*. Doesn't that look fabulous. Would you like to share it?"

Jared sighed. "Okay, no more talk of finances and, yes, let me help you with that." He slid a fork into the rich chocolate cake dripping with raspberry sauce. "Here, open." He held the fork to her lips.

"Mmm." Kendra closed her eyes with pleasure as the sweet chocolate melted on her tongue. When she reopened them, the slow seductive smile he gave her made her toes curl and her palms go damp.

"I used to love to feed you chocolate, remember?" His voice was deep and his eyes full of passion.

As he fed her another bite, she felt the junction

between her legs growing damp, but she couldn't tear her eyes from his.

"Good wine, dark chocolate, and a warm bed, and we could pleasure each other for hours."

Visions of the two of them in bed made her pulse quicken and her breath come in shallow gasps.

Jared took the last bite of cake for himself, then leaned forward and cupped the back of her head bringing her mouth to his.

The feel of his tongue and the taste of the chocolate sent her already aroused body over the edge. A low moan escaped her lips as the exquisite release flowed through her. When he broke the kiss and her eyes fluttered open, she saw the triumph in his smoldering eyes. "Baby, that's only the first one," he whispered. "You know I can give you many more."

Mortified, her cheeks burning, Kendra attempted to gather her wits. *Oh, sweet mother, I just sat here and came in Antoine's.* She swallowed hard and with every bit of dignity she possessed got to her feet. "Pay the check. I'm going to the Ladies' room. I'm ready to leave."

His lips twitched as he tried to hold back a smile. "Sure thing."

Kendra's legs felt as if they were made of rubber as she made her way across the restaurant. She couldn't look any of the other diners in the face. *Deanne and Loren were right. I should have never allowed myself to be alone with him.* She stopped in front of the sink and splashed cold water on her face. Patting her face dry with a paper towel, she studied her reflection in the mirror. Her eyes were too bright and her cheeks were blushed a rosy pink. *How could I have sat there and allowed that to happen?*

She could almost hear the chorus of Deanne and Loren's voices. *"Because when it comes to that man, you have no shame."*

Get control of yourself. You haven't done anything but have dinner, kiss him, and have one little orgasm. All you have to do now is go home, thank him for dinner, and go up to your apartment alone. She groaned. *I can do this. I can. I just got caught up in the moment, that's all. I got it out of my system and it won't happen again.*

Frantically she tried to recall the spell to ward off unwelcome advances. Even though it was a little late, with a triumphant smile she recited the words.

A soft breeze filled the warm night as they left the restaurant. The streets were alive with the sights and sounds which were New Orleans. Horse-drawn carriages clattered past. Music from jazz to rock blared from open bars. A spicy mix of cooking aromas filled the air, and laughing people crowded the streets.

"Let's walk back by way of Bourbon Street and see what the masses are up to," Jared said.

Kendra nodded and allowed him to guide her around a group of street musicians. When the saxophone player let loose with a sexy blues number, Jared took her in his arms and swayed to the music.

"Relax, *cher*," he said when she stiffened in his arms. "Just feel the music."

Kendra couldn't help but laugh. How she loved this city. Where else could you dance in the middle of the street and no one cared? She gazed into Jared's eyes and knew he was daring her to stay in his arms. Well, she'd show him. She could do this. What was one dance? Besides, they were surrounded by people. She was in no danger from him or her own emotions. So she gave him her most seductive smile and wrapped her arms around his neck, losing herself in the gentle beat.

She did her best to ignore the feel of his arms as they tightened around her waist. She fought the thrill that ran up her spine as his fingers moved up her bare back. When his lips found the sensitive spot beneath her ear and the familiar desire heated her blood, she knew she was in serious trouble. To her relief, the song ended. She stepped out of his embrace and gritted her teeth at his amused grin.

Damn the man. And damn her traitorous body. She turned on her heel and hurried down the street, cursing under her breath at the sound of his low chuckle behind her. She knew now for certain she should have never gone out with him. She had to get away as quickly as possible. As sure as the sun would rise tomorrow, she was about to do something she shouldn't.

When they finally stopped at the street entrance to her apartment, Kendra paused, gathering what self-control she had left. Intending to thank him for dinner and tell him goodnight, she turned, her words dying on her lips. The sexual magnetism between them was so strong it seemed to be forcing them together. *No,* Kendra silently pleaded as she struggled to suppress the passion building inside her. *I can't do this.*

Jared stepped close and gently cupped her face. "Baby, we can't fight what's between us. Just let it happen. I love you. I've *always* loved you."

Kendra gave one last gallant attempt to pull herself away, and then his lips were on hers.

When the explosion of passion ignited between

them, they could do nothing but cling to one another and ride the wave as it carried them higher and higher.

The rough wall against her back cleared Kendra's mind enough to gasp, "We need to get inside."

Jared fumbled with the doorknob. "For the sake of Odin, where's the key?"

Kendra's breath came in tiny gasps. "In my purse."

"Then find the damn thing before I take you right here on the street."

She frantically searched her bag while Jared's mouth kissed his way up her neck. When his teeth grazed her ear, chills of delight rippled across her skin. "Oh, the hell with it, Jared. Just open the damn thing."

He flicked his wrist and the door flew open. They stumbled through, Jared slamming the door shut behind them. His belt and her shoes were the first articles of clothing to litter the stairwell as they stumbled up to her apartment. Jared's kisses were hot and demanding while his hands touched and caressed. They'd made it half-way up when she tore at the buttons of his shirt and he tugged at the strings of her halter dress. She fisted her hands into his hair. "Jared, for the love of the Gods, I can't wait, do something."

"Sweetheart, if you don't care we're on the stairs, neither do I." With one quick yank, the top of her dress fell away revealing her breasts. "*Mon Dieu*, Kendra," he whispered, as his mouth closed over one pink swollen nipple.

Kendra was panting for breath when her cell phone rang. "Jared?"

"Ignore it," he growled, as he ran his hand up her skirt, jerking down her bikini panties and plunging two fingers into her welcoming heat.

Any coherent thoughts vanished, replaced by the exquisite sensations he was creating inside her. She dug her nails into his back as her climax built.

"That's it, baby. Come for me."

"Jared," she cried as her orgasm consumed her. Before she could catch her breath, she felt herself lifted off her feet.

"We need to get off these damn stairs." Jared made it up two steps when screeching tires and a woman's piercing scream filled the quiet night.

"What was that?" Kendra asked.

"It doesn't matter."

She wriggled in his arms. "Jared, put me down. Someone could be hurt. We have to see if we can help."

"Kendra, the streets are full of people. Someone will call 9-1-1. You're not a healer. There's nothing you can do. I'm the one who's hurting and needs you."

"But, Jared, we can't just ignore…"

"Oh, yes, we can." When his mouth covered hers, his kiss was hard and unyielding.

Once again under the magic of his kiss, her resolve crumbled like dust. Her fingers were on his zipper when another scream from outside wrenched her back to reality. "Jared, let me go. I have to see what's happened."

Swearing colorfully in French, he did as she asked.

Kendra straightened her clothing, retied her top, slipped on her shoes, then ran down the stairs and out onto the sidewalk. A crowd had gathered around a prone body in the middle of the street. Sirens wailed in the distance.

"It was incredible," a woman said when Kendra stopped beside her. "She had just stepped off the curb."

She pointed to the woman lying on the ground. "And a black car came out of nowhere and hit her and didn't stop."

"I got half of the license plate number," a man said.

Before Kendra could step into the street, Jared gently grabbed her elbow.

"It's okay. See." Jared nodded toward a man who was kneeling next to the woman.

Kendra instantly recognized him as a healer from their coven.

"He'll take care of her until the ambulance gets here," Jared reassured her. "There's no reason for us to stay."

Kendra nodded and they weaved their way through the crowd back to her apartment. At the street entrance, she turned.

He gave her a slight smile. "I have a feeling we're not going to continue where we left off."

Furious with herself for how easily she'd let down her guard and reacted to his touch, she shook her head. "Don't think for one minute that because of what happened I've forgiven you or want you back. I lost my head. That's all. Trust me, it won't happen again."

"You can't ignore what we have together. You said you'd let me explain, and I intend to do just that."

"Thanks to you, Jared, what we had is gone. As far as listening to what you have to say, I'll think about it."

He took a step toward her, pinning her between him and the door to her apartment. "You think what we had is gone? I don't think so, love." He bent low until their lips were a breath apart. "Tell me you didn't come alive in my arms. Tell me you didn't feel the heat between us. Tell me you didn't want me as much as I wanted you. Tell me you don't love me."

When she opened her mouth to reply, his lips covered hers. Her traitorous body reacted to his kiss, and she knew that unless she found the strength to stop him, they'd end up in her bed. With every ounce of willpower she possessed she broke the kiss. "Jared, I never said I wasn't still attracted to you. But there has to be more than sex. There has to be trust, and I don't trust you anymore. You told me you didn't love me and weren't coming back. That's not something easily forgotten or forgiven."

Jared angrily stepped back. "You know what? That's just fine. If you ever decide you'd like to know the truth, call me. Or better yet, why don't you ask your friend." He turned and with long strides disappeared into the night.

Chapter 16

Adam Montief shook with the effort to control his rage. He stood opposite Kendra's apartment and watched as she and Dupre went inside. At the thought of the bastard's hands on Kendra, dark energy flashed from his fingertips.

The last thing he'd expected was to actually fall in love with the little witch. He spotted a woman with a walker at the end of the block. He waited until she had shuffled halfway across the street, waved his hand, and the car that was slowing down for her suddenly sped up.

As bystanders' screams filled the night, Adam smiled with satisfaction and increased the car's speed until it was out of sight. If the driver was a conscientious person and came back, well, it would be up to him to explain why his car had accelerated, then sped off. Adam stayed where he was as Kendra hurried out her door and ran down the street to where people were gathering around the woman.

"Did you see what happened?" a young man in a Saints cap asked Adam.

"No, I just got here."

"It was the most terrible thing I've ever seen. That poor woman," the man continued, indicating the crumpled body, "was crossing the street when a car just ran her down. The driver must be drunk or something.

He didn't even slow down when she bounced off the hood."

"That's terrible," Adam said. "I hope she'll be all right."

"I doubt it. I can't imagine anyone surviving a hit like that."

Dismissing the woman and her fate, Adam turned his attention to Kendra's apartment. He stood in the shadows as Kendra and Dupre returned. Soon they were having a heated discussion, then the slut was back in Dupre's arms. Adam's eyes burned like smoldering coals. How to stop them? Jared suddenly turned and stomped away, his aura a bright red. *Well, well, well, perhaps Dupre's reunion with his love isn't going as planned.*

Lights in Kendra's apartment flickered on, and Adam debated whether to knock on her door. It could be the perfect opportunity to take advantage of the situation. She might be vulnerable enough, and mad enough, and aroused enough, to allow him to comfort her in ways he could only imagine. Adam started across the street but quickly stepped back as Loren and Deanne pulled up in Loren's car. He raised his hand to strike them both down but realized that would cause more problems. He cursed all women and waited to see if Kendra would let them in.

Ten minutes passed and it was clear the girls were staying. What were they saying? Concentrating, he sent a listening charm toward the apartment window. When it bounced back, he tried again. Dupre must have put a security charm on the building.

Adam smiled without humor. Did Dupre really think he could keep him out? He doubled his efforts.

Nothing. *Bastard.* He tried one last time. When the security charm still held, he stood, fists clenched, as lightning struck around him, thunder rattled windows, and a sudden downpour filled the streets of the French Quarter.

On Julia Street, outside the Quarter, Adam slammed the door of the apartment he'd rented. His long walk back in the rain hadn't lessened his temper in the least. *Damn Dupre.* He could put up all the security spells around Kendra he wanted. Spells were made to be broken, and by the devil's horns, Adam was just the witch to break them. He picked up his crystal ball from the table and hurled it across his apartment. It cracked the drywall, then bounced across the thick carpet.

"I would have thought, after being bested by Dupre once, you would have learned an uncontrolled temper will not help you succeed."

At the sound of the raspy voice, Adam froze. Tentacles of dread spread up his spine. Before he could turn, the voice spoke again.

"Perhaps I was wrong in giving you a second chance to exact our family's revenge."

Adam, knowing he must remain calm and never show weakness, took a steadying breath and turned, facing the fearsome image in the ancient mirror. "Grandsire, I was just letting off a little frustration. You know you can depend upon me to fulfill my duty and destiny."

"Does that include the needless killing of a mortal female?"

Adam swallowed. "I—"

"No excuses," Augustus Montief shouted, his visage vibrating with his rage. "Because of your attraction for the girl, you lost control and interfered with outsiders. Our fight is between the Montiefs and the Dupres. You are not to use mortals to achieve your goal."

Adam gritted his teeth and silently cursed. He didn't give a damn if mortals died. In the past, he'd entertained himself for hours toying with the pathetic creatures as they tried to escape his little torments.

"Now Dupre is back, you can finish this and return to Black Island," Augustus stated, interrupting Adam's thoughts. "Even though I wished to have his death occur on Montief soil, that will not be possible. Since you allowed him to kill Daman, it is your responsibility to take charge of the compound."

The reproachful tone in Augustus' voice drove Adam's temper to the boiling point. Even though Adam was devastated by his uncle's death, his grandsire took every opportunity to remind him it was his fault. It took all Adam's powers of concentration to remain calm and not let Augustus see his fury. "Killing Dupre here isn't as easy as doing it on Black Island," Adam said. "Kendra may know of my connection to Dupre. If he were to turn up dead, the police might question me. I need to take my time and do it properly."

Augustus scowled. "You can kill Dupre and be back on Black Island before the authorities know who you are. It is not Dupre who is keeping you in New Orleans, it is the pretty little witch. Do not let your lust for her distract you or cause you to lower your guard. Dupre is no fool, nor is he weak. He will do all he can to protect her. Use her to flush him out if you have to but destroy Jared Dupre for good this time."

"Yes, Grandsire." When the image faded away,

Adam stood in front of his large picture window. As he stared at the street below, a young girl's fiery red hair caught his attention. What began as a desire to take what belonged to Dupre had turned into his own passion for Kendra. Bending her to his will was proving more difficult than he'd anticipated.

He'd achieved some success by sending her the crystal bottle with its special scent, but he hadn't accomplished the final seduction. The gullible little witch had an unusually strong resistance to him. Well, this scenario wasn't over. He'd made it back to New Orleans before Dupre, but now he was here, Adam was running out of time to bring her totally under his control. He'd soon find a way to break through Kendra's defenses.

He needed to make sure Dupre remained unable to convince her of the truth. A thought struck him and he smiled. *Yes, that's it.* He laughed aloud, flicked his wrist, and a bouquet of black roses appeared. He waved his hand, and a cut crystal vase now sat upon the table. Adam placed the flowers in the vase and went to a cabinet where he withdrew a vial containing a clear liquid. *This should do nicely.* He carefully poured tiny drops of the liquid on the blooms while murmuring,

As their fragrance fills the air,
There is not one to compare,
She will only trust in me,
As I will, so mote it be.

As the sweet fragrance of the roses intensified, they slowly turned from black to blood red. He nodded with satisfaction. *Perfect. It won't be long before Kendra is mine.* How satisfying it would be, while watching the bastard die, to give Dupre a vivid description of the many ways he'd had his intended bride.

Adam headed for the bathroom and stripped off his clothes. Before getting into the shower, he glared in the mirror at the faint traces of scarring left on his body. He should have ended this with Dupre that night on Black Island. The triumph on Dupre's face when his falcata had pierced Adam's chest still enraged him. He knew he was a good swordsman; it had been Dupre's damnable luck that he had been able to wound him.

Or had it? Adam frowned and touched the scar near the center of his chest. For a second, before he'd felt Dupre's blade, he could have sworn he'd seen the image of a woman standing behind him.

Adam had a scraggly pine growing out of the side of the rocky cliff to thank for his life. The tree had briefly broken his fall, giving him time to focus his energy and slow his descent. Although his injuries were severe, with the last of his strength he crawled along the rocky shore to a small inlet where an opening in the rock led to an underground chamber beneath the school. He dragged himself inside and, before he passed out, sent a spear of energy through the tunnel to summon his people to rescue him. The healers had worked on him for hours, and they hadn't been sure they'd be able to save him.

Adam turned the shower on high and stepped under the cold stinging spray. He wasn't about to give Dupre another chance. The next time they met would be the last. As for Kendra, tomorrow he planned on surprising her by taking her to lunch. Would she admit she'd been with Dupre? Although it really didn't matter if she lied or told him the truth, he'd soon teach her the exhilaration of mixing pain and pleasure.

****

Jared stomped into his suite at the Dupre Hotel slamming the door behind him. The evening with Kendra had fueled his fury all the way home. How for the love of Odin was he supposed to explain to the stubborn woman why he'd left if she wouldn't even listen to him?

As he passed his desk, he noticed the message light on the phone blinking. He cursed again as he checked the caller ID. A confrontation with his father would make this fucked up night complete. Jared sat down heavily in his high-backed chair and stabbed the replay button on the answering machine. While he waited for his father's message, he flicked his wrist and a cold beer appeared in his hand. He'd driven back from Black Island and arrived late the night before. Anxious to see Kendra, but apprehensive over her reaction, he hadn't slept well. He'd expected his reunion with Kendra to be difficult, but how in the hell was he to get her to listen to him?

"Jared, this is your father," a deep voice from the machine announced.

"No kidding," Jared murmured, tipping up the bottle.

"I'm back from Baton Rouge. I wish to speak with you. I'll expect you in my office first thing tomorrow morning."

Yeah, and I want some answers from you. Beginning with Angelique and what you know about the Montiefs. Jared switched off the phone recorder and leaned back in the chair. Growing up, he'd heard the story of how Angelique and Jean Dupre escaped the Haitian revolution. Once safe in New Orleans, they had opened the hotel. He didn't recall ever hearing about anyone in his family killing someone named Augustus Montief. If it were true, it had to have happened during Angelique's time.

But why would a vengeful spirit wait two hundred years? Why would Adam care what happened to his relative so long ago? Jared shook his head. Tomorrow, he'd do some research into his family history. He glanced at his mirror on the desk. Perhaps he could just ask Angelique.

He picked it up and said, "Angelique, I need some answers." The glass remained dark and Jared repeated his words. When she didn't appear, he laid the mirror down and, frustrated, flicked his hand for another beer.

Throughout his life he'd seen a number of spirits who called the Dupre Hotel home. The portly gentleman in a dark frock coat and silk top hat who enjoyed changing the time on the grandfather clock in the lobby was one of his favorites. Or the pale, dark-haired flapper who sat at the bar smoking cigarettes, blowing kisses to passing men, and occasionally pinching their asses. But he hadn't encountered Angelique until she appeared to him in the mirror.

As far as he knew, other than Angelique, himself, and Philippe, no other Dupre had possessed magical powers. He frowned. Why not? It was true Jean Dupre had been a mortal, but magic could be passed down even if only one parent, Angelique for instance, had magic. It was unlikely two centuries had passed without anyone having the gift.

Thinking back, he recalled how relieved his mother had seemed when Jared was able to use the mirror. He sipped his beer. *Curiouser and curiouser*. Thoughts of his mother made him smile. When he and Philippe were children, she would entertain them by making their stuffed animals dance across the room, or she would create miniature castles for them to play in. His father would watch with amusement, but never participate.

He sighed. It was after her death that Philippe had started down his path of self-destruction. His father had grieved so deeply that instead of welcoming their efforts to comfort him, he'd shut his sons out. If only he'd realized they were as devastated as he was.

Jared's eye fell on a framed photograph of Kendra and him taken while they vacationed on Martinique. As he held the photo, the fear he'd had earlier came rushing back. Had Adam had enough time to begin weaving his spell over her? Is that why she was so reluctant to listen to him? *If the son-of-a-bitch thinks I'll just stand by while he draws Kendra into his weird cult, I'll damn well show him otherwise.*

The next morning Jared made his way down the dark-paneled hall to his father's corner office. Not bothering to knock, he opened the heavy oak door and stepped in. His father, a man of medium stature with short-cropped salt and pepper hair, sat behind an antique walnut pedestal desk. On the wall behind him hung a portrait of Jean Dupre, a handsome man in a white lace cravat and a dark blue velvet coat, his dark brown hair tied back with a black ribbon.

Without saying a word, Jared sat down in a worn oxblood leather chair across from the desk. A few seconds of silence passed while father and son studied one another. Then Jacques spoke, a definite edge to each word.

"I've grown to expect this type of behavior from

your brother, but not from you. I would appreciate it if you would explain where you've been, where your brother is, and what you two have been up to. Also, I'd like to know how you could have done such a despicable thing, leaving that girl two days before your wedding."

Jared's jaw clenched as he held onto his temper. "First, *that girl's* name is Kendra, which you're perfectly aware of. Second, I intended to be back for my wedding. Third, for the time being, Philippe is living on Black Island. And as to where we've been and what we've been doing, we've been trying to stay alive."

Again, Jacques studied Jared, then sighed. "Is your brother all right?"

"He is now."

Jacques sat back in his chair. "I'm listening."

Jared relaxed his taut muscles, crossed one booted foot over his knee, flicked his wrist and a cup of coffee appeared.

His father scowled. "Do you have to do that? If you'd like some coffee"—he pointed to a cherry wood and brass tea cart—"there's a fresh pot over there."

Jared sipped the hot brew. "That's where this came from."

Jacques tapped his pen on the green desk blotter, a sure sign his patience was running short. "Are you here to have a civilized conversation with me or do parlor tricks?"

Jared's mouth formed a grim line. "Father, I'm a witch. Don't you think by now you'd be used to it?"

Tap, tap, tap went Jacques's pen, before he tossed it aside. "Would you like to begin?"

"All right, this is what happened."

When he'd concluded with Adam being back in New Orleans, Jacques leaned forward, crossed his arms on his desk, and in a tone of suppressed anger said, "Unlike your sister, you're not one for melodrama. So I'll assume what you've just told me is the truth."

Jared nodded.

"Your wounds have healed, and you're all right?"

"It took some time, but I'm fine."

Jacques's nostrils flared. "And during this time you couldn't call me in person? You have some strange woman call to tell me you and Philippe were severely injured, but you both were showing signs of improvement. Although you hadn't regained consciousness. Imagine my horror when I asked what hospital you two were in and learned you were being taken care by Wiccan healers. I asked where you were and was told some island off the coast of Connecticut, and I'd be informed of your progress, but never got another call. I had no idea what your condition was, or why you and your brother were up there. I also had no idea when you were coming home. I had this trip to Baton Rouge planned and expected you to be here to take care of the hotel."

"Father, I'm sorry. I wasn't conscious or aware of my surroundings for weeks. Once I began to heal, I should have called. By then I didn't want to explain over the phone. If I had to do it over again, I would have done things differently."

"Is this Adam person still a threat to my family?"

"No, it's me he is sworn to kill."

Jacques lifted his hands and let them drop. "Oh, well, that makes me feel better. What about your sister?

If this monster likes to go after young women, she could be in danger. Annette didn't inherit your mother's powers. She couldn't begin to defend herself."

"As long as Annette stays in Michigan, she'll be fine."

"I don't understand how in the hell your brother could have gotten himself mixed up with such a person. I wish to God neither of you had been born with your mother's curse."

Jared saw the pain in his father's eyes and gentled his tone. "Father, Mom never thought of her Wiccan gift as a curse. Most Wiccans are good, hardworking people who use their gift to help, not harm. But like any culture there are those who are cruel and evil. Adam Montief has twisted his gift into something ugly and I plan on stopping him."

"Why does it have to be you? If Adam is such a threat, then I would think men of the Wiccan Council could track him down and destroy him."

"Unfortunately, it's not that easy. Wiccans can't use magic to kill, and the Council can't sentence someone to death without cause."

"You've just told me he tried to kill you and Philippe, and he's known to have tortured people to death. Isn't that enough to have him arrested or whatever the Wiccans do with their criminals?"

"That's the problem. Those people are dead. You'll not find anyone still under his control to testify against him. Father, the men of my coven are aware of what Adam is and what he's done, and they'll be alert, but it's me he's after. He says he's out to avenge the death of someone named Augustus Montief. Do you have any idea who he is?"

"Since this man is a witch, I would assume it's your mother's family he's talking about, not mine."

"He's perfectly clear it was the Dupres. How much do you know about our family?"

"I know Jean made his fortune in sugar cane and opened this hotel in 1802."

"The sugar cane plantation was in Santo Domingo wasn't it?"

Jacques nodded.

"And he left there with Angelique?"

Again, Jacques nodded.

"Well, supposedly whatever happened took place there and involved Angelique."

"That would have been over two hundred years ago."

Jared finished his coffee and placed the cup on the desk. "I know."

"You're telling me some crazed witch is after you because of something that happened two centuries ago? That's insane."

"Be that as it may, he's here. He wants me dead and Kendra for his own, but he'll have to kill me first."

Jacques rubbed his temples. "For God's sake, son, would you please stop talking about dying. I don't think I could take losing any of my children."

A stillness came over Jared. Suddenly Jacques's face revealed all his sixty years. Displaying affection used to come easy to his father, but following his wife's death, Jacques had become cold and aloof. Jared relaxed and in a quiet tone said, "Father, Philippe is fine, and Annette is safe. As for me, Adam had his shot at killing me, and he failed. I'm not about to give him a second chance."

Jacques hesitated, then cleared his throat. "Jared, we've had our differences, but I want you to know I love you, and I've always been proud of you. That's why I wanted to speak with you about taking over the Dupre."

Jared swallowed back the emotion clogging his throat. He knew how hard those words were for his father to say. In an unsteady voice, he managed, "I won't let you down. But right now, I need you to tell me everything you know about Angelique and Jean Dupre."

"Who did what way back when has never interested me. I care about preserving the hotel. It was your mother who enjoyed family history. Try the display cases in the library. They're full of memorabilia from the hotel's past. Also, there are old books. Perhaps you'll find something that can help you."

"I plan on going through what's there, but those are mostly about New Orleans. I need something more personal, like a diary or journal."

Jacques shook his head. "If there is such a thing, I have no knowledge of it." He paused. "Although, I do recall your mother talking about some old photographs and papers she had come across."

Jared's pulse quickened. "Where are they?"

"They could be anywhere. There are still boxes of her things in her closet. And more boxes and trunks in the storage room."

"Great, Father, thanks. I'll see what I can find. I have one more question. What can you tell me about Angelique's mirror?"

A pained expression filled Jacques's eyes before he looked away. "I don't know anything about that mirror, nor do I want to."

It was apparent from his father's reaction that he did know something, so why act as if he didn't? Annoyed, Jared took the mirror from his pocket and placed it on the desk. "Like it or not, Father, you are descended from a witch. Why you and mother kept this from your children is beyond me. I also find it hard to believe that other than Philippe and myself there haven't been any other witches in the Dupre line. As eldest, the mirror was given to me on my eighteenth birthday. It has the ability to show me what I ask. In fact, Philippe and I have both the mirror and Angelique to thank for saving our lives. I'd like to know, am I the only Dupre who could make the mirror work?"

Jacques stared with distaste at the elaborately carved wood frame, cracked and stained with age, the glass within dull and gray. "Jared, I loved your mother, but as you know, I was never comfortable with magic."

"I understand and I'm sorry to have to involve you, but the answer to why Adam Montief wants me dead is in the past. So, if you know anything, please tell me."

Jacques stood and crossed to a small Louis XV side table where a carafe of water sat upon a silver tray. Pouring himself a glass, he stared up at Jean Dupre's portrait and sipped the water. "You said Angelique helped you and your brother survive. How is that possible?"

Jared settled back into the chair. "I used the mirror to track Adam when he took Philippe, and when I fought Adam, though I know you will doubt this, Angelique gave me power. I might not have survived otherwise."

Jacques turned, a resigned set to his mouth. "You

think it was your mother's death that set me against the Wiccan people, but my dislike of magic began long before I met Justine. I loved her so much that when I learned she was a witch it didn't matter, though my biggest fear was that our children would inherit her powers. When we realized both you and your brother had, I was terrified." He glanced at the mirror. "I honestly don't know much about Angelique, but I can tell you something about that damn mirror." He placed his empty glass on the tray and resumed his seat behind the desk. "As you know, neither of my parents had magical power, but my brother and uncle did."

Jared's brows rose in surprise. "I didn't know you had a brother. I thought there was just Aunt Sybil?"

Minutes passed while Jacques silently stared at the mirror. When his eyes met Jared's, they reflected a deep sorrow. "William was two years older than me, and my uncle a few years older than William. Both of them died long before I met your mother."

Jared knew his father's way of dealing with emotional pain was to hold it deep inside. But not to even let them know he'd had a brother? Whatever had happened must have been devastating to him. "Father, how did they die?"

"I'll get to that. For generations the mirror has been shown to male Dupres on their eighteenth birthday."

"I wonder why it's just the male members of the family?" Jared mused.

"I have no idea," Jacques said with impatience. "Perhaps during your search of family history you'll discover that. Anyway, neither William nor my uncle could make the mirror work, but they were determined to try. The mirror was kept in a small wooden chest."

185

Debby Grahl

He held up his hand. "And before you ask, I have no idea where the chest is. Your mother put it away after the mirror was given to you."

Jared held back a smile and nodded.

"One night, William and my uncle found the chest and took the mirror. What we didn't know was that my uncle had recruited William into a group that practiced dark magic. My father discovered the empty chest, but William and my uncle were missing. He was about to go looking for them when a pale frightened young man showed up at our door. He told us there'd been a terrible accident and we needed to come with him. My mother was frantic and wanted to go, but my father insisted she stay with my sister. He took me instead. I was sixteen at the time and scared to death at what we would find."

Jared saw the effort it took his father to relive this part of his life. He wanted to tell him he didn't have to continue, but his need to know the past was too strong.

"The young man took us to a secluded spot in the marshes by Lake Ponchartrain where rituals were held," Jacques was saying. "Even though I don't have magic, the evil I felt there chilled me to the bone." He took a deep breath. "We found William and my uncle dead on the ground, the mirror clasped in William's hand."

Jared shook his head. "That must have been horrible for you, but I can't imagine Angelique killing one of her own."

Jacques's jaw tightened. "I didn't say Angelique had anything to do with their deaths. The cult leader had insisted they give him the mirror. When they refused, he killed them. Then he tried to grab the mirror. A flash of light shot from the glass and his hand burst into flame. At least that was the story the young man told us."

Jared's mind took him back to Adam's compound and the old man called Daman who had one hand. "*Merde*," he murmured.

"What's wrong?" Jacques asked.

Jared shook his head and tried to clear his mind of the feel of his sword sinking into human flesh. He swallowed back bile. "Father, do you know the leader's name?"

"No. Why?"

"I had to kill a man called Daman in order to save Philippe's life, and I think he was the same man who killed William and your uncle. He had lost his right hand."

Jacques's eyes closed then opened. He took a deep breath before he was able to speak. "You took another human being's life?"

Jared rose and paced across the thick carpet. "I'm not proud of that fact, but trust me, I had no choice. I did it to save Philippe's life." He halted in front of his father's desk. "Killing innocent people is as wrong in the witch community as it is in the mortal one. But destroying evil has to be done in both. Witches have ways of punishing those who commit nonviolent crimes, but don't have prisons like mortals do. So they have to execute their monsters themselves. I wasn't kidding when I said I plan to destroy Adam."

Father and son stared into each other's eyes until Jacques sighed wearily and motioned toward the drinks cabinet. "It's a little early in the day, but fix me a scotch, then tell me why you think this Daman person killed William."

Jared fixed two drinks, handed one to his father, then resumed his seat. "I'm beginning to think the Montiefs were interested in our family long before this business with Adam and myself. I also think Angelique and her mirror are here to protect us."

Jacques placed his palms on the desk and leaned forward. "If it hadn't been for that mirror, my brother would still be alive. As far as I'm concerned, no good can come from it. As for help from Angelique"—he gestured with his hand—"that's nonsense."

"Father, this hotel is crawling with ghosts. You can't tell me you've never seen them."

"I have seen your magic, but how can I be expected to believe in something I can't see and doesn't exist?"

Jared opened his mouth to tell his father that a young black girl with a feather duster was at that very moment standing behind him but decided to keep it to himself.

"No matter what I say, you're going to do as you wish," Jacques continued. "And if you're convinced that mirror and Angelique can keep you safe, well, then, God be with you." His voice took on a steely tone. "But I expect to be kept informed of events as they happen."

Jared rose. "No problem. I'll go see what I can find in the library."

Jacques waved him back into his chair. "I'm not done. You need to know I purchased that small hotel in Baton Rouge I told you about. I plan on moving as soon as we can get the transition in order. So I suggest if you're serious about taking charge here, you make time to discuss it with me."

Stunned, Jared sat back down. "I didn't realize things had progressed to that point."

"You know I haven't been happy here since your mother passed. I need to get away from New Orleans and all the memories. Besides, the hotel should have the changes you've suggested, and I don't have the will or desire to see it through. The hotel in Baton Rouge is small and quaint and isn't expected to have hot tubs, wireless access, or video games."

Jared tried to hide his smile. "Father, the modernizations I plan on doing to the hotel will in no way affect its appearance or our standards. You can trust me on that. I love this old place as much as you do and would never do anything to destroy its history."

"That's why I'm putting it in your hands. Now, are you ready to go over the details with me?"

"Sure, I'll do my research in the library after we've finished."

Chapter 17

Kendra carefully wrapped the blown glass unicorn in tissue paper and slipped it into a silver bag. "He should be a nice addition to your collection," she said as she rang up the sale.

The young woman, slim with a smooth mocha complexion, nodded, and her tight braids swayed. "It will. I've collected seven so far. I love your store, and I'll definitely be back."

Kendra smiled and handed her the bag. "Thank you. We hope to see you soon."

When Kendra turned to help the next customer in line, her smile died on her lips. In front of her stood someone Kendra despised. "Hello, Kathleen. How can I help you?"

Kathleen Leblanc glanced around the store. "Well, I just dropped in to see your little shop. It's rather"—she hesitated—"quaint, isn't it?"

Kendra gritted her teeth. "We like it. Is there something you needed?"

"No, not really. I get all my supplies from Minerva. Actually, Kendra"—she leaned in close and gave her a taunting smirk—"naturally, working at the Dupre, I know Jared's back, so I came in to see if what I heard is true."

"And what would that be?"

"That you were seen all cozy with Jared last night

at Antoine's.''

Remembering just how cozy she and Jared had been, Kendra silently groaned. There were times she wished she could be downright mean because right now she would like nothing better than to turn Kathleen into a warty toad. Kathleen had a trim curvy body, lots of curly blonde hair, and cat-green eyes set in a heart-shaped face. Their dislike for one another dated from the third grade when Kendra had been chosen over Kathleen to play the part of Queen of the Fairies in their school pageant. In retaliation, Kathleen had changed Kendra's fairy dust into itching powder. Their animosity toward one another had increased as they grew older. "Yes, he's back and we had dinner. So what?"

Kathleen shrugged. "Nothing. It's your business if you want to make a fool of yourself again."

Kendra knew she should just ignore the comment, but she couldn't help asking, "Make a fool of myself how?"

Kathleen laughed mockingly. "By taking back a man who dumped you on your wedding day. I mean honestly, Kendra, have you no pride?"

Kendra dug her nails into her palms. "You've been trying to get Jared back since he chose me over you. Talk about not having any pride. As for Jared's and my relationship, I really don't think that's your, or anyone else's, business. So why don't you do both of us a favor and get the hell out of my face?"

Kathleen's eyes narrowed and her nostrils flared. Before she could speak, the bells above the door jingled. Kendra glanced up to see Thaddeus holding a vase of red roses. She smiled as he caught her eye.

"This is a surprise," she said as he stopped in front of the counter. "I didn't expect to see you today."

"I thought since we weren't able to have dinner last night, I'd bring you these." He handed her the flowers. "And take you for a celebratory lunch." He nodded toward Kathleen. "But if you're busy, I can come back later."

"No, don't go on my account," Kathleen said. "I was just leaving."

As she literally fled through the door, Kendra stared at her disappearing back. She turned to Thaddeus and grinned. "I don't know what you did to make her leave but thank you."

He shrugged. "I don't know what I did either, but since it put such a pretty smile on your face, I'll be happy to do it again."

"These are wonderful. Thank you. I love roses." She inhaled the flowers' sweet aroma. "Mmm, they smell incredible."

"I'm glad you like them. Now how about that lunch? We could go to Antoine's. You haven't been there lately, have you?"

Kendra felt her face flush as she stammered, "Ah, well, I don't know if I can get away."

"Aren't both Loren and Deanne here?" he asked. "I'm sure they can handle things for a short while."

Deanne joined them at the counter. "Oh, what pretty roses." She smiled at Thaddeus. "Hey, where ya't?"

"Fine, Deanne. How are you?"

Deanne grinned. "Fine as frog hair." She turned to Kendra. "Speaking of frogs, I'm starving. How about if I go get us some po-boys for lunch?"

"Well," Kendra hesitated.

"I've just asked Kendra to lunch at Antoine's to celebrate your success," Thaddeus interjected. "I was hoping you wouldn't mind covering for her for a while."

Deanne's face took on a thoughtful expression. "Well, let me see, if I had a choice between po-boys and Antoine's, hmm…which would I choose?" Her eyes opened wide. "Gee, I think I'd choose Antoine's."

Kendra laughed. "Me, too."

"Okay, I'll go get our pitiful lunches, then you can go enjoy your fabulous one," Deanne said.

"Now I feel like a real jerk," Thaddeus interjected. "I should have invited all three of you, not just Kendra. Why don't we do dinner instead? Then you can all go."

Deanne shook her head. "That's nice of you, but you and Kendra go ahead. Loren and I will see you at the party on Saturday."

"Party?" Thaddeus asked.

"Don't you remember? I told you Saturday is when we're having our grand opening party," Kendra said.

Deanne nodded. "At my parents' restaurant, Baby Blues, on Basin Street in the Treme. It has great down-home food because my mom is the cook and killer blues because it's my brother's band."

Thaddeus' face cleared. "And you still want me to come?"

Kendra cocked her head. "Of course, I want you to come. Why wouldn't I?"

Thaddeus hesitated. "Because I know Jared Dupre is back in New Orleans, and I'm not sure where that leaves me."

After they'd met, Kendra had been amazed at how

quickly she'd felt comfortable enough with him to explain about Jared and what had happened on her wedding day. Thaddeus had been sympathetic and understanding. He'd told her he wouldn't rush her into anything she wasn't ready for and she should tell him if he came on too strong.

Now there he stood looking like a puppy about to be thrown out into the cold. When Kendra heard Deanne's intake of breath, she knew she was about to make a derisive comment about Jared, so she gently stepped on her foot. "Deanne, why don't you go get those po-boys? We don't mind waiting until you get back."

Deanne gave her a sour expression and hurried off.

When they were alone, Kendra laid a comforting hand on Thaddeus' arm. "Jared Dupre hurt me deeply. As far as I'm concerned, our relationship is over."

Thaddeus glanced away, then back at Kendra. "Ah, not according to him."

"What do you mean?"

"I had an unpleasant encounter with him yesterday."

Kendra narrowed her eyes. "What happened?"

"I was sitting enjoying my beignets and coffee and he approached me. He made some crazy accusations, then told me to stay away from you."

Kendra silently recited a calming charm. "What kind of *accusations*?"

"Kendra, it was a lot of nonsense that really doesn't matter."

"Thaddeus, it matters. Please tell me."

"Okay. For some reason he's decided I'm a dark witch named Adam who tried to kill both him and his brother. Kendra, I have no idea what he's talking about. I'm not even from New Orleans. How could I know either of them? Besides the fact I'm no killer."

He sounds so sincere. How could he be lying? Still, she had to know. "I can't tell you how sorry I am this happened. But I don't understand how Jared could have thought you were someone else."

He shrugged. "He said something about seeing me here yesterday and assumed I was this other man."

An idea struck her. Bizarre as it might be, it could be the answer. "I don't suppose by any chance you have a twin?"

"No. I have a younger brother who doesn't resemble me. And he's no killer either."

Kendra sighed. "They say everyone has a double somewhere. I was hoping…"

Thaddeus took her hand. "Kendra, I enjoy being with you, but I don't want to create problems for you. And to be honest, I don't want to find myself caught in the middle of some love triangle. Nor do I want some jealous hothead who thinks I'm capable of murder after me."

She looked into his warm, tawny eyes. *He truly is a kind, thoughtful man who couldn't be the person Jared claims he is, but could I ever feel toward him the way I felt about Jared?* Could she give herself so totally to another man?

Right now, love was the last thing she was feeling toward Jared Dupre. She went up on her toes and lightly kissed Thaddeus' cheek. "I'll take care of Jared. He won't bother you again. Now, here's Deanne. Let me get my purse and we can go. How about the courtyard at Brennan's instead of Antoine's? I feel like sitting outside."

Thaddeus nodded. "That sounds good."

****

The afternoon breeze was mild. They sipped Brennan's signature Bloody Marys seated in a courtyard fragrant with spring blooms. Kendra pushed Jared from her mind as she enjoyed the gentle sound of the fountain and the spiciness of her drink.

"So were you able to get a good night's sleep?" Thaddeus asked. "Considering the crowd waiting to get into Enchantment when I left, I could understand why you were so tired."

Instant images of what she'd been doing the previous night made Kendra's cheeks burn. What if he'd seen her out with Jared? She mentally shook her head. No, he didn't live in the Quarter so she was probably safe. She cleared her throat. "Actually, yes, I did. I turned off my phone and fell asleep."

Seeing the doubt in his eyes, Kendra inwardly groaned. *I'm a terrible liar. Should I just tell him the truth?* Damn Jared anyway. This situation was all his fault. If he'd just left her alone, she wouldn't be sitting here feeling like a fool.

"Would you like another drink?" Thaddeus asked, breaking into her thoughts.

She shook her head. "These are very good, but I have to go back to work with a clear head." That reminded her of something she'd wanted to ask him. "Thaddeus, you said you're a teacher on sabbatical, but you've never told me what you teach or where."

"Haven't I? Well, that's easy to remedy. I teach medieval history at a small private college up north. But my passion is the persecution of witches by the church."

Kendra scrunched up her nose. "That's a little creepy considering you're a witch. Personally, I can't bear to read anything that has to do with the Salem trials."

Adam shrugged. "It's a subject close to my heart. In fact, there's an exhibition on witch trials and medieval torture at Minerva's museum tonight. I was going to ask you if you'd like to go?"

"That sounds pretty gruesome." *Damn,* she silently cursed when disappointment filled his eyes. Still guilt-ridden over her lie, she sighed. "Well, perhaps it wouldn't be too bad."

Thaddeus smiled. "History can be gruesome, but it is all a part of our past."

"I suppose. Although Minerva can be pretty weird at times. I can't imagine what she's come up with."

"Trust me, it will be an experience you won't forget. I can pick you up after work. We can go to the museum, then eat at the Louisiana Pizza Kitchen."

Kendra laughed. "Well, how could I turn down an offer like that?"

When Kendra got back to Enchantment, Loren and Deanne were bursting with questions.

"So, what else did Thaddeus say about Jared after I left?" Deanne was the first to ask. "After what Jared told you about Thaddeus, I can't wait to hear his side of the story."

Kendra placed her purse behind the counter, then repeated her and Thaddeus' conversation.

"Jared has a hell of a nerve telling Thaddeus to stay away from you," Deanne said. "Like he still has any right to."

Kendra snorted. "Well, he might think he has the right, but he's going to learn otherwise."

"I still can't believe Jared thinks this Adam person and Thaddeus are the same," Loren said. "And that he's a deranged monster. But on the other hand, why would he make it up?"

Deanne threw up her hands. "Because he's crazy." She turned to Kendra. "Right?"

Kendra was rearranging the roses from Thaddeus she'd left sitting on the counter.

Deanne tapped Kendra on the shoulder. "Hello, we're talking to you."

"Aren't these wonderful?" Kendra inhaled deeply. "I don't think I've ever smelled roses this sweet."

"Yeah, they're real nice, but will you stop fooling with them and pay attention?" Deanne asked in exasperation.

Kendra reluctantly turned from the intoxicating aroma of the roses. "Sure, what were you saying?"

"We were talking about how Jared is making all this stuff up."

Kendra shook her head. "I honestly can't put the awful things he told me together with Thaddeus. He's one of the most thoughtful men I've ever met."

Loren shrugged. "Perhaps it's as simple as mistaken identity."

"I'm beginning to think that must be the answer. Jared may be a jerk, but he wouldn't make up a story like that. He had a bad experience with someone, just not Thaddeus."

Deanne placed her hands on her hips. "Something's telling me more happened last night between you and Jared than you're letting on."

Kendra busied herself straightening an already neat display of tarot cards.

"Jared got you all soft and gooey, didn't he? Now you're going to put your blinders back on and let him convince you to take him back, aren't you?"

"Jared did not get me all soft and gooey. And I didn't say I was going to take him back either."

"Girl, you lie about as well as my little sister when she denies eating cookies while her mouth is ringed with chocolate. So spill it, what happened?"

Kendra let out a long breath. "I didn't go to bed with him, if that's what you're getting at." She sighed. "But I came close."

"I knew it," Deanne said. "I could tell by the way you were acting last night."

Memories of her body's response to Jared's touch made Kendra turn away. "I didn't want to say anything because I didn't want to hear what a fool I am. But I've learned from my mistakes and it won't happen again. Until I feel I can be alone with him and not want to rip his clothes off, I have to stay away from him."

Deanne giggled. "Well, if your problem is having an itch that needs scratched, I'll bet Thaddeus would be more than willing to help you out."

"Since Jared is the only man I've ever been with, it's not easy thinking about sex with another man."

"Who knows; Thaddeus might rock your boat more than Jared," Deanne said.

"I can't imagine that, but sex isn't my biggest problem right now. Thaddeus has asked me to go with him to Minerva's witch museum tonight. She's having some kind of display on torture and the persecution of witches, the thought of which freaks me out."

Just then the bells over the door tinkled, and a short, plump woman came in.

"Hello, Mrs. Bass," Kendra said. "How are you?"

"Hello, girls, I'm just fine," she replied. "I heard all about your shop and wanted to come see for myself."

"Well, we're glad you stopped by," Kendra said. "Let us know if we can be of any help."

Loren lowered her voice. "I can't imagine why anyone would want to see Minerva's torture display."

Deanne nodded. "She's some weird witch."

"Are you going to go?" Loren asked.

"I told Thaddeus I would, but I have this strange feeling I shouldn't."

"Then tell him the exhibit isn't something you're comfortable seeing," Loren suggested.

"He was so pleased when I agreed to go. It would hurt his feelings. I'm just being silly. Who knows; the exhibit might be very interesting."

"There are rumors Minerva is involved with dark magic," Deanne said.

Loren shook her head. "That's just because she's different. I'm sure she's no more into dark magic than Thaddeus is."

Three teenage girls, all in paisley scarf skirts, entered the shop and headed for the display of blown glass figures. "I'll go help them," Kendra said. "You two see if Mrs. Bass needs anything."

"Good grief," Loren said agitatedly, when the store was again empty. "I didn't think Mrs. Bass would ever make a decision on what herbs she wanted. I swear she kept picking the same ones up and putting them back down."

"Mrs. Bass bought some of our fresh herbs?"

Kendra asked.

Loren nodded.

Kendra watched through the plate glass window as Harriet Bass flicked open her cell phone before hurrying down the street. "She's got one of the finest herb gardens in New Orleans, so why is she buying them from us?"

Loren shrugged. "Perhaps she's just being nice and trying to help us out."

"Oh, what does it matter," Deanne said. "A sale is a sale. I'm more interested in what Kendra is going to do about the two men in her life."

Kendra smiled. "I'm going to go out with one and tell the other one where to go."

Chapter 18

Outside the Dupre hotel library, Jared thanked Mrs. Bass and disconnected his phone. Woodrow had done as he'd asked and told the coven about Adam. They were keeping an eye on Kendra. Jared knew if she ever found out he had asked the coven to watch her, his ass was dead meat, but it was for her own safety.

He frowned. Harriet Bass had told him she overheard the girls talking about Kendra going to Minerva's museum tonight. He shook his head. He couldn't imagine Kendra agreeing to go to such a place. A cold dread knotted in his stomach. Could this be another manifestation of Adam's control over her? Why else would she agree? Damn, just what he wanted to do, spend his evening in some spooky house of horrors, but he wasn't about to allow Kendra to be there alone with Adam. He'd stay out of sight and watch.

The grandfather clock in the lobby behind him struck the hour. "*Merde.*" He'd been with his father longer than he'd planned. Well, he had a little time to look through the display cases before he needed to leave.

Whenever he entered the hotel library, it was as if he'd stepped back in time. Tall, narrow French windows which led out onto the courtyard ran along one wall. Opposite them stood floor-to-ceiling bookcases stuffed with leather-bound books. A portrait of a beautiful, olive-skinned, raven-haired woman hung above the marble mantel of a brick fireplace flanked by glass-topped display cases. Delicate spindle-legged tables held Tiffany lamps. Overstuffed couches and chairs sat upon a thick Turkish rug. The room smelled of lemon furniture polish and aged port.

Removing a ring of brass keys from his pocket, Jared unlocked a display case and lifted the lid. Among the memorabilia was an assortment of tintypes depicting nineteenth-century Dupres, the original deed to the hotel, the dining room's first menu, an 1804 map of the Vieux Carre, and a page from an 1858 register listing S. L. Clemens as a guest.

Not seeing anything he thought would help, Jared opened the other case. This held a lady's lace and ivory fan, a silver-plated brush and comb, a black and gold feathered Mardi Gras mask, opera glasses, a man's gold pocket watch, and delicate gold and silver jewelry. Jared recalled his mother telling him the lady's items belonged to Angelique.

He was about to close and lock the case when a silver brooch, tarnished with age, caught his attention. Lifting it from its bed of velvet, Jared crossed to the windows where the light was better. Studying it closely, Jared discerned an intricate, thin circle of silver surrounding an interwoven pentacle.

As he stared down at the brooch, the air around him stirred. He turned, his eyes locking with those of the portrait. A shaft of sunlight streaked through the window illuminating the silver brooch pinned to her bodice. Jared moved closer and his pulse quickened. There was no doubt. The brooch he held in his hand was identical to the one Angelique Dupre wore in the portrait. When Jared's eyes again met hers, he swore and took a step back. Angelique's eyes glowed with a dark intensity.

"Okay, you definitely have my attention. So give me some answers. Who is Augustus Montief, and what did you do to make his descendent want to kill me?"

When Angelique didn't respond, Jared, frustrated, silently cursed.

"You know I never had the chance to thank you for saving my life on Black Island, so thank you."

Still no response.

"I can't deal with this situation without answers. You appeared to me once, and I was told by some street spirit you held the truth and could help me." The brooch vibrated in his hand. Jared's eyes widened in surprise when the circular center loosened. Carefully, he opened it the rest of the way. Inside was a miniature portrait of an older mulatto woman holding a white baby. The woman was identical to the spirit who had led him to Congo square. He read the inscription: "My beloved grandmother, Taneen, and my treasured son, Anton, 1792."

Trying to process the implications of what this meant, Jared's eyes shot back to Angelique's portrait. "Are you telling me the spirit I saw was my great-great something grandmother?" He laughed out loud. No wonder she was so bossy. He smiled down at the brooch. "Well, I'll be damned."

Jared waited to see if Angelique would show him anything else. When nothing happened, he placed the brooch back into the display case, and his eye fell upon the Mardi Gras mask. He studied the woven design of the gold thread. Once again, a pentacle took shape next to the right eye. As he stared at it, he realized the thread that ran across the top of the mask was different. Running his finger along it, he discovered it wasn't thread but thin metal. He turned the mask over and felt along the seam. "And what do we have here?" His fingers touched something hard beneath the fabric. Gently he passed one finger back and forth over the object. "That's it, loosen for me, so I can see what you are."

He smiled with satisfaction when the tiny gold key nestled inside revealed itself. As he held it in his palm, the image of a small, carved wooden chest flickered through his mind. *Okay, we're one step closer.* Closing his fist around the key, Jared again went to stand before Angelique's portrait.

"I don't have time for a treasure hunt, so I'd appreciate it if you'd just tell me where the chest is and if it's of any importance to my understanding the past." He waited, but nothing happened. He tried not to let his impatience show. "Can you at least give me a clue?" His mirror appeared in his hand. He glanced from the portrait to the mirror.

"Show me the chest," he commanded. The glass went dark, then a room appeared. He peered closer. "Show me more." When it didn't change, he took the mirror and sat in a high-backed chair where he concentrated on the image within it. Visible above a brick fireplace was a painting of the hotel courtyard resplendent with summer blooms. Next to this stood a gilded table between two casement windows covered by lace curtains. Ornate crown molding ran along the ceiling, and the edge of a faded oriental rug lay on a hardwood floor.

The room must be in the hotel, but Jared couldn't place where. It wasn't one of the guest rooms nor did he think it was his parents' suite. Considering his father had said his mother had put the chest away after giving him the mirror, it had to be a room she would have used. He'd show it to his father. Perhaps he'd recognize it.

As he sat, possibilities playing through his mind, the image suddenly changed. Jared watched as Kendra paused in front of Minerva's shop. Damn it, he'd lost all track of time. He waved his hand and his jacket appeared. Slipping it on, he left the library and was halfway across the lobby when someone called his name. Turning, he saw Kathleen Leblanc coming toward him.

Damn, he didn't have time for this. "Hey, Kathleen," he said when she stopped in front of him. "I'm sorry, but I'm in a hurry."

"Jared, we have a problem with one of tomorrow morning's deliveries."

"Can't you handle it?"

"He insists on speaking with either you or your father."

Jared sighed with exasperation. "Then get my father."

"He's not here. I have the person in charge of the delivery on the phone."

Jared swore colorfully in French and took the phone from her outstretched hand.

****

Minerva's Metaphysical Sundries and Museum of Witchcraft occupied a two-story frame house on St. Claude in the Faubourg Marigny, a neighborhood bordering the Quarter that was less touristy but coming into its own as an arts community and nightlife venue.

When Kendra and Thaddeus arrived, the sky was darkening, and the air smelled of rain. Before going in, they stopped in front of the display window. Glowing pillar candles of black, red, white, yellow, green and blue were arranged upon tiers of black velvet. Scattered among these, blown glass gnomes, trolls, gargoyles, and hissing coiled snakes twinkled eerily in the candlelight. Across the top hung grotesque masks depicting horned beasts and sneering devils.

"It's certainly not like Enchantment's window display," Kendra said.

Thaddeus chuckled. "But still eye-catching."

Kendra smiled. "I can't deny that. It didn't look anything like this the last time I was here." She paused. "It was the day I met you." She'd needed supplies for Enchantment and had stopped by Minerva's to see if she had anything they could use. Thaddeus had walked out of Minerva's back room, and when his eyes met hers, a warm comforting feeling came over her. Her emotions still raw from Jared's betrayal, she found herself drawn to him. Minerva introduced him as a friend from out of town. She and Thaddeus talked for quite a while. He asked her about places to see in the Quarter, and she offered to show him around. She'd enjoyed his company, but even though he'd tried to deepen their relationship, she hadn't allowed it to go any further.

"Minerva said she wanted to grab people's attention, and I think she's achieved that," Thaddeus continued. "She also had to rearrange the store so she could put the museum on the second floor."

Kendra pointed at a double-edged thin-bladed knife with a black handle. "What do you think that's used for? It's not a *boline* for cutting herbs or a ritual *athame*."

Thaddeus bent closer to the glass. "I'm not sure. It might be some kind of sacrificial knife."

"Great," Kendra murmured with a shudder. "Okay, well, I guess we should go in."

Thaddeus nodded. "After you." He held open the solid wood-paneled door.

The musky smell of sandalwood and patchouli engulfed Kendra. As her eyes adjusted to the dim candlelight, an undercurrent of negative energy put her senses on alert. A small gathering of people moved among the array of voodoo dolls, silver chalices, incense, ritual kits, and strange objects in glass jars Kendra had no interest in knowing about. When a beaded curtain in the rear of the store was drawn back, a collective gasp filled the room.

Kendra understood why. Minerva in bright daylight could be startling. Minerva in this setting was downright unnerving. Her hair, dark as pitch, coiled like snakes high upon her head. Her face was long and pointed and her skin so pallid as to appear translucent. Her heavy-lidded eyes were lined in coal black and her lips painted blood red. Her clinging black dress reminded Kendra of Morticia's from the Addams family. Tiny silver serpents dangled from her ears and from a twisted silver chain around her neck.

"Good evening," Minerva said, her voice low, with a slight eastern-European accent that Kendra thought fake. "*Velcome* to my exhibit." Her smile showed a row of tiny white teeth like small ivory chisels. "Before you see the exhibit, please help yourself to some hors d'oeuvres and a vonderful spiced punch of my own concoction." She gestured toward the curtained doorway. "Everything is in the next room. Due to limited space upstairs, I have to ask that no more than three of you go up at a time." She flung out her arms. "Now, enjoy."

Minerva sent the first group up the enclosed staircase, then, noticing Kendra and Thaddeus, headed their way.

She turned so Thaddeus could kiss her cheek. "Thaddeus, velcome. How vonderful to see the two of you. And Kendra, how nice of you to come."

"Hi, Minerva," Kendra clasped the claw-like hand she held out. "The shop is quite something."

"Oh, thank you. Vait until you see my exhibit. I hired a man who would put Madam Tussauds to shame." A woman's scream floated down the stairs, and all heads turned that way. Minerva laughed. "Everyone, don't be alarmed. Some of the figures depicting the persecution of vitches are extremely lifelike and may startle you."

Perfect, Kendra thought. *I can't* vait.

"Let me fix you each a glass of my punch and a plate of hors d'oeuvres," Minerva said. "Then after the final group you can go up, and you'll be able to take your time."

Before Kendra could decline the food and drink, Thaddeus spoke. "That sounds good. I could use a bite, and I was hoping we could go up last."

"Vonderful." Minerva headed in the direction of the adjoining room. "Follow me."

Stretching out each syllable, Kendra mimicked,

"*Follow me*."

Adam frowned.

She gave him a sheepish grin. "Sorry, I couldn't resist. She is a bit of a cliché, you have to admit."

Kendra declined food but accepted a glass of greenish punch from Thaddeus. As she sipped the frothy brew, she studied her surroundings. Fat candles burned in wall sconces. A crystal ball sat on a cloth-draped table beside a deck of tarot cards. Bags of herbs filled a counter, and bowls of colored crystals were set around the room.

A display of books caught her attention. In order to read the titles, she stepped closer. Considering Minerva's reputation, she wasn't surprised to see the majority of the books had to do with the occult: *The Magus*, *The Grimoire of Abrahmelin*, *The Malleus Maeficarum*. Mixed among these, the *Pharmakeia of Love Potions and Aphrodisiacs* caught her eye and she took it down.

"A stimulating read," Thaddeus said from behind her.

Lost in the book, Kendra jumped and slammed it shut. Mortified, she quickly replaced it on the shelf. "Yes, well, Minerva has some interesting reading."

He smiled. "If you're ready, it's our turn."

Kendra glanced around, surprised to see the room was empty. "Where is everyone?"

"They've all gone. We're the only ones left."

"Really? I didn't see anyone leave."

Amusement danced in his eyes. "You must have been too enthralled by your reading."

Her cheeks burning, she busied herself with setting down her nearly empty glass, then took a deep breath.

"Okay, let's go."

"You can finish your punch. I'm not in that big of a hurry."

She shook her head and lowered her voice. "I don't know what Minerva put in it, but it's awfully sweet."

"Did you think so? I thought it was rather tasty." He took her arm and guided her toward the stairs.

Minerva was nowhere in sight as they headed up the narrow staircase. Suddenly feeling lightheaded, Kendra clung to the banister. *I should have had something to eat,* she thought as she stepped through the door at the top of the stairs into utter Hell.

Low moans of pain and agony filled the air. Other than a few candlelit wall sconces and an eerie glow coming from what Kendra assumed to be the exhibits, the rest of the room was in darkness.

Her dizziness increased. She blinked to try and clear her mind as Thaddeus led her to the first display. A gasp lodged in her throat when she saw a woman swinging from a gallows, wrists and ankles bound, her face grotesquely distorted by bulging eyes and a protruding tongue.

"No," Kendra murmured taking a step back.

Thaddeus put his arm around her. "It's all right, I'm here," he whispered in her ear as he guided her down the room.

Unsteady on her feet, she was about to ask him if Minerva's punch was laced with alcohol when the words died on her lips. In front of her was a woman stripped to the waist, her back streaming with what looked like real blood, as a man with a whip slashed her flesh open. Kendra swallowed back the bile that rose in her throat. "Thaddeus, I've seen enough. I'd like to leave." She frowned. Had she slurred her words?

Thaddeus held her tight against the front of him and kissed the side of her face. "It's all right, sweet. I'll protect you."

His hard member pressed against her backside. She shook her head. It must be her imagination. He couldn't possibly be aroused by this. In front of them now was a woman in stocks, with people jeering and throwing rotten fruit at her.

A slight buzzing began in Kendra's ears. The exhibits went in and out of focus.

"Are you all right?" Thaddeus murmured in her ear. "I'm sure I can find a place for you to lie down if you're not feeling well."

"No, I'm fine," she managed to say through numbed lips. "I just want to leave."

He ran his hands up and down her arms. "Perhaps just a short rest. There's a room right over here. I know I can calm your fears." He kissed her neck.

Kendra grasped at her gold unicorn, but she couldn't make her fingers close around it. With every bit of will power she possessed, she tried to come up with the words for a clarity spell, but her mind was blank. Panic clawed at her chest. Minerva's punch had to have been spiked, but with what? There were times when she'd had too much to drink, but she'd never felt like this. Again she tried to clear her head. Her breath came in shallow gasps. She wasn't sure what was real. *Oh, sweet Mother of the Gods, help me,* she silently cried.

"Here we are, the last exhibit," she heard Thaddeus say just before a scream ripped from her throat.

A naked woman was lashed to a post, her mouth

opened in a silent wail of agony as flames licked at her legs, slowly working their way up her body until they totally engulfed her. Kendra could have sworn she felt the heat and heard the woman's screams.

Thaddeus stood behind her, his body molded to hers, his words coming to her from a distance. "Pleasure and pain are closely intertwined. The greatest pleasure is in experiencing them as one. Come with me, sweet. I'll show you."

Voices and images swirled around her. Hands gently stroked her breasts through the silk of her shirt. The juncture between her legs ached for release.

In horror she whimpered, "No, please, no." Mentally she fought back with everything she had. In a brief flash of clarity, by the light of the flames, she made out what she hoped was a door. Breathing hard, half-crazed, she summoned all her remaining will and struck out with a blast of energy, knocking Thaddeus off his feet. She heard a thump and a curse but didn't look back.

Kendra stumbled toward the door, her high heels making her progress erratic. With hands that shook uncontrollably, she fumbled with the knob. When she finally managed to get it open, she clung to the banister, praying she wouldn't fall as she careened down the stairs. She tripped on the last step, her calf-length skirt tangling around her legs, pitching her hard onto the sidewalk.

Tears streaming down her cheeks, she heard Thaddeus calling her name. The cool night air and the gentle rain hitting her face began to clear her head. With scraped hands, she pushed herself to her knees, then rose unsteadily to her feet and tried to run.

Chapter 19

Delayed by the delivery mess at the hotel, then unable to find a parking place, Jared turned the corner by Minerva's shop. Kendra weaved toward him, random energy shooting around her.

He slammed on the brakes and leapt out of the car, leaving it in the middle of the street. Protecting himself as well as he could from her energy spikes, Jared caught her as she was about to go off the curb.

Seeming not to know who he was, she struggled to get out of his arms. "Let me go." She screamed.

When he held her tighter, she sent an energy charge through him that about knocked him on his ass.

Regaining his balance, again he fought off the spears of energy. "Kendra, it's me." He gave her a shake. "What's wrong with you?"

Her pupils were dilated and her breath came in tiny gasps. Jared could tell she was trying to focus on his face.

"Jared?"

"Yeah, baby, it's me."

"Get me out of here." Her words came slightly slurred.

"Sure thing, but first you have to bring the energy back in. Come on, you can do it. Concentrate. That's it." As the energy around her lessened, Jared helped her into the Porsche. He glanced in the direction she'd come from. He saw Adam disappear around the corner and yelled, "Cowardly fucker."

When they were both in the car, Kendra lay back against the headrest, her breathing settling back to normal.

His stomach in knots at the thought of what Adam might have done, he tentatively asked, "What did he do to you?"

She shook her head. "Who? What?"

"That man you call *Thaddeus*. What did he do?"

"No, not him. Minerva."

Jared frowned. "What?"

"Jared, please, I think something was in the punch. Please help me clear my mind."

"They drugged you?"

"In the punch."

"I'm going to need you to sit up."

She did as he asked. He held her face between his hands and looked into her eyes, then cursed. Her pupils were still dilated, but as hard as he tried he couldn't penetrate through. He gritted his teeth. There was another way he could give her his power. He pulled her close and covered her mouth with his.

When he felt her relax and her breathing become more regular, he broke the kiss. "Better?"

She nodded. "Thanks."

He brushed the hair from her face. "You were pretty out of it. That kiss was strictly for medicinal purposes. Can you tell me what happened?"

"Not here. Take me home."

"Okay." He noticed her bleeding hands and swore. "I'm not very good at this, but I'll try." He took each one in his, murmuring softly, until the scrapes faded.

"That should do for now."

For the first time since he'd found her, she gave him a tremulous smile. "My shining knight."

"Always." He put the car into gear and pulled out onto the street. Traffic was light so it was a quick trip to her apartment.

She led him up the stairs and into the open airy room that Jared thought was totally Kendra. Napping in a chair, Clementine raised her head, stretched, and yawned, then jumped down and hurried over to rub against Jared's leg. He crouched down and scratched her behind the ears. "Well, at least *she* still likes me."

"She likes anyone who will give her some attention."

Jared rose. "Typical female."

Kendra placed her purse on the kitchen counter next to a vase of roses.

Jared frowned. *That asshole 'Thaddeus' probably sent them.* Not wanting to upset Kendra any more than she already was, he kept quiet.

To Jared's disbelief, she turned and fell into his arms.

"Hold me, Jared. Just hold me."

"Sure." He wrapped his arms tightly around her. "Do you want to tell me what happened?"

She shook her head. "I don't want to think about it now." She wound her arms around his neck. "Make me think of something else."

"I'd be happy to." His mouth covered hers.

****

Kendra lost herself in the taste of Jared's kiss and the incredible way he made her feel. In the back of her mind, she knew she was about to make a huge mistake, but for now she didn't care. She wanted nothing more than to lose herself in the wonderful sensations only Jared could excite in her.

Breathless from his kiss, she gazed into his eyes, dark with his need and his desire. Remembering how he could make her body sing with pleasure, she whispered, "Love me, Jared."

"I thought you'd never ask." The wicked smile he gave her had her tingling with delicious anticipation. "Where's your bed?"

Her pulse quickening, she pointed to an open door.

He picked her up and carried her into the bedroom. The walls were painted pearl gray with white trim. On one wall was a large watercolor of a sunset over Lake Pontchartrain. The furniture was from her apartment, and a rattan fan rotated slowly over her four-poster bed.

"You've had this bed for a long time."

She nodded. "It holds lots of memories."

His grin widened. "That it does." He fell with her onto the quilt covered mattress. "I remember sneaking into your bedroom at your parents'. And how I had to muffle your screams."

"My screams? What about...?" The rest of her words were silenced when his lips covered hers. The kiss was a tangle of tongues as their hunger for each other grew.

Jared fumbled with the buttons of her blouse. "We need to get out of these clothes."

"I agree." She unsnapped his jeans and tugged at his shirt. When his chest was bare, she ran her fingers through his thick chest hair.

He skillfully unclasped her lacy bra. "You have no idea how much I've missed you," he said as he placed kisses along her neck. "I've missed the taste of you, the feel of you." He ran his thumb across her taught nipple. "Baby, you have to know how much I love you." He bent and took one swollen peak between his teeth and tugged.

She moaned his name as her body reacted to this sweet torment. He squeezed and caressed her while taking her nipple deep into his mouth.

Her breath caught. "Jared, I want…"

"You want what?" He circled her nipple with his tongue.

She squirmed, trying to wriggle out of her skirt. "More."

He nipped at her nipple with his teeth. "We should take this nice and slow."

"Jared."

He chuckled and ran his hand down her stomach, over her hip, and across her backside and slowly unzipped her skirt.

She kicked off her shoes as he slid the soft cotton down her legs and tossed it onto the floor. He ran his hand back up her inner thigh to cup the junction between her legs. "Mmm, what do we have here?"

Kendra gritted her teeth. "Damn it, Jared."

"What, love?" Through the fabric of her panties, he made tiny circles with his thumb. "You like that?"

Her climax building, she gasped. "Stop that and take them off."

His grin was pure devil. "I'd be happy to." He slid her panties down, then, as she watched through a haze of passion, he unhooked his belt and let his jeans fall. When he stood before her naked and aroused, her throat went dry. She opened her arms. "Come to me."

But instead of doing as she asked, he knelt at the side of the bed and spread her legs. "I know what you want. Open for me, baby. Let me taste you."

"Oh, Mother of the Gods." Kendra whimpered as she dug her nails into his bare shoulders. His tongue and teeth tasted and teased her female bud until she was writhing against him. "Jared, please."

He chuckled low. "I'm trying to please you. How's this?" He slid two fingers inside her and watched her body convulse as she screamed his name. "That's it. Come for me."

Before her mind cleared, Jared was over her. "Wrap your legs around me," he demanded, and in one quick thrust he buried himself deep inside her.

Kendra entwined her fingers in the thick hair at the base of his neck. They moved together until as one their magic merged. A magenta mist blending with dark blue emanated from them, becoming more vibrant as their heat increased and their passion rose.

"Give me all you've got, sweetheart," Jared rasped, his gaze boring into hers as the mist swirled faster and faster. "That's it; come over the edge with me."

Kendra let his magic fill her, until as one they soared into oblivion.

Jared buried his face against her neck, as they tried to regain their breath. "Well, that's a good start. Give me a minute and we'll take it slower this time."

"Hmm." Kendra hummed contentedly as she ran her hand down his back. "I'm perfectly happy right now."

"I can make you even happier."

She chuckled. "I doubt that."

"Is that right? Let's see."

"Jared," she gasped when his warm mouth found the sensitive spot just beneath her ear.

"See, I told you."

In the kitchen, Clementine's ears twitched as Kendra's cell phone rang.

****

Adam slammed his phone shut and threw it across the living room. Blood red energy pulsed from his body. The little bitch wasn't answering her phone because she was too busy fucking Dupre. The drops of datura he'd put into her punch were just beginning to take effect when she'd freaked and ran from him. It should be him pounding into her, not Dupre. He'd been so aroused as he stood behind her, watching the horror on her face as she looked at the exhibits, he had wanted to take her right there.

He'd planned it all perfectly. Kathleen was to keep Dupre busy and Minerva had agreed to leave and allow him access to the upstairs bedroom. By the time the night was through, Kendra should have been his. He ground his teeth. His cock was getting hard just thinking of the ways he'd meant to have her. He hadn't thought she'd be clearheaded enough to knock him down and escape.

His eyes narrowed. Well, she'd pay for using magic against him. When he'd rounded the corner and seen her in Dupre's arms, he should have killed them both. A smile spread across his face. No, that would have been too easy. Before he killed him, he was going to make Dupre watch as he fucked the little bitch silly. He'd keep her until he tired of her, then she could join her love in the afterlife.

He retrieved his phone from the floor. He needed

to work off his lust and anger, and he knew exactly how he wanted to do it. He punched in a number. "Kathleen, get over here."

Chapter 20

Predawn light filtered through the shuttered windows while the sounds of the French Quarter coming to life filled the room. Car horns blared, delivery trucks rumbled past, and a carriage clattered by on its way to Jackson Square. Kendra stretched contentedly as memories of their passionate night played gently through her mind. She turned to the man sleeping beside her, brushed the hair from his forehead, and sighed.

How could she have been so incredibly stupid as to throw herself into his arms? But she knew the answer too well. Jared was the one person she knew would keep her safe and make her forget the horrors she'd seen. But by giving into her desire for him, she'd just set herself up for more heartbreak.

Idiot, idiot, idiot, she chastised herself. *The first time you're upset and scared, what do you do but play right into his hands? If you want to keep your heart in one piece, and not have history repeat itself, then last night can't be anything more than a night of comfort and great sex. If you don't want to spend the rest of your life crying over him, you'd better end this now.*

With determination Kendra flung back the covers. As she sat up, a strong arm went around her waist pulling her back.

"Where are you going?" Jared held her close

against his naked body and nuzzled her neck. "I have an excellent idea how we can begin our day."

The physical manifestation of his idea pressed hard against her bottom as he caressed her breast. "You feel so soft and so good," he whispered in her ear. "I think we should spend the day right here." He ran his hand over her hip. "It's been a long time, and we've got a lot of catching up to do."

"And whose fault is that?" Kendra pushed his hand away and reached for her robe.

"Whoa. Come back here." Jared gathered her against him. "I thought we worked our way past this last night."

"Well, I guess you were wrong. Now let go of me. I need to get ready for work."

Jared glanced at the bedside clock. "It's six-thirty in the morning. We have plenty of time to finish this conversation. So tell me how we got from what we had last night to you being pissed at me all over again."

Kendra ground her teeth. The arrogance of the man was incredible. Did he honestly think all it would take was a night in his arms for her to forgive and trust him again? The presumptuous ass was in for a surprise. She may have let her fear and passion rule last night, but the shield around her heart was still intact.

"Who said I wasn't still pissed at you? Just because I let you make love to me doesn't mean I've forgiven you. In fact, I'm far from it. I had a need, and you fulfilled that need. Don't read any more into it than that. As far as I'm concerned, last night was nothing more than two old friends enjoying good sex."

Jared braced himself on one elbow and glared down at her. "Two old friends enjoying sex? What the hell is that supposed to mean?"

She willed her voice to sound calm and steady. "We had a night of great sex and that's all. Don't assume because of that you're back in my life."

His eyes darkened with suppressed anger. "You can look at me and tell me that what we felt last night meant nothing to you?"

Behind the anger, Kendra heard the hurt in his voice. It took every bit of willpower she possessed not to throw her arms around his neck and tell him she still loved him and wanted him back. But she'd shed too many tears and there was too much remembered pain for her to take that chance. Swallowing back the lump in her throat, she whispered, "Yes."

His jaw clenched, a myriad of emotions flickering in his eyes. He demanded, "Then explain to me why you wanted me last night? If all you needed was sex"—he smiled coldly—"then why didn't you stay and allow your friend Adam, or, sorry, I mean Thaddeus, to comfort you? Why were you running away from him like the hounds of hell were at your heels?"

"I wasn't trying to get away from Thaddeus. I wanted to get as far from Minerva's horrible exhibit as I could."

Jared snorted. "Is that right? Do you remember you were drugged out of your mind?"

"Thaddeus had nothing to do with that. Minerva must have laced the punch with something."

He shook his head. "Minerva is a weird witch, but why in the hell would she drug her punch? Did you notice anyone else acting doped?"

She'd been so enthralled by the book on aphrodisiacs, they could have all been prancing about naked and she wouldn't have noticed. "No, but that doesn't mean they weren't. I wasn't paying attention to everyone. Besides, if something was added to the punch, anyone that was there could have done it."

"Did your boyfriend seem drugged?"

She opened her mouth to reply but closed it again. Had Thaddeus acted strange? She didn't think so. Her memories were mostly jumbled unfocused images. From what she could remember, she thought he'd been kind and wanted to help her. She frowned. There was something, but as hard as she tried it wouldn't come. She shook her head.

"Well, was he?"

"No, he acted perfectly normal. As much as you'd like to think Thaddeus is some kind of bad guy, I'll have to disappoint you. He did nothing wrong last night. I ran because I was scared. I needed comfort and you just happened to be there, and things between us went too far. That's all."

The smile he gave her chilled her to the bone. "You know, love, considering the way you were all over me, I'd say not only is your new boyfriend the scum of the earth, he must not be much of a man. I can hardly wait to tell him I had to step in and satisfy his woman."

At that moment Kendra was so mad, she wanted nothing more than to slap the smug look off his face. Her intentions must have shown because his eyes narrowed and in a low voice said, "Don't try it."

She gritted her teeth. "Don't tempt me. You're being disgusting and vulgar."

They glared at each other. Kendra tried to regain her composure. She let out a long breath. "Jared, Thaddeus is a good and decent man who, I'm sure,

225

given the chance, wouldn't leave me and break my heart. I'm not going to lie here and listen to you put him down."

"Is that right? Well, you should learn more about someone before you let them into your bed. For your information, your boyfriend uses his power to brainwash his victims into doing despicable acts that would make you violently ill."

"Stop it." Kendra placed her hands against his chest. "You don't know anything about him. You're just saying this because you're angry he's in my life. What did you expect me to do, Jared, just sit around hoping you'd come back?" She held back the tears that threatened to fall. "I believed you when you said you loved me, and what did you do? You left and told me you didn't want me anymore." Her breath came in tiny gasps. "And now you're here, and you expect me to forget what you put me through. The hell with that. You've got a long way to go before I'll ever trust you again. In the meantime, I'm seeing Thaddeus, and you'll just have to get used to it."

Jared's words came out in a growl. "If anyone has to get used to something, it's you. Like it or not, your boyfriend is exactly what I said he is and more. The bastard recruited my brother into his demented cult and threatened to come after you as well. Saving my brother and keeping that asshole's hands off you are why I had to leave. Damn it, Kendra, I love you. I told you I've always loved you. Can't you understand it's because of my love for you I had to do what I did?"

"Jared, I don't want to hear this. If you loved me that much, why did you call me and tell me you couldn't marry me?"

"If you calm down, I'll try again to explain. In order to keep you safe, I had to break all ties with you. Your boyfriend threatened to kill Philippe if I didn't call you and tell you we were through. I had to make sure he wouldn't use you to get to me, and now he's doing just that. As I told you, Adam has vowed vengeance against my family and those who are close to me.

"Damn it." He rolled off her and sat on the edge of the bed. "I don't know how the bastard survived the fall, but it must have taken some powerful magic. His being here now is not a coincidence. He's pissed I lived and got Philippe away from him, and now he's here for you." He turned to where she still lay. "How did you meet him anyway?"

Kendra thought of telling him that it was none of his business, but instead she said, "At Minerva's."

Jared laughed. "You picked him up in a store dealing with the occult. For the love of Odin, Kendra, shouldn't that tell you something?"

Kendra frowned. "Minerva's shop doesn't just deal in the occult. A lot of people go there. In fact, before we opened Enchantment, I went to ask her about some of her suppliers. And I'm certainly not into dark magic."

"Tell me, what does your boyfriend do for a living?"

Kendra's frown deepened. "He told me he's a teacher on sabbatical. What does that have to do with anything?"

Jared snorted. "He's a teacher all right. For your information, his school is in a secure compound on Black Island and he teaches young people how to become as evil as he is."

Kendra sat up, the sheet falling away to reveal her breasts. When Jared switched his attention to her chest, she quickly covered herself. "Thaddeus told me how you threatened him. He told me he'd never met you and had no idea what you were talking about."

Jared shook his head. "Did you expect him to tell the truth?"

"Isn't it possible you have him confused with someone else?"

He let out a frustrated breath and, naked, got to his feet. "No, Kendra, I haven't confused him with someone else."

Kendra's eyes were drawn to the traces of scars on his body that until now, she hadn't noticed. "Oh, Jared." Now on her knees, she lightly traced her finger along the jagged line that ran below his ribs. "What happened to you?"

He smiled without humor. "Your friend did that to me."

She shook her head. "No, he couldn't."

"Yes, he could."

She fell back against the headboard, her mind reeling. Was he telling her the truth? Could Thaddeus be the monster he claimed? Could she have been so easily misled into believing Thaddeus was a kind man who truly cared about her? Or was this all just a horrible misunderstanding? But she couldn't deny Jared's scars. Obviously, some of what he was telling her was true. In the past, if asked whether Jared was capable of deceiving her, she would have said it was impossible. On the other hand, if told he would leave her days before her wedding, she would have said that wasn't possible either. Now she didn't know who or what to believe. What she did know was that she needed time to sort this all out and have a chance to talk to Thaddeus.

She sighed. "Jared, I need time to absorb all you've told me."

He sat back down on the bed. "Fine, but while you're doing so, promise me you'll stop seeing him."

Kendra shook her head. "I'm not making you any promises."

He shifted so he lay back on top of her. "Everything I told you is the truth. He's a very dangerous witch. You have to stay away from him."

"I told you I need time to think this through. Now get off me."

"Damn it, Kendra, why won't you listen to me?"

She gritted her teeth. "Jared, I'm going to count to three and if you haven't moved, I'll send your ass flying into the next room."

The smile that spread across his face begged her to try it.

Before she could do so much as flick one finger he had both her hands pinned above her head. "You want to play, then let's play."

His mouth came down over hers. His warm lips dared her not to respond. Just as her resistance weakened, a pounding on the front door jerked her back.

"What the hell is that?" Jared growled.

"My salvation," Kendra panted.

"Their timing is fucking incredible," Jared mumbled as he rolled onto his back.

Kendra glanced at the clock and gasped. "It's

probably Deanne wondering where I am. Thanks to you, I'm late for work." A rather loud feline howl came from the other side of the bedroom door. "And poor Clementine is starving."

Jared got out of bed, stretched, and picked up his jeans before he headed for the door. "That cat could live off her fat for days, but I'll take care of her."

By the time Kendra realized his intention, it was too late. "Jared, don't you dare answer the door," she called, hurrying after him while throwing on her robe.

When Kendra came into the room, Clementine was contentedly eating her morning crunchies. Jared, wearing nothing but his jeans, stood smiling, while Deanne, hands on hips, glowered from the open door.

"What the devil's been going on here?" Deanne demanded, stomping into the room, glaring from Jared to Kendra.

"If it isn't Miss Mary Sunshine," Jared said, closing the door after Deanne stormed past.

Deanne turned an accusatory finger at Jared. "What did you do to Kendra?"

Jared smiled, leaned against the couch, and crossed his arms. "I did everything she asked me to do and more."

Deanne scrunched up her nose. "You're disgusting."

Jared lifted one brow. "Don't hold back, Deanne. Tell me what you really think."

Deanne stomped away, then back toward Jared until she stood directly in front of him. "I think you took advantage of Kendra's feelings for you, and I'd like nothing more than to slow roast you over a pit. And don't you dare laugh at me." She raised her hand and a ball of energy appeared in her palm. Jared was quicker.

"No Jared, don't," Kendra cried, but she was too late. As she watched, Deanne sailed past her to land with a thump in a padded rocker.

"For the love of Odin, Jared, how could you?" Kendra hurried to Deanne's side. "You could have hurt her."

Jared gave Kendra an exasperated look as he slipped on his shirt. "She's fine. I wasn't going to hurt her."

"I can't believe you used your power against her." Kendra planted herself in front of Jared. "What's wrong with you?"

"What the hell was I supposed to do, stand there and let her do who knows what to me? She's not exactly a timid witch."

"I don't know what kind of people you've been with but using power against women is not acceptable behavior in civilized covens. I want you to leave and don't come back!"

"Damn it, Kendra, I told you I didn't have any intention of hurting her. I just wanted her out of my face."

Kendra pointed toward the door. "Leave, now."

"Fine." Jared cursed colorfully in two languages as he gathered up his things. When he was fully dressed, he stopped in front of Kendra and bent down until they were nose to nose and held her arms. "Your boyfriend is the one who likes to hurt women. Remember that." He turned toward Deanne. "If you're such a good friend and want to protect her, keep her away from him. He's the one out to hurt her, not me."

Kendra's eyes flashed. She was so angry she could

hardly form a coherent thought. Finally, she managed to speak between gritted teeth. "Jared, take your hands off me." When he just glared through stormy eyes, Kendra sent a strong jolt of energy soaring up his arms.

"Fuck." He cursed. As fury suffused his face, she took a few steps back.

"Jared, I told you to take your hands off me and I meant it."

Not saying a word, he came slowly toward her.

Eyes narrowed, she took another step back and held up her hand. "Jared, stop right there. If you didn't want me to use magic on you, you shouldn't have manhandled me like that."

The cold grin he gave her had Kendra licking suddenly dry lips. Out of the corner of her eye she saw Deanne begin to rise from her chair. Before she could tell her to stay where she was, Jared flicked his wrist and Kendra felt the protective shield surround them. Kendra knew Deanne could still see them but couldn't penetrate the shield. Even though she knew Jared would never physically harm her, her unease grew as he stopped in front of her and placed his hands on the wall pinning her between them.

"Manhandle you," he said, glaring at her through eyes shining like blue shards of ice. "Sweetheart, if I ever actually manhandle you, trust me you'll know it. As for using magic against me, don't ever do it again."

Kendra knew he had every right to be angry, but damn it, she was angry as well. "Then when I ask you to do something, I expect you to do as I ask, not act like some barbarian. Now, I'll tell you again, leave."

He opened his mouth, closed it again, then shook his head. "Sure, love, I'll leave. Just remember your boyfriend is the true barbarian. If you don't believe me, try using magic against him and see what you get." With a flick of his wrist the shield lifted. With a final scowl he slammed out the door.

Kendra let out a long breath and turned to where Deanne still sat. "Are you sure you're all right?"

"I'm fine. The prick got the jump on me, that's all. Next time I'll kick his ass."

"No you won't, because there isn't going to be a next time. Deanne, you saw his temper. I've never seen him that angry and provoking him won't accomplish anything." Kendra rubbed her temples. "Mother of the Gods, I need coffee, and we have to get downstairs and open the store."

"No, we don't. Loren is there."

"Good." Deanne was right on Kendra's heels as she went into the small kitchen.

"What do you mean there isn't going to be a next time? Are you telling me after the performance we just witnessed you've finally seen what he truly is?"

Kendra scooped dark roast coffee into the coffee maker. "What I mean is that I understand you and Loren are trying to protect me, but I don't want to be protected. Now let me finish before you explode. I couldn't have gotten through the past weeks without your help, and I appreciate all you both did for me, but I need to handle this on my own."

"Girl, what are you talking about? Obviously, Loren and I were right. You can't even be around him without ending up in the sack. Not to mention letting him treat you like he's some domineering macho witch."

Kendra slapped down the lid of the coffee maker.

"Last night was nothing more than sex, and it's over. And I didn't let him treat me like a domineering macho witch. I fought back."

Deanne chortled. "Yeah, right. As soon as he became aggressive, you backed down. As far as sex, it hasn't been over between you two since the first time he put his hands on you. I've never seen two people who couldn't stay out of each other's pants like you two. How many times did we have to cover for you while you snuck off with him to the Dupre Hotel? For the sake of the Gods, Kendra, you almost flunked out of Tulane because you couldn't stay out of his bed."

"That was a long time ago." Kendra paused, slid the vase of roses out of the way, and slammed two coffee cups and the sugar bowl down on the counter. "I'm determined history won't repeat itself."

"Oh, really? So when did this determination begin? The first chance you get, what do you do but hop into the sack with him. How do you know he doesn't have someone waiting for him back wherever he's been? Maybe he's just using you because he knows he can."

The thought of Jared touching another woman the way he touched her made her sick to her stomach. It was out of spite that she allowed Jared to believe she'd been with Thaddeus. The truth was that each time Thaddeus tried to make love to her, Jared's face filled her mind and stopped her. "There can't be anyone else because Jared told me he's here to stay." *And he still loves me and wants me back.*

"He's here to stay? Oh, that's just what you need. Talk about the devil's temptation."

"Deanne, just because I let him back into my bed doesn't mean I'm naive enough to let him back into my life. Like I said, it was just sex."

Deanne cocked her head. "You're telling me one night with Jared has gotten him out of your system?"

Kendra nodded.

Deanne rolled her eyes. "I'll believe that when I see it." She brightened. "I know, you can get Thaddeus to tell him to leave you alone. When he doesn't, Thaddeus can kick the crap out of him." She paused. "Speaking of Thaddeus, what was that Jared was raving about?"

"I thought you'd never ask. But before I tell you what Jared said, let me tell you what happened to me last night."

"Damn, I'm sorry. I forgot about you going to Minerva's. How creepy was it?"

Kendra popped a bagel into the toaster and held up the pack. "Do you want one?"

"Sure."

While they heated, Kendra described what she'd seen and that she thought Minerva may have drugged the punch, ending with Jared finding her and bringing her home. "So you see, I didn't just jump into bed with Jared. I was scared and freaked out and needed comfort. And I know what you're thinking—that's no reason to go to bed with him, but last night it was exactly what I wanted."

Deanne was speechless. She opened and closed her mouth before she finally said, "Holy crap. That bitch drugged you? Where the hell was Thaddeus?"

"You know how Minerva is. She probably put some herb in the punch thinking it would add to the drama of her horrible exhibits." She placed Deanne's bagel on a plate and poured her a cup of coffee. "And you know how susceptible I am to alcohol. It could have affected me more than anyone else. What I do feel bad about is running out on Thaddeus. I know he was coming after me, and if he saw me with Jared, well, Jared may not have to worry about me being with Thaddeus any longer."

Deanne sipped her coffee and looked thoughtful. "I don't know. Minerva has done some crazy things, but intentionally drugging people? If someone got hurt, I would think she could get into a lot of trouble."

Kendra set down her butter knife. "That's true, but something definitely happened to me. If it wasn't Minerva's punch, then what?"

"I think we need to ask Loren about hallucinogenic herbs. Then you need to talk to Thaddeus. If you were as out of it as you say, he must have noticed. Perhaps he knows something."

"Jared told me Thaddeus is really Adam, a demented dark witch who almost killed Philippe and tried to kill Jared. And now is after me."

Deanne snorted. "What bull. We both know he said that because he's jealous."

Chapter 21

Jared slammed into his room at the hotel, threw down his keys, and headed for the bathroom. He was so pissed, he hoped a shower would cool him off. He couldn't understand why the hell Kendra was being so thick-headed. He stripped off his clothes and turned on the spray. He knew he'd hurt her, and she had every reason to be upset, but for the love of Odin, they'd been together for years. Wouldn't you think she'd trust him more than Adam?

He let the hot water pound the back of his neck. His muscles were so tight, he should have gone to the gym. Punching his fist into a bag and pretending it was Adam's face might have been the best way to work out his anger. He turned off the water and reached for a towel. Somehow, he had to convince Kendra that what he'd told her about Adam was true before it was too late.

Dressed and with a strong cup of coffee sitting in front of him, he got out Angelique's mirror. The most constructive thing he could do was discover what the Montiefs' vengeance was about. He looked into the glass. "Show me where the chest is," he commanded. When the image he'd seen before reappeared, he sat back in his chair and studied the room in the glass. Still nothing seemed familiar. Jared tapped his coffee cup in thought. Had Angelique and Jean lived somewhere besides the hotel? It would have been a lot smaller during their time, but as far as he knew they'd been right here. He narrowed his brows. He'd always assumed his parents' master suite had been part of the original hotel, but perhaps not.

Again, he studied the room. His mother had never been a lace curtain and gilt furniture kind of person. She'd preferred damask and dark woods. Frustrated, he sat glowering at the image. "Damn it to hell, Angelique, I'm tired of games. Just show me where the fucking chest is."

"*Merde.*" He covered his head with his arm as books hurtled off the shelves toward him, pictures flew from the walls, and lamps toppled from tables. "Okay, okay, I'm sorry. Stop."

Tentatively he lowered his arm and glanced around. "Christ," he murmured. *Never piss off a ghost.* He looked to where he'd dropped the mirror and silently cursed. Angelique was staring back at him, her eyes blazing with rage. With trepidation, he bent and picked up the mirror. When he opened his mouth to speak, she cut him off.

"I will not tolerate being spoken to in such a disrespectful manner. Nor do I play games. I showed you where the chest is hidden. Go retrieve it."

His own temper, which hadn't cooled much since that morning, resurfaced. "I'd be glad to retrieve it, if I knew where the…" He swallowed back the expletive he was about to use and continued, "Where it was located. I don't recognize the room. Is it in the hotel?"

She scowled. "Certainly, it's in the hotel. It was my private sitting room."

"Well, it's not here now." With surprise and a

certain amount of unease, he watched as she disappeared from the mirror to reappear in full manifestation right in front of him.

A dark-haired beauty, with deep blue eyes and an olive complexion, she wore the rose silk dress from the portrait. High-waisted and with a high gathered neckline, it had puffy sleeves and was trimmed along the bottom with dark roses.

Irritation showed in her eyes as she stood, hands clasped in front of her. "Jared, what are you talking about? It's located off the second-floor gallery overlooking the courtyard."

Jared could feel the power emanating from her. He spread his arms. "I'm sorry, but there isn't anywhere in this hotel that resembles that room."

Deep in thought, Angelique paced, her dress swirling around her feet. "Could they have destroyed it during my absence?"

Jared's brow rose. "Absence?"

She cocked her head and gave him a slight smile. "Though I have been waiting for the one who could use my mirror, I have not spent the last century and a half in this hotel. There are many changes here. Perhaps my sitting room has been turned into something else."

Jared nodded. "That could be. Throughout the years the hotel has been remodeled. We now have fifty guest rooms and this floor with the family suites."

She glanced around the room, waved her hand, and the books, pictures, and lamps were all back in place. Then she glided over to one of the long casement windows. "When my papa passed, Jean and I decided to turn the house into this hotel. We began with ten rooms and that included our quarters. When we," she hesitated, "moved on, there were twenty. With pride I have watched as generation after generation of Dupres have advanced the hotel, but still maintained our standards."

Finding it more than a little disconcerting to be sitting there having a conversation with a ghost, Jared cleared his throat. "Will you tell me what happened on Santo Domingo and why Adam Montief wants me dead?"

She turned and sighed. "You have no idea how much I regret that my actions have placed you in such a dangerous position, but if I had to do it all again, I would. Augustus Montief was a cruel man. I had no choice but to escape with my son. I knew Augustus would not rest until he fulfilled his vow of vengeance. I also knew that the one who would carry this out would be as evil as he was. What I didn't know is who it would be or when it would happen. When you were given the mirror and could make it work, I knew the time had come."

Jared shook his head. "But why me?"

She smiled. "When is your birthday?"

"August fourteenth. Why?"

"Do you know the date of the slave rebellion on *Saint-Domingue*?"

"No."

She glanced to where a widescreen television hung above the fireplace and pointed. "Am I correct that it is possible to project images upon that?"

Confused, Jared nodded.

She waved her hand. "Watch and you will understand. Then find the casket. It will help you destroy Adam Montief. It is August 14, 1791." The television flickered, and a very young Angelique appeared on the screen. Jared felt lightheaded. He had the sensation of being drawn into the scene, and into Angelique's mind and heart as well.

****

Wispy tentacles of smoke seeped in from the upper gallery and beneath the closed double-louvered doors. In the stifling heat, Angelique Montief flicked her wrist and set the bamboo ceiling fan spinning. Kneeling on a woven mat with sweat coating her body, she lifted a small wooden brass-bound casket from the bottom of a large trunk, inserted a gold key, and opened the lid. Inside two objects lay wrapped in thick cloth. She carefully unwrapped the smaller bundle to reveal a pentagonal mirror, a gift handed down to her by her grandmother, its ancient oak frame carved with tiny pentacles. She glanced over her shoulder at her locked bedroom door, then stared into the mirror and whispered, "Show him to me."

When the glass remained blank, fear clutched at her chest. Again, she said the words, and the image of a plantation house engulfed in flames appeared. "No, please, he can't be dead." Tears blurred her vision. The fiery image changed to reveal a human form lying beneath flowering bougainvillea.

Hope rising, Angelique peered closer.

"Show me his face."

She saw his indigo blue eyes blink open.

"I'm coming, my love."

He couldn't hear her, but she hoped that in his heart he knew she would find a way to get to him.

As the smoke in the room thickened, she knew her time was running out. She rewrapped the mirror and placed it into the smaller casket among cloth bags of herbs and potion-filled vials. Relocking the lid, she hung the key on a chain around her neck, dropped a jeweled dagger into her pocket, and tucked the casket under her arm.

Crouched beneath the smoke, with the sound of shouting coming closer, she considered the quickest way to reach her son and escape. She'd be too exposed on the gallery. Anton's room was two doors down the hall. With any luck, she could make her way to him without being seen.

Most of the servants and slaves had joined the Marrons' rebellion, and her husband was fighting to keep them off the sugar plantation. Augustus Montief was a powerful witch, but not even his powers were strong enough to hold back the murderous hordes she could hear coming for their masters' blood.

Augustus had locked her in, placing what he thought would be an impenetrable shield across both doors. Angelique coughed, choked by the darkening smoke. Her husband's biggest mistake was underestimating her. Along with her grandmother's gift of healing, she had inherited strong magical powers.

Facing the heavy wooden door to the hallway, she allowed the magic to pulse through her right hand. She threw a ball of energy and watched with satisfaction as it shattered the lock.

Out in the hall, the smoke was denser. In fear for her son's life, she crawled to his room. When she tried to turn the knob, she realized Augustus had placed a shield across Anton's door as well. Angelique hit the lock with another blast of energy.

She had known that for her own safety, he could

never discover the truth of her abilities. Soon after their marriage it had become horribly apparent Augustus wasn't the gentle, kind person she'd thought, but a cruel monster who only wanted her for her dowry and the sons she could produce. But if Augustus Montief planned to let her die in flames while he escaped with their son, he would learn just how powerful she truly was.

She hurried into the room slamming the door behind her. A tall, imposing woman stood guard in front of her son's crib. The woman's face was delicately boned with striking turquoise eyes and skin the color of creamy chocolate. An intricately wrapped snowy white tignon covered her head. Earrings of shell and beads dangled from her ears, and copper bracelets encircled her arms. "Taneen, thank the Gods it's you."

"It about time you get here. I about to take the baby and go."

"I could not leave my room until I knew Augustus was out of the house. Did he lock you in with Anton?"

Taneen snorted. "You tink I allow dat son of Satan to lock me up? I wait 'til he left, den let myself in from da gallery. Now we need to go. Most of da slave quarters and half da house is burnin'."

"I know, but how? We cannot allow Augustus to see us, and we dare not be caught by the renegade slaves."

"I already tought of dat. I should take da boy wit me, and you leave on you own."

When Angelique opened her mouth to object, Taneen held up her hand.

"If dat bastard catch you, how you goin' to fight him wit a baby in your arms? And if da slaves see me wit you, dey kill us both."

"But if you're caught with a white baby, the Marrons will murder him."

"I already tought of dat. See." She stepped away from the crib where Anton slept, his normally smooth pink cheeks now a dusky hue.

Angelique gasped. "What did you use?"

"Just a little burnt ash mixed with some cream. I also brought dis."

She held up a sturdy woven basket and opened the hinged lid to reveal it was lined with a soft cotton cloth.

"He fit fine inside."

Angelique hesitated. Taneen was right. They would probably do better if they left separately, but could she ever live with herself if harm came to her son and she was not there to try and save him? On the other hand, Taneen could probably slip right through unnoticed. If she were stopped, Angelique knew Taneen would die herself before allowing her great-grandson to be harmed. Angelique took a deep breath. "All right, you take the baby and head for La Maison plantation, and I'll meet you."

Taneen cocked her head. "I heard it already burnt. Why we goin' dere?"

"Jean Dupre is the one person I can trust to get us to New Orleans."

"How he doin' dat?"

"He keeps a small sloop anchored in a cove below the plantation. I looked in the mirror. Jean may have been wounded. One of us must get to him as soon as possible." Angelique shook her head. "I don't understand; Jean has always treated his slaves well."

"He a white master. Dat all dat matters. You tink

Augustus goin' to stand by and watch his wife and baby get on a ship and sail away wit another man? And once Dupre learns you a witch and your *grandmère* is mulatto, you tink he still goin' want you?"

A steely determination entered Angelique's eyes. "Jean Dupre loves me. Nothing will break our bond. My ancestry will be of no consequence to him." She gently wrapped Anton in his blanket and held him tight. "We are going and I don't intend on giving Augustus a choice. This revolution is horrific, but you cannot treat people the way the plantation owners have treated their slaves and not expect them to rebel. Are any of my own servants still here?"

Taneen nodded. "All de house servants are hidin' outside and dere's a few field hands still loyal to you."

"Good. Take them with you." Angelique froze. Heavy boots could be heard running up the interior staircase. She gave the wooden casket she still held to Taneen, kissed her son before placing him into the basket, then hugged her *grandmère*. "If something happens to me, Jean Dupre will help you and Anton."

While Taneen hurried along the outer gallery, Angelique arranged another blanket in the crib to make it seem as if Anton still slept, then turned to face the door just as Augustus threw it open and halted, a cloud of black smoke surrounding him like an evil aura. Surprise, then rage, filled his cold dark eyes. Angelique stiffened her spine and readied herself for the hardest battle she'd ever fought.

He stepped into the room and closed the door behind him. "Well, my dear wife, it seems I should have also placed a guard at your door to keep that darky bitch from helping you escape." He waved his hand.

"Saving the house is no longer possible. There is no stopping those murdering savages. I've come to take my son to safety. As for you, my slut of a wife"—he sneered—"your lover is dead. There is no one to save you now." His grin dripped smug satisfaction. "That's right, whore. Did you really think I wouldn't find out you've been spreading your legs for that mortal coffee planter?"

Angelique tried to hide her shock. She thought she'd been discreet, but none of that mattered now. The longer she stalled, the better chance Taneen had to get away. She braced herself and steadied her voice. "I will not allow you to take my son."

Augustus's bark of laughter was without humor. "You will not, will you? You have no choice. Your simple healing powers are no match for me. I'm the Powerful One. Your purpose was to give me sons. Since one was all you produced, and since you have betrayed me, I have no further use for you."

His face twisted in disgust. "The boy is lucky he resembles me, or I would kill him as well. You're a stupid woman, but even you must know I married you for your dowry. My powers are great, but even I can't conjure wealth. Saving this plantation is what truly mattered to me, and now it's about to be destroyed."

The intensity in his eyes put Angelique's senses on full alert. She took a calming breath and gathered her power. "I'm not as stupid as you think, Augustus. Anton is not going anywhere with you. As far as I'm concerned, you and your plantation can burn in Hell."

When he lunged, his arm outstretched to cast a powerful blow, she was ready. Angelique flicked her wrist and sent Augustus flying against the wall. Before he could retaliate, she flung up her arms to encase herself in a protective bubble and grabbed the bundled blanket from Anton's bed. She ran through the gallery doors and down the outer stairs. He bellowed in rage. She lifted her skirts in a dead run toward the sugarcane fields. Mortals couldn't see her in the bubble, but to another witch the outline of her body was visible.

Patches of drifting smoke swirled around her as she crossed the harvested cane fields, the stubble whipping at her ankles, threatening to trip her. If she could make it to the band of thick vegetation that divided her husband's plantation from La Maison, she might have a chance. At the sounds of heavy breathing and pounding feet behind her, Angelique increased her speed.

Gasping, her side burning and her legs aching, she shot her fist in the air and flames erupted across the path behind her. She prayed to all the Gods her luck would hold and the firewall would slow Augustus down. Ahead were fifty yards of open field before she could reach the safety of tangled sea grape, wild orchids, and coconut palms.

Suddenly the shield around her shattered and she was hurled to the ground. The breath knocked out of her, she lay on her stomach, Augustus's laughter coming closer.

"I've got you now, whore."

Sheer panic forced her to her knees, then to her feet. On shaky legs, she glanced over her shoulder. His arm was raised and a flash of light speared toward her. With a strength she did not know she possessed, she flung up her arm, deflecting the blow with an energy shield. Augustus cried out in pain.

When she entered the thick foliage, she waved her

hand in front of her clearing a path, making sure it closed behind her. With her breath coming in short gasps, she slowed her pace and tossed aside the loose, empty bundle. In a few more yards, she would reach La Maison's rows of coffee trees and safety.

As she broke through the sea grape into the clearing, something slammed into her back knocking her off her feet. She used her right hand to break her fall, crying out in pain as the fragile bones in her wrist snapped. With Augustus almost upon her, she managed to rise. Dizzy and nauseous as excruciating pain shot through her wrist, she managed a few steps before Augustus clamped his hand around her upper arm.

His mouth inches from her ear, he growled, "You dare to run from me, bitch." He turned her toward him and slapped her face, snapping her head back. "You dare to hide your powers, then use them against me." He slapped her again.

Her head spun, and blood trickled down her chin from her split lip. As she tried to gather her wits, again he growled, "You think you can hide my son from me?" He lifted his fist to deliver another blow. "I'll never let you have him. Where is he?"

Half-crazed with pain and fury, unable to use her right hand, Angelique mustered what strength she could and kneed him in the groin.

"Bitch, I'll kill you."

"Not if I can help it." With her uninjured hand, she snatched the jeweled dagger from her pocket and plunged it into his chest.

"Rot in Hell, you bastard."

Without glancing back, she hurried toward the rows of coffee trees. When she entered the clearing where La Maison plantation burned, relief flooded over her. Ahead stood Taneen holding her son, surrounded by a few loyal servants. Jean Dupre limped toward her.

Before she could reach the man she loved, an icy chill surrounded her. She glanced over her shoulder and a scream lodged in her throat. Augustus Montief stood a few feet behind her, the bloody dagger in his raised left hand. Fear such as she'd never known kept her rooted to the spot. For the man, his eyes ablaze with hatred, was no longer flesh and blood, but a shimmering translucent image.

When Augustus spoke, his hollow voice seemed to penetrate her very soul.

"Angelique Montief, I curse you and all those who may come from you and Dupre. Beware. Someday the one who carries my blood will avenge my death."

He drew back his arm and in a flash of light sent the dagger hurtling through the air. Its bloody point pierced the ground at Angelique's feet.

Chapter 22

"*Merde.*" Jared stared at the blank television screen as the room spun around him. He'd never experienced anything so intense. "Angelique?" he whispered, but she was gone.

He squeezed his eyes shut and pressed his fingers to his temples, his head reeling. He had no idea how Angelique had made that happen, but it was as if he'd been a part of her. He'd known her thoughts, felt her terror, smelled the smoke, and known her pain. He took deep breaths to calm his heaving stomach. "Next time you want to hurl me through the looking glass, Angelique, I'd appreciate it if you'd warn me first."

After a few minutes, he rose unsteadily and, on shaky legs, headed for his liquor cabinet. He poured two fingers of bourbon into a glass gripped in trembling hands and downed it in one swallow. Slowly his body calmed. "Damn."

That was way too weird. But now he knew the truth and what he needed to do. He set down his glass and went to where the mirror lay on a table. Angelique's sitting room was still visible. He'd begin by showing the image of the room to his father and hopefully he'd be able to tell Jared where it was. If not, at least he had one clue. Angelique had said it was located on the second floor. Thankfully that was where they had their private rooms, so he wouldn't be poking around among the guests' things.

Knowing his father would be in his office, Jared headed for the elevator. When he entered the lobby, the aromas coming from the dining room reminded him he hadn't eaten anything since last night. Deciding to grab a quick bite before seeing his father, he changed direction. He'd taken only a few steps when Carla Delany, the daytime restaurant hostess, stopped him.

"Oh, Mr. Dupre, I was just going to call you. Kathleen hasn't come in for work. When I tried her cell, she didn't answer. I was wondering if you know where she is?"

Jared frowned. "I have no idea. See if Anna can get Leon to come in and cover for her until she shows up."

She hesitated.

He tried to keep the impatience from his voice. "Carla, what is it?"

"Mr. Dupre, I'm sorry to bother you with this, but I'm afraid something's wrong. Kathleen and I are good friends. She'd never miss work without telling me why."

Jared recalled the mix-up with the delivery from the night before. "I saw Kathleen last night and she was fine. Perhaps she had some kind of family emergency?"

Carla shook her head. "I talked to her mom, and she hadn't heard from her either."

Jared knew firsthand how much Kathleen enjoyed partying. If she was having a good time, she'd stay up all night, but never before a work day. "I tell you what. If you don't hear from her by this afternoon, let me know."

"Thanks. I really appreciate your help." She gave him a wan smile. "If I could use magic, perhaps I could find her."

Jared squeezed her shoulder. "That's where I come in. Don't worry. I'm sure she's fine."

Hours later, after painstakingly searching every inch of the second floor, Jared, tired and disgruntled, stood in what had been his sister Annette's bedroom. Married and living in Michigan, Annette still used the room when she came to visit. She probably wouldn't appreciate him poking around in here, but this was the last place for him to search. His father had glanced at the image, shaken his head, and handed the mirror back.

As Jared stood there hoping for some kind of inspiration, a disheartening thought came to him. If the sitting room no longer existed when she gave him the mirror, his mother would have hidden the casket somewhere else. He groaned and flopped down in a padded wicker chair. That would mean it could be anywhere. Rubbing his hands across his face, he shook his head. No, the mirror showed him what he asked, so the room must be here.

Perhaps some fresh air would clear his head. He rose, opened one of the casement windows, and stepped out onto the balcony. Below him the courtyard, with its central fountain, wrought-iron benches, and flowering plants, made a tranquil setting. The hotel was U-shaped with the main entrance on Royal and a rear entry via the *port cochere* that led into the courtyard.

An older couple sat on one of the benches holding hands. Jared smiled as the man bent down and whispered something in her ear making her laugh. It was obvious that they were still deeply in love. Someday that could be Kendra and him. For a few minutes, he stood lost in thought, then sighed. If he didn't rid their lives of Adam, Kendra and he might not have a future.

As he stepped back through the window, a painting which hung over the bed caught his eye. He stood staring, then swore. There, in the painting, was Angelique's sitting room. Someone must have painted the picture before Annette's room was remodeled. He lifted the painting from the wall. Behind it the plaster was smooth and showed no signs of ever concealing a safe. He rehung the painting and cursed colorfully in French. He took a step back and studied the wall. Behind it was the bathroom. Shaking his head, he went to look.

Above the marble sink was a beveled glass mirror. When he tried to lift it down, it wouldn't budge. He ran his fingers along the sides and smiled with triumph when he discovered a tiny latch. He held his breath as he swung it open. "Yes," he exclaimed when the safe was revealed. His excitement was short-lived when he saw it had a combination lock.

"You're not keeping me out," he said through gritted teeth. He was about to hit the lock with a spear of energy when he noticed the tiny strip of yellowed paper taped to the back of the mirror. Smiling with satisfaction, he read the faded numbers and twirled the lock.

Jared sighed in relief when the safe door swung open. Inside sat the casket, its wood dark with age. He lifted it out and returned to the bedroom. He set it upon a small Queen Anne desk and raised the lid. A gasp lodged in his throat as he recognized the dagger Angelique had used to kill Augustus Montief. The hilt, encrusted with sapphires, rubies and emeralds, glowed brightly. For several minutes he could only stare, then reverently he lifted the weapon.

The jolt of energy that shot through him almost knocked him off his feet. "Holy Mother of the Gods," he whispered. Swallowing hard, he watched as the jewels pulsated in his hand.

"Okay, you've got one hell of a punch." He planted his feet and tightened his grip around the hilt. When the intense energy flowed through his arm, a slow grin spread across his face.

****

After closing the store, Kendra, Deanne, and Loren sat upstairs in Kendra's apartment enjoying what had become their customary after-work glass of wine.

"Another successful day of sales," Kendra said. "I've even taken orders for items we've run out of."

Deanne sat on the couch, slipped off her shoes, and scratched Clementine who curled up next to her. She sipped her wine. "We are so kicking ass. We're going to give Minerva major competition."

Loren turned to Kendra. "Speaking of which, from what you told me, I'd say it was datura, commonly known as jimson weed, that you were given last night. But I still can't see Minerva putting something like that in her punch."

Kendra frowned. "Isn't that some kind of poison?"

Loren nodded. "It can be highly toxic if given in large doses or used without proper knowledge of its potency. It's also a love potion."

"Holy crap," Deanne said. "Minerva must have lost her mind to put something like that in her punch. She could have killed someone."

"She's a good herbalist and would have known

how much to use," Loren said. "My question is why would she do it? I mean she can be pretty strange at times, but to drug her guests." She shook her head. "Like I said, I can't see it."

"And she couldn't have been sure how much any one person might get, just putting it in a punchbowl. It would be nuts," Deanne countered.

"Then if not Minerva, who?" Loren asked.

Both girls turned to Kendra who sighed. "Jared thinks it was Thaddeus."

"Well, I don't think it was him either," Deanne said. "Like Minerva, why would he do it?"

Loren bit her lower lip. "I hate to say this, but we can't rule Thaddeus out." She held up her hand forestalling Deanne's objection. "I know we're all upset with Jared…"

"Not all of us," Deanne interrupted, glowering at Kendra. "One of us spent the night in bed with him."

Kendra rolled her eyes. "Honestly Deanne."

"Okay, obviously I've missed something," Loren said.

Kendra refilled her wine glass, took a deep breath, and explained.

"Yeah, and if he ever tries that with me again, his ass will be the one flying across the room," Deanne stated after Kendra had finished.

"As I said earlier, no you won't. Antagonizing Jared will not help." Kendra turned to Loren. "Will you please tell her?"

Loren nodded. "Kendra's right, Deanne. Angering Jared won't accomplish anything. And I can't say I'm surprised to hear he spent the night."

"Neither of you has any idea how horrible that

exhibit was," Kendra said. "I was scared and upset and Jared showed up. I told Deanne it was nothing more than comfort sex and it won't happen again."

Loren grinned. "I kind of doubt that, but before you say anything, let me continue. I think we need to consider what Jared said about Thaddeus. Yes, he seems to be a perfectly nice guy, but what do we actually know about him?"

Kendra set her glass down and rubbed her arms. "It gives me the absolute willies to think I've been going out with someone as cruel as Jared has accused Thaddeus, or 'Adam', of being. How could he come across as a perfectly normal person and hide that much evil inside?"

Deanne snorted. "Girl, Dexter seems like a nice guy, too."

Kendra shivered.

"Before we accuse Thaddeus of anything, we need to see what we can find out about him." Loren turned to Kendra. "Have you heard from him today?"

"No, he's probably upset with me for the way I ran out on him. If he saw me with Jared, well, I may never hear from him again."

"That would solve one problem," Deanne said.

Kendra opened her mouth to reply, shook her head, then closed it again.

"In a way Deanne is right," Loren said. "If you don't hear from Thaddeus, we've nothing to worry about."

Kendra stepped to the counter and picked up the bottle of wine next to the vase of roses. She refilled their glasses. "As I told Jared, there were other people at Minerva's last night. One of them could have fooled around with the punch."

"That's true," Loren said.

"Maybe. If they were some of Minerva's wacky friends," Deanne said. "It could have been someone's idea of a joke."

"Did you recognize anyone?" Loren asked.

Kendra shook her head. "Honestly I didn't pay attention. She's totally changed the store and it's really creepy. The only light came from candles and a few wall sconces. She had hors d'oeuvres and the punch in the room she uses to do her readings." Kendra sucked in a breath.

"What is it?" Loren asked.

"While I was waiting for our turn to go upstairs, I took a book from Minerva's bookcase," she paused. "The title was *Pharmakopeia of Love Potions and Aphrodisiacs*."

Deanne laughed. "Girl, if you looked like Minerva, how else would you get a man?"

Loren almost choked on her wine. "Oh, my, Deanne."

"What? It's true. She runs around looking like an extra from the Addams family."

Tears of laughter streamed down Kendra's cheeks. "You're so right."

"Okay, okay, enough," Loren said. "We're missing Kendra's point."

"Which is?" Deanne asked.

"That, if I had to guess, the book explains herbs that can be used as aphrodisiacs, including jimson weed."

Kendra's cheeks turned pink as she recalled some of what she had read. "It did."

"You have our full attention," Deanne stated.

"I couldn't get through all of it, but there were some pretty explicit descriptions of what some herbs can make you do."

"Oh, do tell," Deanne said.

Loren waved her hand. "Not now. We need to keep on point."

Deanne rolled her eyes. "Yes, professor."

Loren ignored Deanne and continued. "Minerva knows what herbs to use, but if she's selling a book like that, well, anyone could have known what to add to the punch."

"So we're right back where we started," Kendra said.

Deanne set down her wine glass and stood up. "Since we suck as detectives, let's go get something to eat. I'm starving. How about burgers?"

Loren cleared her throat.

"Oh, all right, Miss No Meat. What about red beans and rice? We can go to the Gumbo Shop and hold the andouille."

Loren smiled. "Sounds perfect."

"I have to work the nine o'clock haunted hotel tour tonight," Kendra said. "So that works for me."

As they gathered their things to leave, Kendra's phone rang. Glancing down at the caller ID she saw it was Thaddeus.

"What should I do?" she asked.

"Answer it," Loren said. "See what he has to say."

Chapter 23

Kendra took a deep breath and answered. "Hello."

"Kendra, it's Thaddeus."

"Thaddeus, hi."

"I'm calling to apologize for last night. I wanted to make sure you were all right."

"I'm fine. I'm the one who should apologize. I feel awful about running away like that. It's just, well, Minerva's exhibit really upset me, and I just freaked."

"I totally understand. I hadn't seen the exhibit and had no idea how graphic it was. I'd like to take you to dinner to make it up to you. That is if you want to see me again."

"Dinner?" She turned to Loren and Deanne for their reaction. They both vigorously nodded. "Of course I want to see you again, and dinner sounds nice. I'm working tonight, so I have to be done by eight-thirty."

"No problem. I'll pick you up in half-an-hour."

Kendra ended the call and let out a breath. "Okay, hopefully I'll find out some answers. But I have to tell you, thanks to Jared, the entire time I'm with Thaddeus I'll be wondering if he's some kind of psychopath."

Deanne knitted her brows. "Should we follow you?"

"I don't think that will be necessary. I have my unicorn." She touched the glass figure at her neck. "And we'll be in a restaurant. But to be on the safe side,

Loren, can you put some protection together for me?"

"Sure, I'll run downstairs and make an herb sachet for your purse. If we haven't sold it, we have a bracelet of amber, amethyst and red tiger's eye you can wear."

A short time later, Kendra opened her door to admit Thaddeus. "Hi, come on in. I have to feed Clementine. I'll just be a minute."

Thaddeus stepped into the apartment. "That's fine, take your time." He glanced around the room. "Do you realize I've yet to meet your cat?"

Kendra turned to where Clementine had been sitting by her dish patiently waiting for her dinner. "That's strange, she was right there a minute ago. She never leaves when she thinks food is coming." Kendra shrugged. "She must have seen a bird or something and is in the bedroom window."

"I'm glad to see your roses are still holding up." Thaddeus nodded to where the vase sat on the coffee table.

"They're perfect, thank you again." She gazed into his soft brown eyes and had the sensation of being drawn into their dark depths. *Jared is wrong about him. He's a kind, decent man who would never harm me.* When he held her in his arms and kissed her, she sighed and opened her mouth to him. He deepened the kiss and held her close, caressing the back of her neck. A floating sensation came over her, as well as a sudden overwhelming need for sexual release.

The tension inside her built until she dug her nails into his shoulders. From a far distance she heard him whisper, "That's it, feel my pleasure, let it surround you, now let it come."

She could do nothing but cling to him while the

orgasm that erupted throughout her body consumed her.

The next thing she knew she was standing in her bedroom, blinking in confusion. She heard a high-pitched howl followed by Thaddeus's cries of pain. In horror, she saw Clementine wrapped around Thaddeus's leg, her claws penetrating through his slacks.

"Clementine, no, stop that." She hurried to pull the cat away. "Oh, Thaddeus, I'm so sorry. I don't know what came over her. She's never done anything like that before. Sit down and let me see how bad it is."

Visibly holding onto his patience, Thaddeus waved her away. "I'm fine. I'll just go into the bathroom and take care of it."

"It's through there." She pointed. "Again, I'm sorry."

He gave her a tight smile. "Don't worry about it. We must have startled her, that's all."

When Thaddeus shut the bathroom door, Kendra knelt next to the cat and stroked her trembling body. "It's okay, sweetheart. Did he scare you? I'm a little shook-up myself." Embarrassment over her reaction to Thaddeus's kiss mixed with her unease. She'd had some pretty explosive orgasms with Jared, but nothing like that. Especially over a kiss. It had been almost scary in its intensity.

"Are you ready to go?" Thaddeus asked.

Startled, she winced. "What?"

"I asked if you were ready to leave."

She stood. "Sure. Are you all right?"

This time his smile was full of warmth. "I'm fine. Please don't let it bother you."

Kendra licked dry lips. She had to mention the kiss

and her reaction. "Thaddeus, about…" She felt the color staining her cheeks.

He took her hand in his. "Kendra, there's nothing to be ashamed of. We're two adults attracted to one another, though I'm afraid Clementine has spoiled the mood. Let's go on and have a nice dinner."

She nodded gratefully. "Let me get my purse." With Thaddeus behind her, she headed out the door.

Once they were down on the street, he said, "We'll go to Dickie Brennan's, if that's okay with you?"

She hesitated. The restaurant was around the corner from the Dupre Hotel and a favorite of hers and Jared's. Could she take a chance they'd run into him?

"If you don't like it there, we can go somewhere else," he was saying.

"No, Dickie Brennan's is fine." If they saw Jared, well, then she'd have to deal with it.

"It's quite a ways." He took her arm and steered her toward a black BMW. "I thought we'd drive."

When he opened the passenger door, a jolt of fear and foreboding startled her and she paused.

"Is there a problem?"

She tamped down the urge to jerk her arm from his grasp. What was wrong with her? Wasn't she just in his arms? If he wanted to harm her, he'd had the perfect opportunity. She frowned. All Jared's wild accusations had her emotions whirling like some crazed carnival ride. Still, a voice in her head told her to be cautious. She turned to Thaddeus and smiled. "I've been indoors all day and would love to stretch my legs. Do you mind?"

He shrugged. "Whatever you like."

They made their way up Chartres and turned right

onto Iberville. Kendra kept her eyes straight ahead as they passed Royal and the Dupre Hotel. Once in the restaurant they headed down the steps to their table, waiters and hostesses greeting Kendra.

"You seem to be well known here," Thaddeus said.

"Ahh, yes, well." Kendra stammered. "You happened to choose one of my favorite places to eat."

Thaddeus smiled. "I'm glad to hear that. Would you like a glass of wine?"

She shook her head. "Since I have to work tonight, I'll just have a soda, thanks."

After the waiter took their order. Thaddeus clasped her hand. "Kendra, again, I'd like to apologize for taking you to Minerva's. If I'd had any idea the exhibit would upset you that much, I would have never invited you to go."

Here was the opening she'd been waiting for. "Thaddeus, it wasn't your fault. Minerva is a little weird, and I should have expected the worst, but there is something I'd like to ask you about."

"Sure, what is it?"

She gazed directly into his eyes. "Did Minerva spike the punch with some kind of hallucinogenic herb?"

His brows rose. "What?"

"Minerva. Did she put something in the punch to heighten our experience viewing the exhibits?"

Thaddeus shook his head. "Not that I'm aware of. Why are you asking me such a thing? Not only would that be dangerous, I'd think it would also be illegal."

Kendra sipped her water. He truly seemed outraged. She set down her glass. "So you felt no ill effects from the punch?"

"No, why? Did you?"

She nodded. "If it wasn't Minerva, then someone else did. Because I was certainly drugged."

Consternation filled his face. "Are you telling me your behavior was caused by a hallucinogenic herb?"

She shrugged. "Or something."

"Kendra, please, I'm trying to understand, but why would someone give you drugs?"

"I haven't the slightest idea. I assumed they were given to everyone, but evidently not. Thaddeus, I was so out of it, I hardly remember anything."

He stared into his wine glass before replying. "Your behavior was odd, but I thought you were just agitated over the exhibits. I'm so sorry. I didn't realize what was happening." His mouth formed a thin line. "And you'd better believe I'm going to ask Minerva about it. I've never heard of anything so reprehensible."

Kendra folded and unfolded her napkin. How could someone as evil as Thaddeus was supposed to be sound so sincere? She'd never experienced the dark side of magic, but on the other hand her instincts were usually pretty good. She thought Thaddeus was exactly what he seemed, a nice guy who cared for her.

Thaddeus sipped his wine. "I wonder though."

"What's that?"

"If it turns out not to have been Minerva, then who?" He studied her closely. "Kendra, I don't want you to think I'm doubting you, but you're sure you weren't just reacting to the exhibits?"

"Definitely not. But you bring up a good point, that anyone there could have done it. Again, I have to ask, why? Some people have a strange idea of what's fun. Maybe I should be the one who talks to Minerva. She may not even know what happened."

He hesitated. "If you like, but do you honestly want to go back there?"

The thought of going anywhere near Minerva's shop made her skin crawl, but she wanted to discover the truth. "Not really, but if she or someone she knows is drugging people with her punch, they need to be stopped."

"How about if we go together? I'd like to hear what she has to say. Unless…"

"Unless what?"

He took a deep breath. "Unless you'd rather go with Dupre."

Kendra couldn't speak. He must have seen her with Jared. Before she could think of a response, he continued.

"When you ran out of the museum I was concerned, so I followed and saw you get into his car." He paused, looked away, then back. "Kendra, I enjoy being with you, but I don't want to be in competition with Dupre. So if you two are trying to patch things up, perhaps I should step aside."

The hurt in his eyes tore at Kendra's heart. Her earlier apprehension was nothing more than jumpy nerves. She placed her hand on his arm. "Thaddeus, last night I was scared and not in my right mind. Jared happened to be there and I let him take me home, that's all." She saw the skepticism on his face, but she continued. "Jared is under the impression that we'll eventually get back together but considering that I'm not sure I can ever trust him again, I don't see how that's possible."

Thaddeus smiled. "So I can take that to mean I

might have a chance?"

Before she could respond a female voice said, "Why, Kendra, hello."

Kendra turned to see Monique Frost, a member of her coven, standing next to the table.

"Hey, Monique, how are you?"

"Fine, thanks. I'm here with Barb, Sherry, and Shelley and I saw you sitting here." Without waiting for Kendra to introduce her, she held out her hand to Thaddeus. "Hi, I'm Monique Frost."

Thaddeus smiled and took her hand. "Thaddeus Marsh."

"Nice to meet you," Monique continued. "Are you visiting New Orleans?"

He nodded. "For a while."

"Great, I'm sure Kendra can show you all our wonderful sights."

Thaddeus squeezed Kendra's hand. "I'm hoping to take up a lot of Kendra's time."

Monique's smile suddenly turned brittle. "Well, I'd better get back. Enjoy your dinner."

Kendra watched as Monique wove her way to her table until, taking a seat with her back to them, she took her cell from her purse and made a call.

"Is she a friend of yours?"

"She's part of my coven."

"I don't think she likes me being with you. Is she also a friend of Dupre's?"

"We've known her for years, and she's usually very friendly."

"Kendra, I…"

"Thaddeus, it's all right." She stopped him before he could continue. "Jared and I were together for a long time, and people don't know how to react when they see us with someone else. What I don't understand is why I'm the one getting the icy stares? It wasn't me who left Jared." The servers arrived with their food and Kendra was glad for the distraction.

After coffee and a rich mousse Kendra knew she shouldn't have had, she glanced at her watch. "Dinner was wonderful. Thank you, but I need to get going."

"I was wondering if I could join the tour. I'd naturally pay for my ticket. I think visiting haunted hotels would be interesting." He smiled. "Especially if you're the guide."

Kendra silently groaned. Since her mother added the Dupre Hotel to their list of stops, they'd decided to begin the tours there. Seeing the eager expression on his face, she cursed Jared for putting her in this position. Damn him anyway. If Thaddeus wanted to go on her tour and Jared didn't like it, then that was too bad. "I'd love to have you join us, but I have to warn you that we begin the tour at the Dupre."

Thaddeus shrugged. "I have no problem with that if you don't."

"Then let's go."

As soon as they turned the corner onto Royal, Kendra was surprised to see police cars parked in front of the hotel. "I wonder what's going on. We have a few minutes before people start arriving for the tour—let's see if we can find out anything." She led Thaddeus across the street and halted on the sidewalk where she spotted Jared speaking with a police officer. When Jared turned and saw her with Thaddeus, she braced herself.

Jared said something to the officer, then headed

their way. "What the hell are you doing with *him*?"

Kendra bristled. "Jared, that's enough. For your information, I'm waiting to begin my tour, and Thaddeus is joining us."

"Isn't that nice. You don't listen very well, do you?"

Kendra gritted her teeth. "You're not my keeper."

Thaddeus touched her arm. "Kendra, I should leave."

Jared stood, his body tense. Anger blazed in his eyes and his mouth had a grim set to it. "Good idea, fucker. Leave."

"Jared, stop it. You're acting like an ass. And Thaddeus, stay right there."

"You know what, Kendra, I've got other problems right now. So go have fun, and if he turns you into one of his zombies, you can't say I didn't warn you."

As Jared turned away, Kendra grabbed his leather-jacketed arm. "What's going on? Why are the police here?"

"Kathleen LeBlanc is missing."

"What?"

"She didn't show up for work this afternoon, and her family hasn't heard from her since she left yesterday. It seems I may have been one of the last people to see her."

Even though she disliked Kathleen, Kendra didn't want any harm to come to her. "Is there anything we can do?"

"Considering she's an adult, normally the police wouldn't put out a missing person's report on her for seventy-two hours, but her parents are so worried they agreed to investigate. I've notified the coven, and there are groups out searching for her."

"Does anyone know where she hangs out? Or who her friends are?" Kendra asked.

"Carla said she was seeing someone but didn't know who. She said Kathleen was being extremely secretive about this man. Carla also was afraid she'd gotten mixed up with some bad people." Jared's attention shifted to Thaddeus.

"You wouldn't know anything about this, would you?"

"Jared, why would he?"

"Because controlling and hurting women is something he likes to do, that's why."

The hostile sparks of energy pulsating from the two men were frightening.

Thaddeus's face was rigid with anger when he said, "Dupre, I don't know who you think I am, but I don't hurt women. I'm getting tired of you trying to convince Kendra I'm some kind of monster, so back off."

"You lying son-of-a-bitch." As the two men lunged at each other, Kendra threw up her arms to block them with an energy shield. "Stop it. Both of you just stop it. For the love of Odin, we're out on a public street, there're police officers a few feet away, and I'm sure the last thing they want is a couple of witches battling it out in front of this crowd."

The NOPD and the Wiccan community got along well enough as long as the witches were discreet and didn't interfere with the mortal members of the community or flaunt their magical abilities in front of tourists. Kendra glanced quickly over to where the police stood to see if they had observed their tiff and let out a breath of relief when she saw their backs were to them.

Jared and Thaddeus glowered at her as if this was all her fault. Well, she'd had enough. "You know what, I have a tour to conduct, so I'm leaving." She turned to Thaddeus. "You're still welcome to join us, if you'd like."

Thaddeus looked from her to Jared and nodded.

"Good." She turned to Jared. "Please let me know if there's any word on Kathleen."

"Sure thing. You two have a nice night."

Kendra opened her mouth to respond, decided to ignore his sarcasm, and crossed the street to join her group.

Chapter 24

When Kendra was out of earshot, Jared faced Adam. "You may have her fooled now, but I'm going to expose you for what you are. Then I'm going to send your demented ass to Hell."

Adam grinned. "By the time you've so-called "exposed" me, Kendra will be mine, and she'll see what a pathetic weakling you really are. Then it will be me sending *your* ass to Hell."

As Adam turned away, Jared's fist clenched, itching to slam into that arrogant face. The bastard would make a mistake, and Jared planned on being there when he did.

But now, he needed to find Kathleen.

He'd first met Kathleen when she'd come to work at the hotel. She soon let him know she was interested in him and ready and willing to have a good time. Still in turmoil over his mother's death, he had taken comfort in her arms. They'd had a passionate six-month affair.

Then he'd met Kendra, and his life had changed. He'd gone back to college and broken it off with Kathleen. At first, she'd been pissed, and the animosity between her and Kendra hadn't helped, but eventually she'd come to see he loved Kendra, and they'd been able to remain friends.

Now it seemed she may have gotten herself into

something way over her head, and he would bet everything he had that Adam was involved. He'd attempted to use his mirror to find Kathleen but nothing had happened. The images were being blocked, and as hard as he'd tried he hadn't been able to break the hold. Adam was the one witch he knew of with that kind of power.

As he entered the hotel, Kendra was telling her group about the nineteenth-century madam who wandered the halls knocking on doors. A plump middle-aged woman with short dark hair and skepticism written all over her face asked, "I also heard there are witches that live here. Is that supposed to be true as well?"

Kendra smiled. "There're all kinds of unexplained happenings here in New Orleans. Some could be magic. It's up to you to believe or not believe."

"Well, I believe in both witches and ghosts," a young guy wearing a Pat O'Brian's T-shirt said. "In fact, I can feel the temperature dropping right now. Isn't that supposed to mean there's a ghost present?"

"I can feel it, too," another woman said.

"Oh, God," a teenage girl squealed. "Let's get out of here."

When the chandelier swayed back and forth, a balding man with a New Jersey accent demanded, "Barbara, give me the camera. We don't want to miss this."

Jared watched as Kendra's smile wavered. They were right, it was freezing. What the hell was going on? Yes, the ghosts were there, but as far as he knew, they weren't known to put on a show like this. Then he noticed the shock on Adam's face, followed his line of vision, and silently cursed.

Angelique stood on the mezzanine, staring directly down at Adam, hatred blazing in her eyes.

Jared scanned the crowd to see if anyone else could see her and thanked the Gods when it seemed no one else did, including Kendra, who had her back to the mezzanine. Before he could decide what to do, Angelique spoke, each blistering word echoing throughout the room.

"Adam Montief, your dark soul is not welcome here. Leave my home and never return, or know my wrath."

Jared cursed fluently in French when the prisms in the chandelier danced like castanets. But to his relief the only people who had heard Angelique were himself and Adam whose face had turned a sickly white. Jared smiled. Good, she was scaring the crap out of the bastard.

Some of the tour group, along with guests of the hotel, headed for the exit. Others snapped pictures of the chandelier while a few stood paralyzed, their mouths hanging open. Kendra caught Jared's eye, the expression on her face a silent plea for help.

When his father entered the lobby, Jared wished he could join those leaving. Instead, he checked to see if Angelique was gone, sighed gratefully that she was, and went to meet his father.

"Jared, what in the hell is going on?" Jacques Dupre asked. "And why is it so damn cold in here?"

Deciding the truth would be worse than the lie, Jared said, "I'm not sure, but I think the air-conditioning must have turned on. I'll get it checked."

"It's February. Why would the air-conditioning

come on?'

Not allowing Jared to reply, his father continued. "Isn't that Kendra?" Jacques pointed to where Kendra was trying to gather her group. "What is she doing?"

"It's her haunted hotel tour. She told me you gave permission for her to use the Dupre."

Jacques frowned. "Is she making this happen in order to entertain her group?"

"No, she has nothing to do with it."

"Then I suggest you take charge and restore some semblance of decorum to this hotel." Jacques turned on his heel and marched away.

Jared let out a long breath and met Kendra as she hurried across the lobby. "What in the world was that?" she asked. "Half my group are elated, some are heading for the bar, and the rest have disappeared."

"Angelique decided to put on a show." He looked over to where Adam had been standing, but he was gone. "Where did Adam go?"

Kendra waved away his question. "I haven't the slightest idea. What do you mean Angelique? Was she here?"

"Yes, but no one saw her except me and Adam."

Kendra frowned. "Thaddeus. Why him?"

"I don't know, but I think she scared the hell out of him and that's why he left."

"Oh, for goodness sakes, I doubt that. I have to go finish the tour with those I have left." She grinned. "Spectral New Orleans will probably get great reviews from this. I'll call you later."

Jared discreetly waved his hand. The chandelier stopped swaying, and the temperature in the room rose. The hotel employees were calming the guests, and things were as much in control as they were going to get. He wanted to find Angelique so he headed for his rooms.

Once upstairs, he grabbed his mirror and, trying to keep the irritation from his voice, said, "Angelique, I'd like to speak with you." The mirror remained dark and he ground his teeth. "Please, I have something to talk to you about other than what just happened."

The air around him crackled and she appeared.

"What was that man doing here?" she asked before Jared could speak.

"He was part of Kendra's tour."

"You will make sure he never enters this building again. Do you understand?"

Jared held up his hands. "Hey, I had nothing to do with that, but after your performance, I don't think he'll be back."

Her eyes flashed. "My performance was minor compared to what will happen if I ever see him again."

"Okay, okay, I understand. Now, I have a problem. A friend of mine is missing and my mirror is blocked. Can you help me?"

She frowned. "I don't understand."

"The mirror won't show me where my friend is."

"That's impossible. No one can stop you from seeing."

Jared shook his head. "There are times when Adam Montief can. He also has the ability to know when I'm watching him and project his own image to me. I have a feeling he's involved with my friend's disappearance, and that's why he's blocking me."

Her eyes opened wide. "He has that much power?"

Jared nodded.

"This is Augustus' doing. He's helping the boy. We will see about this. He will not thwart me. Place the mirror on the desk."

He did as she asked and she laid her hand on the glass and whispered, "*Grandmère*, once again I need your help." The glass shimmered, then in a brilliant silver flash the spirit of the mulatto woman Jared had met on the street appeared.

Without preamble she asked, "What happen now?"

After Angelique explained, Taneen glared at Jared. "I tought you goin' to take care of dat man."

One dead ancestor was enough. Dealing with two of them was setting Jared's teeth on edge. Annoyed at getting a scolding from a ghost, he snapped, "I stabbed the bastard and sent his ass over a cliff. What more could I have done? I can't help it he survived. But he did, and now he's here, and I think he's involved with a friend of mine. So wasting time criticizing me isn't going to help me find her or destroy Adam."

"You gettin' feisty wit me, boy, ain't goin' to help either."

"Enough. Jared, I know none of this is your fault." Angelique turned to Taneen. "*Grandmère*, are you ready?"

Taneen nodded and the women grasped hands, then placed their fingers from the other hand upon the mirror. Their faces were rigid in concentration. Tiny sparks of smoky black light danced within the glass. They chanted words Jared couldn't understand, and the light gradually faded to gray, then to white.

They released their hands, and Angelique, her mouth set in a firm line, said, "Augustus tried to fight us, but the spell is broken. The mirror is yours to command."

"Thanks," Jared replied. "Will he be able to block it again?"

Taneen narrowed her eyes. "Dat son-of-a-serpent strong, but not as strong as us."

"He may have a protective spell around himself that keeps you from seeing him, but nothing else should be hidden," Angelique added before they disappeared.

Jared picked up the mirror. "Show me Kathleen." The imaged that appeared revealed his worst fears. She lay stretched out on a stone slab, moonlight casting an eerie shadow across her battered face. Her bruised arms were crossed over her chest and her bloody hands folded. His stomach heaved and he swallowed back the bile rising in his throat.

"Where is she?" The image changed to show him a crumbling tomb, its iron door open. "Damn it, which cemetery?" he yelled. The sign for Lafayette No. 1 appeared and Jared took off.

****

Adam had to keep himself from running the entire way back to where he'd parked his car in front of Kendra's. Breathing heavily, he wrenched the driver's door open and flung himself in. With trembling hands, he started the engine and screeched away from the curb. He'd never experienced anything that unnerving, and he hoped never to again.

He'd become used to seeing Augustus' face in the mirror, but to actually be confronted by an enraged Angelique made his skin crawl. He took deep breaths. He had to regain his self-control before he got home. He could never allow Augustus to detect any weakness in him.

Entering his apartment, the control he'd tried so hard to maintain shattered when he saw not just a face in a mirror, but Augustus standing in the middle of the floor.

Spears of light ricocheted off the walls as Augustus bellowed, "What have you done?"

Adam opened and closed his mouth before he was able to say, "Grandsire, I didn't know you could materialize out of the mirror."

"Because you were out with that O'Connell wench, I had to fight Angelique and that mulatto bitch alone. They have broken your spell on Dupre's mirror and he's probably on his way to the cemetery to find the LeBlanc girl."

Desperate to hold onto his self-control while reassuring Augustus, Adam said, "Grandsire, there isn't anything to worry about. No one will connect Kathleen's death to me."

"You had better hope not. Your inability to control your temper and your lust has now jeopardized your final goal. Once again, you have allowed your jealousy of Dupre to interfere with your task. You are here to destroy Dupre, not chase after his woman or kill unnecessarily."

Adam's shock upon seeing Augustus faded to anger. He was the one charged with killing Dupre, and by damn he'd take care of it when the time was right. As for Kendra, he wasn't leaving New Orleans without her, and if the Powerful One didn't like it, well, that was too bad.

With increased confidence, Adam waved his hand and a glass of scotch appeared. Taking a large gulp, he turned his back on Augustus and crossed the room to stand in front of the window. In a calm voice he said, "As for Dupre, I'm working on a plan. We'll soon be rid of him."

"You had better hurry. If the police connect you to the LeBlanc girl's death, your time here will be over. I don't need to tell you how displeased I will be if you have to leave New Orleans without completing your task."

Adam felt the air in the room grow warm and still and Augustus was gone. He took another swallow of his drink. He was telling the truth when he said he didn't think he'd be connected to Kathleen's death, but in case Dupre started sniffing around, he'd better finalize his plans. Kathleen's energy strikes had lashed him, leaving ugly welts on his arms and chest that would take time even for him to heal entirely. Damn her. If she hadn't fought him or tried to use magic against him, she'd still be alive. *Subjects are to be subservient at all times*. That was something he thought she understood.

He went to the table where his crystal ball sat. He'd see if Jared had found Kathleen's body. "Where is Dupre?" The mist in the ball swirled, then nothing. Adam cursed. "Show me." Again nothing. *Fucking bastard must have doubled his privacy charm.* Well, to hell with it. He'd hear soon enough if she was found.

He thought of Kendra. If it hadn't been for that damn cat, he'd have had her beneath him, and she'd be one step closer to being his. It had taken everything he'd had not to kill the creature, but he knew that would have put an end to any chance he'd have with her. Now she'd be wondering why he'd left her at the hotel. The vehemence of Angelique's hatred still made him shudder. He'd wait until morning to call Kendra. By then, if there was news of Kathleen, she'd know. He waved his hand and another drink appeared.

****

It was just before midnight when Jared and the head of the Wiccan Council, Woodrow Charbonneau, entered Lafayette No. 1. Using torch light and his mirror, Jared led the way around crumbling tombs deep into the heart of the cemetery. A pale woman in antebellum dress stopped, stared at them, smiled, then drifted away.

Woodrow shivered. "No matter how hard I try, I can't get used to them. How Deanne and the girls go to visit with Marie Laveau is beyond me."

Jared shrugged. "They do take some getting used to." He glanced down at his mirror. "I think we go this way." They rounded a corner and were stopped by a young man in a muddy World War One uniform, the left side of his chest a dark bloody cavern.

"I'm trying to find my brother. Have you seen him?" he asked.

"No, sorry, we haven't," Jared replied.

The soldier's eyes filled with tears and he disappeared.

"For the love of Odin, let's hurry and get out of here," Woodrow said.

"It should be in the next row." Jared stepped past the rusted iron gate and peered into the open tomb. The smell of damp and decay filled their nostrils as they crawled inside. Flaking mortar dust gathered along the walls, but the center of the floor where Kathleen lay had been swept clean.

At the sight of her body, angry red energy pulsated around Jared. "I know that demon bastard did this,

Woodrow. I'm going to hunt him down and make him pay."

Woodrow placed a hand on Jared's shoulder. "Now son, I know how you feel about Adam, but we can't accuse him without proof." He held up his hand when Jared protested. "And I and the others on the Council plan on talking to him. I've already been in touch with the NOPD."

Jared shrugged, knowing the NOPD preferred to let the governing coven handle crimes involving Wiccans or magic.

"First we need to get Kathleen home to her parents. They'll want to begin making arrangements."

Jared flicked his wrist and a blanket appeared. "I'll carry her."

"Wait a minute; I want photographs first." They backed out of the low opening and Jared brushed the dust from his pants. Woodrow withdrew a camera from his pocket and snapped photos of Kathleen, the floor, the entrance, and the outside of the tomb. "All right, that should do. Let's go."

Jared gently levitated Kathleen's still form from the tomb, carefully wrapped her in the blanket, and carried her toward the car, tears blurring his vision. He could tell by the little he could see of her body that she had put up a fight. You couldn't use magic to kill, but you could cause serious damage. Jared was no healer, but if he had to guess, the wound to the side of Kathleen's head was what caused her death.

Envisioning what Adam might do to Kendra sent uncontrollable hatred for the man searing through Jared's veins. Determination blazed in his eyes. If it took all night, he'd make Kendra believe Adam was the monster he knew him to be.

"Do you know where Adam lives?" Woodrow asked.

Jared shook his head. "Kendra might. I'll go see her after we've taken care of Kathleen."

"Son, it's after midnight."

"I don't care. It's time for Kendra to learn exactly what her boyfriend Adam is capable of."

Chapter 25

When Kendra's cell phone rang, she was awake, still dressed and seated on the couch with Clementine. Earlier she'd gathered what remained of her ghost tour and, with an excited group, finished the route. She'd called Deanne and Loren and filled them in on what happened.

Kendra answered on the first ring. "Hello, Jared. Did you find Kathleen?"

"Open the door, I'm coming up."

Puzzled by his brisk tone, she did as he asked. As he entered the apartment, the solemn expression on his face, together with his mussed hair and filthy clothes, told her the news wasn't good. "What's happened?"

"What kind of booze do you have?"

"Nothing but wine. Why?"

"Never mind." He flicked his wrist and conjured a bottle of bourbon and a glass. He set the bottle on the counter, poured a generous portion, and downed it.

"Jared, please tell me what's happened."

He poured another shot into his glass. "Kathleen is dead. Two healers examined her body and said she was raped and tortured before she died. She put up a fight, but whoever killed her was more powerful."

Kendra's stomach heaved while tears gathered in her eyes.

"Where was she found?"

"On a cold slab in a crumbling tomb in Lafayette No. 1."

"Oh, I'm going to be sick."

"You're going to be sicker when I tell you who killed her."

"Who?" But she had a feeling she already knew what he was going to say.

"Your boyfriend."

She held her hand to her mouth and shook her head. As she did, images of her night at Minerva's trickled back. Whispers of things Thaddeus had said were on the edge of her memory.

Jared slammed his glass down. "Damn it to hell, Kendra, what the fuck is it going to take for you to believe me?"

"I don't know what to think," she cried and sat down on the sofa. She lifted Clementine from the coffee table and centered the vase of roses which gave off a sweet perfume. "Jared, I'm a witch with usually good intuition. I've never felt any kind of evil from Thaddeus."

Jared ran his hands over his face. Through gritted teeth he said, "For the hundredth time, Adam and Thaddeus are the same person."

"What proof do you have?"

"The fact I know he's a sick motherfucker who tried to kill me and Philippe, who threatened to kill you, and now has killed Kathleen." He stopped pacing and glowered at Kendra. "If someone else told you what a monster he is, would you believe them?"

"That would depend on who it was."

"How about parents who lost a daughter because of Adam?"

Kendra drew in a deep breath. "Who is that?"

Jared told her about the McBrides and Rose. "Philippe is still on Black Island with them." He stopped in front of her, and his face took on a sour expression. He sniffed. "Where is that sickening sweet smell coming from?"

Kendra scratched Clementine, blinking at his change in topic. "What?"

Without answering he bent to where the roses sat. "It's coming from these."

Kendra smiled. "Aren't they wonderful? Instead of the smell fading, it's getting stronger."

Jared narrowed his eyes. "Are those the roses *he* gave you."

"Yes."

He studied the flowers. "How long have you had them?"

"Just a few days. Why?"

"If they came from Adam, then there's something wrong with them. Well, I can take care of this." He picked up the vase, carried it out onto the balcony, took out one flower, threw the rest into the air, and hit them with a ball of energy that incinerated them.

Unable to believe what she was seeing, Kendra hurried after him. "Jared, what are you doing?" she cried watching as the vase dissolved.

"We'll soon find out if I'm right. I kept one." He flicked his wrist and a small cylinder appeared. He slid the flower in and sealed the end. "I'm going to have this analyzed. Tell me, do you feel any different?"

She hesitated. Was her conviction that Thaddeus was innocent still as strong? Part of her couldn't imagine the man who had been so nice to her being such a monster, but she did feel as if a fog had lifted from her mind. Her inner alarm screamed that Jared was telling the truth. She choked back bile. "I really think I'm going to be sick."

She stumbled back into the apartment, sat down on the sofa, and held her head in her hands.

"Did he give you anything else?" Jared asked.

Kendra swallowed hard before answering. "I think a genie bottle. It's in the bedroom."

Jared stepped into her bedroom and returned holding up the bottle. "Is this it?"

Kendra lifted her head from her hands and nodded.

Without a word, Jared headed for the balcony and Kendra heard the bottle shatter. "That should take care of that," he said, coming back into the living room.

"Jared, how could I have been so fooled," Kendra asked, her voice barely above a whisper. "I'm telling you, he was a perfectly nice guy. He was fun, he had a great sense of humor, and I enjoyed being with him."

"He's both a powerful witch and a great con artist who's fooled a lot of people. Here, drink this." He handed her a glass of water. "But the scary part is that I think he actually likes you. He told me that after he kills me, he plans on having you for his own."

Fury suffused her face and she jumped to her feet. "Not if I have anything to say about it." Now it was her turn to stomp around. "How are we going to bring him to justice for killing Kathleen and keep him away from you and me?"

He sat down in an overstuffed chair. "I have to ask you something."

"What?"

"Did you sleep with him?"

She considered testing his reaction if she were to say yes, but it wouldn't be worth upsetting him over a lie. Besides, if he acted as if he didn't care, that would be worse, so she told the truth. "No. He tried, but I couldn't go through with it."

A thought struck her, and she looked to where Clementine lay snoring on the couch. "Wow, Clementine knew Adam was evil." She explained about the cat clawing Adam's leg, leaving out the part about her orgasm. He didn't need to know everything.

Jared smiled. "Come here." He held out his arms, and she ran to him.

Sitting on Jared's lap, she put her arms around him and buried her face in his neck. "I may have been a fool in regard to Adam, but that doesn't mean I've forgiven you for what you did."

"I know." He ran his hand up and down her back. "And if I had it to do again, I'd do it differently, but I can't change the past. I can only ask you to try and understand."

She raised her head and gazed into his eyes. "I still don't know why you didn't call me and tell me what was happening. I could have gone with you and perhaps helped."

"That's exactly why I didn't call. I had no idea how dangerous Adam was, and I didn't want to put your life at risk. Considering everything we know now, I was right to keep you away. The more I think about it, the more I'm convinced he'd been watching us while working out his plan to take Philippe."

"So he intentionally took Philippe before our wedding to prevent our marriage?"

He nodded. "I believe so."

"How did he get his hands on Philippe?"

Jared repeated what Philippe had told him. "When my mirror showed him to me, it was obvious he'd been beaten. Philippe also told me afterward he'd been drugged."

Her eyes filled with tears. "I'm so sorry I didn't believe you." She sniffed. "How badly was Philippe hurt?"

"He's fine. Like I said, he stayed on Black Island, and he and Violet McBride are getting along well. He thinks she's the girl for him."

"I'm glad. Hopefully she can straighten him out." She took a deep breath. "How close did you come to dying?"

"It was pretty bad, but thanks to Angelique, I survived."

Startled, she asked, "How?"

When he concluded, she shook her head. "This is getting more and more incredible."

He laughed. "Wait until I tell you about my trip through the looking glass."

"What?"

He kissed her. "Nothing. It's a long story."

"We still need to connect Adam with Kathleen's death and get him out of our lives. I'm sure once I explain to Deanne and Loren that Adam truly is the bad guy, they'll be happy to help us."

"No way are any of you getting involved. This is up to me."

Kendra scowled. "Jared, I'm already involved. If Adam still thinks I'm interested in him and angry with you, there'll be a better chance he'll make a mistake."

"Have you not been listening to me? The man is

very dangerous. If he has any inkling that you're trying to trap him, he'll turn on you."

"How will he know? And I just thought of something. We're having our store-opening celebration at Deanne's parents' bar tomorrow night, and Adam is supposed to take me."

"You'll have to tell him your plans have changed and you're going with me."

"Won't that make him suspicious? If we want to catch him off guard, he still has to believe I care for him. I could tell him about Kathleen, and he might let something slip."

Jared shook his head. "He's too smart to fall for that. I need to get him alone and finish this. I'm tired of playing games. I'm going to tell him I want to meet with him."

"He almost killed you once. You can't face him alone."

"Yes, but this time I'll know what to expect."

She stood and placed her hands on her hips. "Why are you being so stubborn? There are plenty of people who would be happy to help."

"Because this is my fight. I'm not about to allow someone else to be hurt or killed. Kendra, I'm not kidding about this. You are to keep out of it."

"What about tomorrow night? I'm not canceling our party. We've invited people, and Deanne's parents are going all out for us."

He also got to his feet and stood so their noses were inches apart. "Listen to me, you won't be at any party tomorrow night, because I've just decided you're leaving New Orleans. You can go stay with the McBrides where you'll be safe until this is over."

She narrowed her eyes. "Are you crazy? I'm not leaving. Adam lied to me, gave me cursed roses, and probably drugged me at Minerva's. I'm not running away like a scared little girl. I'm staying right here, and I'm going to help take him down. So you'd better come up with a different plan."

Jared gritted his teeth. "And who's the one being stubborn?" He threw up his hands. "Fine, if you're going to insist on being at the party, I'll be there as well. But after the party you give Adam some excuse, and you, Loren, and Deanne go to Loren's and stay there until you hear from me."

When she opened her mouth to protest, he stopped her. "Kendra, I'm serious. If you don't do as I say, I'll put you under and take you away myself. And you know I'm strong enough to do it."

Every inch of her body bristled. It took all her willpower not to tell him what she thought of bossy overbearing, arrogant, domineering witches, but she knew her best defense was to agree to his terms. Which didn't mean she had to do as he said. She smiled to herself. She also knew how to distract him. She wrapped her arms around his neck. "All right, I'll do what you want. Now kiss me."

"Kendra." That's all he was able to say before she placed her lips on his and moved her body against him. "Do you really want to talk?" She murmured against his mouth. "Or would you rather?" She ran her hand down his chest, over his stomach and stopped when she cupped his increasing erection. "I think you'd rather do this." She unhooked his belt and flung it to the floor, then slowly unzipped his fly. When his hard penis was exposed, she held him and gently slid her hand back and forth along its smooth surface. "Mmm, nice." When he groaned, she fell to her knees and took him into her mouth.

His breathing became ragged.

She ran her tongue along his shaft then across the tip until he hissed, "You'd better stop."

Ignoring him, again she took him deep into her mouth. Pure female satisfaction filled her, when seconds later he cried her name.

Before she could rise, she found herself lifted off the floor and plopped down on the kitchen counter. The look of primitive lust on his face made her body tremble. "Jared, what are you doing? Let's go to the bed."

He shook his head. "We won't make it. Besides, I've been fantasizing about doing this since the first time I walked in here." He unsnapped her jeans and slid them down her legs, her panties following.

"What are you going to do? Jared, no you can't." But he did. He fell to his knees, spread her legs, and put his mouth on her.

She soon lost any inhibitions of being sprawled there on the counter as his teasing tongue sent delicious waves of pleasure throughout her body. "Oh, sweet Mother of the Gods," she moaned as the climax soared through her. Before the last ripples died away, he thrust his shaft deep inside her.

"That's it, baby, take me in."

Kendra held onto the edge of the counter and met him thrust for thrust. As their rhythm increased, and the energy pulsated from their bodies, Kendra panted, "Jared, I'm going to…" She screamed as another climax rocked her.

Breathing hard, Jared kept moving as her body convulsed around him. The air crackled and the mist swirled. "Baby, I'm right behind you."

As his body arched and he cried out with his own release, Kendra lay spent beneath him.

"That was as much fun as I thought it would be," Jared said on a ragged breath.

"Hmm." Kendra sat up. "Jared, do you realize we always go at each other like two sex-crazed maniacs?"

He laughed. "So what's wrong with that?"

"Nothing, but Deanne and Loren think we have a problem."

He lifted her into his arms and headed for the bedroom. "That's because they aren't getting any, and they're envious." He dropped her onto the bed and lay down next to her.

"Jared, that's an awful thing to say."

He nuzzled her neck. "I really don't want to discuss Deanne and Loren's sex lives." He removed her shirt. "I'd rather be doing this." He took her nipple into his mouth.

She sighed. "So would I."

Chapter 26

"I saw Jared leaving your apartment," Deanne said the following morning, coming into Enchantment carrying a bag of fresh beignets. "I take it he spent the night?"

"He sure did," Kendra replied. "Those smell wonderful. I didn't have time for breakfast." She reached for the bag. "I only grabbed a cup of coffee before I came down."

"So much for getting him out of your system," Deanne said. "Girl, will you never learn?"

"I have a lot to tell you, which includes why Jared spent the night with me, but I want to wait until Loren gets here." Kendra spread napkins on the counter. "I love these, but they're a mess to eat." As she bit into the warm, soft beignet, powdered sugar trickled down her chin.

Deanne sipped her coffee. "Isn't it awful about Kathleen? I couldn't believe it when my dad told us how he and Jared found her. Who could have done something like that to her?"

Just then Loren hurried through the door. "Sorry I'm late. I couldn't sleep last night thinking about Kathleen, then I overslept."

"We were just talking about her," Deanne said. "Under the circumstances, I feel bad about having our party tonight."

"I was with Kathleen's family for a while yesterday, and I mentioned the same thing," Loren said. "They want us to go ahead. They said that, if anything, she loved a good party."

Deanne nodded. "That's for sure."

Kendra brushed powdered sugar from her fingers and took a sip of coffee. "I have something to tell the two of you, and I want to do it before we open." She proceeded to fill them in on everything Jared had told her, including the cursed vase of roses and the genie bottle, and what she'd remembered from the night at Minerva's, ending with, "So you see, he was right, and I was wrong. Thaddeus *is* Adam, and Adam truly is the bad guy."

Seconds ticked past as they stared at her, then Loren spoke, her voice barely above a whisper. "Jared has proof Adam killed Kathleen?"

"Not beyond his instincts and Adam's past behavior."

"I can't believe my dad didn't tell us this last night," Deanne said.

"Jared doesn't want anyone to know Adam's been exposed," Kendra said.

Deanne's hands balled into fists. "What a fool he made out of all of us."

"Tell me about it," Kendra said. "Part of his power is his seductive charm."

Deanne jangled her car keys. "Let's go get the bastard. We'll make him confess."

Loren placed a hand on her shoulder. "Calm down. It's not up to us. This is a job for your father and the Council." She turned to Kendra. "I assume Jared has contacted them?"

"Woodrow is aware of Jared's suspicions, but Jared is planning to take care of Adam himself. That's where we come in."

"Good," Deanne stated. "I can't stand the thought of just waiting around doing nothing. What's our plan?"

"That depends on what Jared does. Last night, he said he would contact Adam and set up a place for them to meet. He also said he'd come to the party. We'll have to keep an eye on both him and Adam. If they leave, we follow."

Loren turned to Deanne. "I suppose we owe Jared an apology."

"About doubting him in regards to Adam, yes, but he still left Kendra and put her through hell."

"He did that to protect me. All we can do now is help him." Kendra smiled. "Without him knowing, that is."

"So you're still planning on going to the party with Adam, or Thaddeus, or whoever the hell he is?" Deanne asked. "How will you be able to sit there and act normal?" She shook her head. "I couldn't do it."

"It'll be hard for us all," Loren said. "But for Jared's sake and our own safety, we have to put on the performance of our lives."

Kendra's cell phone rang. "It's Thaddeus," she said, reading the caller ID. "Now we'll see how good an actress I am." She inhaled deeply, said a calming spell, touched her gold unicorn for strength, and answered. "Hello."

"Good morning," Adam said. "I'm sorry to be calling so early, but I wanted to catch you before the store opened. Did you hear anything about your friend?"

Kendra swallowed hard before she said, "It's nice of you to ask." She hoped her voice sounded normal. "Kathleen was found last night, and"—Kendra paused—"she's dead."

"Oh, Kendra, I'm so sorry. What happened?"

She dug her nails into her palm and silently counted to ten. "All we know is that she was murdered, probably by another witch."

"What? How awful. If there's anything I can do, please let me know."

"Thanks. The Wiccan Council is going to conduct an investigation."

"Do they have any leads? It's such a tragedy. Violence between witches is so rare."

Kendra couldn't believe how sincere he sounded. She wanted to blurt out, "Yes, you sick monster, we know who the murderer is." Instead she kept her cool and said, "I don't have a lot of the details, just that she fought her attacker."

"That poor girl. Again, if I can be of any assistance to the Council, please let me know."

"I will, thanks."

"Are you still planning on having the party tonight?"

"Yes. Kathleen would want us to."

"Do you still want me to come?"

"Of course, but we have to get there early. Why don't you meet us there around eight o'clock?"

"Sure, it's Baby Blues, on Basin Street, in the Treme, right? Oh, and Kendra, I want to apologize for running out on your tour. My encounter with Dupre made me pretty uncomfortable, and when we went into his hotel, well, it just seemed like it would be best if I left before there was more trouble."

"No problem. I understand."

Kendra's hands were trembling when the call ended. She turned to Loren and Deanne. "Oh, what a prick. The bastard was so sympathetic. Honestly, right now I could kill him myself."

****

Frustrated, Jared leaned his elbows on his desk and stared at Angelique's mirror. Try as he might, he couldn't make the mirror show him where Adam lived. He whacked the desktop with his fist and the mirror bounced. *The bastard must have one hell of a privacy charm.*

He was ready to settle this, tonight. He understood that Kendra wanted to help, but he couldn't risk her life. With the blessing of the Council, Jared planned to make Adam pay for the crimes against Rose, against Philippe, and against Kathleen.

Now that Kendra knew what Adam really was, an evil witch with no chance of reform, he worried she wouldn't be able to hide her revulsion and might do something inadvertently that would alert him.

"Hey, asshole," he shouted at the blank mirror. Nothing. Angelique was probably protecting the mirror from Adam, and now Adam couldn't hear Jared summoning him. He glanced over at his cell phone. Kendra would have Adam's number, but if he asked her for it, she'd want to know why. *Damn it to hell, this shouldn't be so complicated.*

He picked up the mirror. "Show me Kendra." The glass shimmered, then Kendra appeared standing behind a display case while two women tried on jewelry. Relieved she finally believed him, Jared thought of their extremely satisfying make-up sex of the previous night and smiled. As he watched Kendra show the girls more jewelry to try on, he hesitated. She'd be busy for a while. Did he dare try?

"Show me her cell phone." Kendra's purse appeared beneath the checkout counter, her phone visible inside. He sighed. Considering they were just back on friendly terms, she'd be furious if she found out. Perhaps there was another way. But who else would have Adam's number? He rolled his eyes and picked up his phone.

"Hi, Minerva, this is Jared Dupre."

"Jared, I knew you would be calling," Minerva purred. "The cards are never wrong."

"Then do you also know why I'm calling?" he asked.

She hesitated. "I'm not sure."

"Minerva, I need Adam's cell number or his address."

"I could never give out personal information like that."

Jared's voice took on a steely tone. "Minerva, I know what Adam did to Kendra at your museum. I know you had a part in it. I don't think the Wiccan Council would look favorably on a witch who allowed something like that to happen."

He heard her intake of breath. "You have no proof."

"Maybe not, but the Council would certainly investigate." He had a thought. "Minerva, did you hear Kathleen LeBlanc is dead?"

"Yes, what a tragedy."

"Did you hear how she died?"

"No."

"She was found raped and beaten in a tomb in St. Louis No. 1. Your friend Adam killed her."

There was silence on the other end, then she whispered, "Jared, is that true?"

"Yes."

"I have to sit down." He could hear the scrape of a chair leg. "Jared, I want you to know my life was threatened if I didn't help him drug Kendra." Her voice broke. "I never wanted to harm her or anyone else. I'll tell the Council what I know about Adam, but I swear to all the Gods and Goddesses, I had no idea he planned on killing Kathleen."

Jared knew she was telling the truth. In all the years he'd known Minerva, she'd never been evil—a little crazy maybe. "The Council would appreciate that. Now I need Adam's cell number."

"If he finds out I gave it to you, he'll kill me."

"No he won't, because I'm going to kill him first."

Seconds later Jared punched in the number, and on the third ring a surprised Adam answered. "Dupre?"

"Yeah, asshole, it's me." Not giving Adam a chance to reply he continued, "It's time to end this. Meet me in St. Louis No.1 tonight."

Adam hesitated. "I have a date with Kendra, so it will have to be some other time."

"I'll be at the party as well. When Kendra is occupied, we'll slip out. This is between the two of us."

"Agreed, but make sure you say your goodbyes to the lady, because you won't be coming back."

Jared scoffed. "I'm not only going to make you pay for fucking with Philippe, you're going down for Kathleen's death, and Rose's too. So enjoy the party. It will be your last." Jared ended the call and, with a determined set to his mouth, went to gather the things he'd need.

****

Adam turned to the mirror where Augustus scowled back at him.

"What did Dupre say?" Augustus asked.

"He wants to meet tonight."

"Where?"

"St. Louis No.1."

"At last my revenge will be complete." Augustus glowered at Adam. "And this time you will not fail me. This will be your last chance. If you do not succeed in killing Dupre, then you must die nobly. If you run like a coward, I will do all that is in my power to make you suffer."

When Augustus disappeared from the glass, Adam silently mouthed, "Fuck you." It wouldn't only be Dupre he'd rid himself of. He'd take great satisfaction in tossing the old man and his mirror into the Mississippi on his way out of town.

Adam scanned the room and made his plans. He'd have his car packed, and when he was sure Dupre was dead, he'd return to the party for Kendra. No one had better dare interfere. He smiled. Unbeknownst to the lady, she was about to take a trip.

Chapter 27

When Kendra, Loren, and Deanne arrived at Baby
Blues, they were greeted warmly by Deanne's parents,
Serene and Woodrow. Colorful congratulatory
balloons, streamers, and banners filled the bar.

The three girls were dressed in identical calf-length
skirts of forest green over knee high boots with two-
inch heels. They wore matching green and white pin-
striped tops with bell-shaped sleeves and a scooped
neck encircled with rows of tiny glittering beads. Their
long hair hung down their backs. Silver hoops adorned
their ears, and sparkling bangles encircled their wrists.

Both excited and apprehensive over what the night
might bring, Kendra followed Deanne and Loren to
where Deanne's parents waited.

"We're so proud of you girls," Serene said. The
slightest aroma of jasmine filled the air as she hugged
each in turn. Serene's café au lait skin and almond-
shaped eyes were so much like Deanne's. But unlike
her daughter, who wore colorful clothes, Serene chose
long skirts and gauzy tops in earth tones.

Woodrow nodded. "I have to say, I had my doubts
when you three told us you planned to open the store,
but you've proven you know what you're doing."

"Thanks to Loren," Deanne said. "She's the brains
behind our success."

Loren blushed. "I just had the idea. It took all of us

pulling together to make it work."

"I wasn't sure how many folks you were expecting, so we set aside an area for y'all in the back," Serene said.

"Perfect, Mama. I have a feeling people will be popping in and out all night."

"My mom promised to stop by between ghost tours," Kendra said.

"My parents are also coming," Loren added.

Serene nodded. "That's fine. I got a big pot of red beans and rice, crawfish gumbo, and a pan of molasses cornbread ready. And bourbon bread pudding for dessert. You just sit yourselves down, and Woodrow will get y'all drinks."

Deanne led the way to their tables. The band, Blues in the Night, consisted of two of Deanne's brothers and three of their friends. They were just tuning up as the girls passed the stage.

"Hey, ladies, where y'at?" Deanne's brother Tie asked.

"Fine, Tie. How 'bout you?" Kendra asked.

"Fine as frog hair," he said with a smile. "If you have any requests, let me know. Tonight is all about y'all."

"I've got one," Deanne said. "How about some Tipitina?" She began to sing and do some quick steps.

Tie strummed an off-key chord. "It's a good thing she doesn't often sing with the band. She usually clears the bar with her screeching."

Deanne snorted. "Yeah, well, it's a wonder you don't empty the place with that ugly face of yours."

Kendra laughed. Deanne could sing as well as her brothers, and people filled the bar the nights she sang.

"Come on you two, enough. We've all heard Deanne sing, and she's great." She turned to Tie. "How about 'Still Got the Blues'?"

"Gary Moore. You got it."

"Thanks." When they arrived at the table, Kendra was surprised to see Derrick and Andre already seated. She glanced circumspectly toward Deanne to see her reaction to Andre's presence. The tightness of Deanne's lips showed her displeasure. Kendra inwardly sighed. For months, Andre had been trying to convince Deanne he still loved her, but Deanne, unable to get past the hurt, would hardly speak to him. Having thought Jared had deserted and betrayed her, Kendra had sympathy for her feelings. Kendra liked Andre and believed he cared for Deanne. She only wished Deanne would give Andre a chance to show her.

Kendra smiled and greeted both men. In their mid-twenties, Andre was of medium height with hair and eyes the color of dark chocolate. He spoke with a Cajun accent and had a smile that could melt your heart. Derrick on the other hand was tall and well-built with dark-blue eyes and sandy-blond hair. He had a tattoo of a dragon on his arm and rode a custom Harley. They were dressed in black T-shirts, black jeans, and low boots.

"It's about time you girls got here," Andre said. "We've started the party without you."

Deanne glowered and took a seat next to Derrick, whose eyes were on Loren.

Andre smiled. "Ah, come on, *cher*, don't sit next to him." He patted an empty chair. "Come over here by me."

Deanne narrowed her eyes. "Not on your life. I'd

rather sit next to a skunk than you." She scowled. "Where's Tarese? Isn't she with you tonight?"

Andre gave her a wounded look. "I told you there was never anything between me and Tarese. You know that."

Deanne snorted. "Yeah, right."

Before Andre could respond, Woodrow arrived with two bottles of champagne.

"These are on the house," he said, popping the cork on one of the bottles.

Serene was right behind him and placed bowls of gumbo, red beans and rice, and hot cornbread in the middle of the table. "Now y'all eat; there's plenty more."

"It all smells incredible, and I'm starving," Loren said.

"Me, too," Kendra added.

"Hey, Thaddeus," Deanne said.

Knowing who stood behind her, Kendra's appetite instantly fled. She clasped her unicorn, took a deep breath, plastered what she hoped looked like a sincere smile on her face, and turned. "Hi, Thaddeus, you're just in time to eat. Have a seat." She hoped her voice sounded normal as she continued. "These are Deanne's parents, Serene and Woodrow, and our friends, Derrick and Andre."

Kendra watched Serene as she shook his hand. A flicker of unease seemed to cross her face before she welcomed him. There was definitely tension between Adam and Woodrow as the two men greeted each other.

"Well, you all enjoy your food," Serene said. "I'll keep an eye out for any more of your guests."

Kendra glimpsed a sneer of distaste pass over

Adam's face just before he smiled and thanked Serene.

Bastard, she thought. *He thinks he's better than everyone here. How am I going to get through this night without giving away my contempt for him?* She jumped as Loren, seated on her other side, kicked her beneath the table. Scowling, she turned, understanding Loren's silent warning. Her face could be an open book. She needed to keep her emotions under control.

"Your parents have a nice place here," Adam was saying to Deanne. "And the food smells terrific."

"Thanks," Deanne said. "The bar has been in my family for over a hundred years. My great grandfather was a jazz musician and used to play here. When the owners wanted to sell, he bought it."

The walls were covered in cypress paneling and wide beams crossed the ceiling. Polished wood covered the floor and hanging brass lamps gave a warm glow.

Friends and family came and went. Both Serene and Woodrow made a point to be close by. They ate, drank, and laughed at Derrick's jokes. Kendra tried to pretend she was enjoying herself, but anger boiled up inside her. This was supposed to be her, Deanne, and Loren's night to celebrate their store opening, and instead they had to pretend to have fun while a killer sat at their table.

Kendra was relieved to see Adam engaged in conversation with Derrick and Andre, keeping her from having to speak with him. She was about to take a bite of bread pudding when Tie's voice coming over the sound system stopped her fork halfway to her lips.

"Ladies and gentlemen. We've got a surprise tonight. There's someone here who's going to play a few numbers with us, and if you've never heard this boy make a guitar sing, you're in for a special treat. So how about a big hand for Jared Dupre."

Kendra slowly set her fork down on her plate and turned toward the stage where Jared was strapping on a guitar. It was about time he got here.

When Derrick and Andre whistled and clap for Jared, she narrowed her eyes. She would bet her best heels Jared had sent them to watch over her until he arrived. They were both big buddies of his and would do anything he asked. For the love of Odin, she was in a public place surrounded by friends. What could happen to her here? Kendra listened in horror to Jared as he said, "This is a tune called "Please Forgive Me." I send it out to the woman I love."

Beside her, Kendra sensed Adam's hostile energy. *Great, now what do I do?* Before she could think of what to say, Adam excused himself and went to the Men's room.

Deanne leaned across the table and whispered. "What's Jared doing?"

"I don't know," Kendra whispered back. "He told me he was coming, but not that he was going to draw attention to himself like this. All he's managing to do is piss Adam off."

"But he does have a sexy voice," Loren added.

Kendra and Deanne stared at Loren, who shrugged. "Well, he does. I wish I had a hunk like that singing to me."

"Oh, for the sake of the Gods, Loren, did you forget what that singing hunk did to Kendra? Besides, he might make Adam mad enough that he starts a fight right here in the bar."

Kendra shook her head. "He likes your parents too

much. He'll wait until he and Adam are outside."

"We need to keep a close eye on the two of them," Loren said. "And here comes Adam."

Kendra was about to reply when Jared's next words hit her like a fist.

"This next one also goes out to my girl." When he started to sing a blues song about making love on a hot New Orleans night, Adam tapped her on the shoulder.

"Would you like to dance?"

Not knowing what else to do, Kendra nodded and allowed him to guide her onto the floor. She felt Jared's eyes boring into her as Adam held her against him. Even though the feel of his arms made her skin crawl, she gritted her teeth and swayed to the music, praying for the song to end. Then to her utter shock, Jared, no longer playing his guitar, a cordless mike in his hand, unceremoniously took her from Adam's arms. Holding her tight against him, they continued the dance while he sang the rest of the song.

The dance floor was packed. Kendra could do nothing but allow him to hold her close while memories of him singing the same song to her in his bed filled her mind. When he finished the song and handed the mike to Tie, Kendra hissed. "What are you doing? You're just making matters worse."

"The bastard had his hands on you. You were supposed to be nice, not hang all over him."

Exasperated, she sighed. "Jared, I wasn't hanging all over him. I'm trying to act as if nothing's happened. I could hardly turn him down when he asked me to dance. Now, go sit at the bar and behave yourself. I'm going to the Ladies'."

She'd barely cleared the restroom door when

Deanne and Loren came in behind her.

"Adam is so mad, he looks like he could chew nails," Deanne said.

Kendra threw up her hands in frustration. "What was I supposed to do? I couldn't make a scene in the middle of the dance floor."

"No, you couldn't," Loren said, "and Jared knows that. What I'd like to know is what he's trying to prove by all this?"

Deanne snorted. "That's easy. He's proving that Kendra belongs to him and rubbing Adam's nose in it."

"You'll have to get rid of one of them before this gets ugly," Loren said.

"Yeah, well, which one do you think is going to back down and leave?" Kendra asked. "Besides, we're supposed to be keeping an eye on the two of them."

Wide-eyed the three of them stared at one another. "And we're all in here," Loren said.

"Shit," Deanne exclaimed as they hurried for the door.

On their way back through the crowd they spotted Derrick and Andre. "What are you doing sitting here at the bar?" Deanne asked.

"Everyone left the tables and are scattered throughout the room," Andre said. "So we decided to sit over here."

Knowing Derrick and Andre knew Adam by the name Thaddeus, Kendra asked, "Where's Thaddeus?"

Derrick glanced toward the door. "He said he'd see you later and left."

A sinking feeling coiled in Kendra's stomach. "And Jared?"

"He's also gone, and he also said he'd see you

later."

"Damn him." Angered at being out-maneuvered, Kendra turned to Deanne and Loren. "He was just waiting for his chance, and we handed it right to him." She turned to Andre and Derrick. "Where did he go? And don't tell me you don't know."

"Hey, *cher*, calm down. We don't know anything," Andre said.

Kendra glowered. "Jared told both of you to keep an eye on me until he got here, didn't he? And I wouldn't be surprised if he didn't also tell you to keep us here until he gets back, right?"

Andre took a long sip of his Blackened Voodoo while Derrick lit a cigarette.

"If you don't tell me where Jared has gone, we're going to cause you real pain," Kendra said as the three girls encircled the two men.

"And we're not kidding," Deanne said planting herself in front of Andre.

Loren folded her arms and stared at Derrick.

"Okay, we were just helping out a friend," Derrick finally said. "But I swear on Thor's hammer, we don't know where Jared went."

"Don't worry, *cher*, he'll be back." Andre smiled at Deanne. "So in the meantime, how about a dance?"

"How about you go to the devil," Deanne replied.

"Come on, *cher*, this is supposed to be a party. You three need to just relax, have a good time, and Jared will be back soon."

"Who left first, Thaddeus or Jared?" Kendra asked.

Derrick frowned. "I think Jared did, but I have to tell you, there was some really negative energy coming from that Thaddeus guy."

Kendra studied both men. How much had Woodrow and Jared told them? Did they already know about Adam? The more she thought about it, the more she was convinced Jared would have confided in them. "All right you two, the time for pretending is over," Kendra said. "I'm sure Jared told you that Thaddeus is really Adam and that he's a monster."

"Yeah we know," Derrick said. "But you shouldn't worry. Jared can take care of himself."

"That's right. He'll kick the bastard's ass," Andre added.

The band had taken a break, and Tie had just joined them. "Are y'all talking about Jared?"

Andre nodded.

Kendra wanted to scream. Didn't they realize what danger Jared was in? She gritted her teeth in exasperation. Of course not. Jared would have made light of it. Telling them it was no big deal. Well, she'd tell them the truth. "Listen to me. Adam is a powerful demonic witch who almost killed Jared and Philippe and did kill Kathleen. If he's not stopped, he will kill again. If you want to help Jared, then help me find out where he is."

Andre and Derrick glanced at each other, then Andre spoke. "Jared didn't tell us any of this."

"If he had, we'd of gone with him," Derrick added.

"What are we going to do?" Tie asked.

"Damn, I wish I had my crystal ball," Kendra said with exasperation.

"Here comes mama, and she doesn't look happy," Deanne said.

"I could see all your auras turning red from across the room," Serene said. "What's going on?"

Deanne quickly filled her in.

"I knew as soon as I shook Adam's hand he was full of dark magic," Serene said.

"If we had a crystal ball perhaps Deanne, Loren and I could break through Jared's privacy charm," Kendra said.

Serene shook her head. "Not in here—there's too much energy bouncing around. You'll need someplace quiet." She turned to Deanne. "Take the girls to the back office." She squeezed Kendra's hand. "Don't worry. We'll find him."

Kendra kissed Serene's cheek, told Derrick and Andre to keep an eye out for Jared, and headed for the office at the back of the bar.

When they entered the small room, Deanne waved her hand and candlelight flickered in the wall sconces.

Deanne went to where her mother's crystal ball sat on a spindle-legged table. "Okay, let's give it a try."

"We're going to have to concentrate as hard as we can," Kendra said.

They each placed three fingers upon the ball and gathering their power said,

"Part the mist and let us see,
If he's far or if he's near,
Show us the picture bright and clear,
As we will, so mote it be."

"Damn it, nothing," Deanne said as the glass remained cloudy.

"Hit it harder," Kendra demanded. Again, nothing happened.

Kendra's hands balled into fists. "Damn him. He's blocked himself to the point we'll never get through."

"Should I get Andre, Derrick and my parents?"

Deanne asked. "Perhaps between all of us we can break through."

Kendra let out a long breath. "I suppose it won't hurt."

"What about trying to see Adam in the crystal ball?" Loren suggested. "He may not think it's important to block himself."

"Great idea." Kendra placed her fingers on the crystal ball. "Give it all you've got."

"Wait a minute. There's something," Loren said.

"What is that?" Deanne asked.

"I'm not sure. It's too fuzzy," Loren replied.

Eyes blazing, determined not to lose Jared to Adam's evil, Kendra poured all her power through her fingers into the ball. "Show us where Adam is."

"Kendra, keep hitting it," Deanne cried. "It's getting clearer. It's a cemetery."

The mist in the ball shimmered and spun, then cleared.

"Which one?" Loren asked.

"St. Louis No. 1," Deanne shouted. "We did it."

"Damn it, it's gone," Kendra said. "I wanted to see Jared's face."

Exhausted from their exertions, the three girls fell into chairs.

"At least we know where to go," Deanne said.

"Yeah, but we have to get out of here without anyone knowing," Kendra said. "If we're seen, you know as well as I do they'll try and stop us."

Deanne smiled and got to her feet. "No problem." She went to a closed curtain and slid it open revealing French doors. "They lead to the courtyard, then into the alley."

"Yes." Kendra clapped her hands. "Let's go."

"Ah, I don't think we want to go tramping through a cemetery wearing dresses and heels," Loren said. "Perhaps we should change first."

"Practical as always," Deanne said. She waved her hand, and three sets of jeans, sweaters, and sneakers appeared.

They quietly made their way across the courtyard, through the gate to the alley, and out onto Basin Street.

"It's really dark out here," Loren said. "And everything is too still and quiet."

"Tell me about it." Deanne glanced over her shoulder. "Something's giving me the creeps and it isn't the ghosts."

They worked their way along the outer wall of the cemetery. Kendra shivered. "I feel like we're being watched. Perhaps we should put a protective shield around us."

"Good idea." Loren lifted her arms, but before she could speak, Kendra, who was ahead of her, suddenly cried out and stumbled back knocking into Deanne.

"Ouch," Deanne said with a grunt.

"What's going on?" Loren asked.

"There's something in front of me," Kendra said.

Loren peered into the darkness. "I don't see anything."

Tentatively Deanne put out her hand. "I can see through it, but it's solid."

"Jared," Kendra said. "He put up barricades in case we followed."

"Bullshit on that," Deanne said. "Let's blast through it."

"The girls reared back and hurled balls of energy at

the invisible wall. When nothing happened, Kendra cursed.

Deanne's brows rose. "Impressive. I didn't know you knew so many naughty words."

Loren shook her head. "Now what do we do? We'd waste too much time going back for help."

"I wish we could levitate ourselves over the wall," Deanne said.

From inside the cemetery, bright flashes of light streaked across the night sky.

Panic threatened to overtake Kendra. "Something's happening. We have to get to Jared."

"What's that?" Loren pointed.

Beyond the invisible shield, a shimmering shape formed.

"For the love of the Gods, it's Kathleen," Deanne whispered as Kathleen Le Blanc's body took shape.

"Kathleen, can you help us?" Kendra called.

"I don't know." Her voice a hollow sound on the wind, her filmy form glowed and pulsating energy surrounded her. She held out her hands and the invisible wall disappeared.

"Kathleen, thank you," Kendra said as the girls hurried toward the cemetery gates.

"Is it just me, or is the temperature dropping?" Loren asked.

"It's always colder here," Kendra said.

Deanne rubbed her arms. "Yeah, but this seems like a different kind of cold than you get from the dead."

"I don't like this," Loren stated. "Something's wrong."

"Stop it," Deanne said. "You're freaking me out."

She glanced around. "What happened to Kathleen?"

"I don't know, but hurry," Kendra said. "Jared could already be hurt."

"Let's find Marie," Deanne said. "We'll be safe once we're with her, and she might know something."

"Wait a minute." Loren flicked her wrist and a burning torch appeared. "Now we can at least see, but watch out for broken pavements."

Their footfalls barely made a sound as they made their way along the rows of pale tombs. Granite angels with broken wings peered down upon them from crumbling crypts. Translucent images flickered outside the pool of torch light.

"There's Marie's tomb." Deanne pointed. "And we're in luck. She doesn't have any other visitors." As they approached, Marie appeared.

"What you girls doin' here? Didn't I warn you?" She narrowed her eyes. "There is bad trouble. You need to leave."

"That's why we've come, Marie," Kendra said. "Jared needs us."

She shook her head. "No, it too dangerous. Them boys already here, and they full of some mean juju."

"Where are they?" Kendra asked.

"They in the back, but you girls not going there. I talked to Jared before the evil one got here. Jared told me what he needin' to do. He asked me to watch out for you three and keep you away. And that's what I'm goin' to do."

"Marie, Jared may not be able to fight Adam on his own. With the three of us helping, we'd have a better chance of destroying him," Kendra said.

The ground shook and bolts of silver light

crisscrossed in the night sky.

Kendra ran in the direction of the light closely followed by Deanne and Loren with a cursing Marie floating alongside. As they rounded a corner, Marie was able to get in front of Kendra and, with a force Kendra didn't see coming, blocked their progress. The three girls stumbled back.

Marie glowered, her hands on her hips. "If you three are determined to get in the middle of this, you're not goin' rushin' in like a bunch of stray hounds after a bone. Now quiet down and stay behind me. You do everything just as I say."

Agitated ghosts swarmed around the girls as they huddled together following Marie deep into the cemetery.

"This is the scariest thing I've ever done," Deanne whispered. "If we don't come out of this alive, I'm going to haunt Jared Dupre forever."

Loren shivered. "For once, Deanne, I'm in total agreement with you."

"We'll be okay," Kendra whispered back. "Jared won't let anything happen to us."

"Hush." Marie waved them to silence. "We're getting closer." A breeze kicked up, raising the dust of the tombs, and the temperature dropped even farther. She turned troubled eyes on them. "I can only hold the evil one away for a short time. You girls are no match for his dark power."

Kendra clutched her gold unicorn and prayed to those who came before her to give her the strength to battle whatever lay ahead. The unicorn began to glow and she felt the strong energy. Love and power. Nothing would stop her now.

"It's all in Jared's hands," Marie said. "You girls stay behind this tomb here. Do not come out for any reason. I'll be in front."

They eased their way around the side of the tomb. The wind howled and swirled. Darkness descended upon them.

A demented laugh filled the night. A light flashed and Kendra screamed.

Chapter 28

Jared stood motionless as a dark mist surrounded him. What the hell? He listened in horror to what sounded like a woman's screams. Was that Kendra? Damn it. How had she found them? Blood running down his face and arms from his wounds, he held his falcata ready, his hands slick with sweat and blood. He tried to see through the mist. When it began to clear, Jared's worst nightmare confronted him. Adam had Kendra, her hands and ankles bound, a knife pressed against her throat.

Fear as he'd never known clawed at Jared's heart. In a voice gone dry as gravel, he demanded, "Let her go, Montief. This is between us. She has nothing to do with it."

A triumphant gleam lit Adam's eyes. "Oh, but she is a part of it. She lied to me and made a fool out of me. I can't let her get away with that. She must learn who her master is, but don't worry, Dupre, I'm not going to kill her. I may have to torture her a little, but she's too tasty a morsel to destroy. I've decided to keep her as my slave, at least until I tire of her. Then I'll give what's left of her to my men to play with."

Jared's blood ran cold. He had to rid his mind of Kendra and concentrate on the man in front of him. Considering the red staining Adam's shirt, Jared knew he'd already managed to inflict some injuries, but he was far from going down. "I'll tell you one more time. Let her go."

Adam laughed. "Or you'll do what?"

"You're a coward, always hiding behind another," Jared taunted. "Your uncle paid the price for that. Now for once fight me like a man."

Adam sneered. "I've always been more of a man than you, Dupre. To prove it, while you lie dying you're going to watch me fuck your bitch over and over again." He jerked Kendra's head back. "I made her come with a kiss. Want to see how it's done? She must be punished for allowing you to put your filthy hands on her, and what better way than to have her fiancé watch her get pleasured beyond limit by another man."

"You couldn't pleasure a dog, Montief."

The blast of energy hit Jared so hard it staggered him back. He heard Kendra's cries as he fought for balance. "Come on, you son-of-a-whore. Stop hiding behind a woman and fight me."

Dirty gray energy pulsated off Adam and his eyes burned like hot coals as he sent another blast.

This time Jared was ready and deflected the blow. "Come on, fucker, you can do better than that."

Adam shoved Kendra away and she fell. Suddenly snakes of every size suddenly slithered around and over her. With her wrists and legs bound, she couldn't use magic to free herself.

Jared knew he couldn't take his eyes from Adam for a second but hearing her screams as she attempted to twist away from the snakes was tearing out his heart.

Marie appeared behind Adam holding the biggest snake Jared had ever seen. She placed the snake on the ground, and it coiled and slid toward Kendra. The other snakes slithered away.

Out of the corner of Jared's eye, he saw Deanne and Loren join their hands in the air and Kendra's ropes fell away. She got to her feet. Instead of running to safety she turned on Adam.

"Kendra, no," Jared yelled, but he was too late. She'd reared back and thrown a ball of energy toward Adam who raised his hand and deflected it back, knocking her hard to the ground. She cried out in pain as she landed in the rubble of a decaying tomb.

To Jared's disbelief, Kendra got to her knees, then her feet. Her left arm hung loose at her side. She clasped her unicorn and her entire body glowed.

Adam, thinking she was down, didn't see her. Energy pulsed around her as she lifted her hand and gold spears of light shot from her fingers directly at Adam's back.

A second before the streak hit Adam, an image of a man appeared behind him. The figure bellowed in rage and deflected the light.

Again, Kendra fell to the ground. Deanne and Loren raced to her side.

The spirit waved his hand and the three girls were enclosed in a cage.

To Jared's shock, the ghost of Kathleen appeared. "Adam Montief," she called. "You will rot in hell."

Seeing the shock on Adam's face, Jared took advantage of the distraction to strike. His steel blade flashed catching Adam on the right collarbone. Adam dropped his knife and conjured a sword of his own in time to partially block the blow. But Adam's grunt of pain told Jared he had connected.

Adam lunged, aiming his gleaming sword point at

Jared's chest. Jared's weapon was high but he swung it downward as he leaped away. His parry pushed Adam's thrust low and the blade bit deeply into Jared's right thigh. He nearly went down to his knee but managed to stumble backward, blood coursing down his leg.

Adam paused to switch his sword to his left hand. Though his arm drooped, a small round metal shield, a medieval buckler with a raised boss in the center, appeared gripped in Adam's right fist.

"That's a bit of cheating, don't you think?" Jared jeered.

"I may be a witch, but I still fight better right-handed. You want to play fair, don't you, Dupre?" Adam circled to his right looking for an opening.

Jared limped away a step or two, then, pushing off with his uninjured left leg, dove low pointing his sword toward Adam's left side. He dropped the blade tip to evade a clumsy parry, then swung it back up as he crossed in front of Adam at a stumbling run. The tip skipped off the shield edge and cut into Adam's chest, penetrating between two ribs.

Adam grunted. A roundhouse swing with the shield caught Jared across his back and knocked him flat, his face in the dirt. As Jared tried to roll onto his side to get his sword out in front of him, Adam—a red foamy spittle dribbling from his mouth—rushed forward, his straight heavy blade held before him like a short spear with his full weight behind it. If Jared couldn't stop him, Adam was going to stake him to the earth like a bug on a pin.

"Jared," Kendra screamed.

His breath coming in shallow gasps, Jared released his sword and fumbled for the jeweled dagger on his belt. It was gone. Jared saw Angelique appear next to him, the dagger held in her outstretched hand, its hilt glowing brightly. "End this curse."

A heartbeat before Adam's blade struck, Jared rolled, the dagger now in his hand, and thrust the steel deep beneath his enemy's ribs. Unable to move far enough away, Jared felt Adam's sword rip into his right side. Adam fell hard on top of him, their blood mingling with the dust of the dead.

Barely conscious, Jared felt the ground shake and heard an unearthly roar. Through half-open eyes, he again saw the image of the man standing over them, his translucent face twisted in hatred and rage.

"*No*," the spirit wailed. "I will have my vengeance."

Jared heard Angelique's voice from behind him.

"Augustus Montief, hear my words. You have failed. Be banished from this world, never to return."

Jared felt himself fading. Before darkness overtook him, he saw Angelique drive the jeweled dagger into the spirit of Augustus who bellowed, then disappeared.

****

Deanne and Loren rolled Adam's lifeless body off Jared. The sword fell to the side of its own weight, blood welling from Jared's wound.

Cradling an injured arm, Kendra knelt next to Jared. "Loren, can't you do something to help him?"

"Move out of the way and let me see," Loren said. "But I'm not an advanced healer. He needs someone with a lot more skill than me, but I'll do my best."

"Help is coming," Kathleen said, as she stared down at Adam's body. Tears fell down her filmy cheeks. "I'm so sorry. I never meant for anyone to get hurt."

Her own tears coursing down her cheeks, Kendra nodded. "Thank you." She turned to see the beautiful spirit, Angelique, who had helped Jared, the jeweled dagger at her feet.

"I can sustain him until help arrives, that's all," Loren said.

Kendra's breath caught. "There's so much blood. You have to stop it."

"I can try." Loren said. She turned to Angelique. "Together?"

Angelique nodded. A silver light glowed around Jared and his eyes fluttered open.

"Jared, oh, Jared, can you hear me?" Kendra frantically cried. "I thought he'd killed you."

In a feeble voice he said, "I'm still here."

"Oh, thank the Gods." She took his face in hers and kissed him. The feel of his pale, cold lips told her he was far from being out of danger.

"Ahem. Sorry to break this up, but I think Jared needs some medical attention."

Kendra glanced over her shoulder to see Woodrow, Andre, and Derrick standing over them.

Jared gave a wan smile. "Hey, Woodrow, you boys missed the party."

"So it seems." Woodrow hunkered down next to Jared. "How you doing, son?"

"He's bleeding," Kendra replied before Jared could answer.

Woodrow's voice was quiet and soothing. "I see that, Kendra. How about I help you up? Then we can take care of him."

She nodded and allowed him to lift her. Blood

soaked her clothing but she didn't seem to care or notice. "Where are you taking him?" she asked as they raised Jared onto a stretcher.

"To a house of healing," Woodrow replied. "They're already waiting."

Kendra swayed on her feet. "I'm coming, too."

Woodrow steadied her with his hand. "Yes, I'd say you need to be seen to as well." He turned. "Deanne, Loren, can you follow us with Kendra?"

Both girls hurried to Kendra's side. "All our cars are back at the bar," Loren said, putting a supporting arm around Kendra.

"Here, take mine." Andre handed Deanne his keys. For a second, a ring of silver light encircled their hands, then disappeared. Deanne and Andre stared wide-eyed at one another, then Deanne jerked her hand away. "Oh, no, not going to happen," she said, backing away.

Her arm throbbing, Kendra's mind didn't register the implications of what had just occurred between the two. She said, "I want to thank Marie and Angelique before we go."

"Angelique is gone," Loren said, "but Marie is over there." She pointed.

Together the three girls went to where Marie stood.

"That boy of yours a brave one," Marie said to Kendra as they approached. "And so are you girls. I'm proud of all you."

"I couldn't have gotten away from the snakes without your help," Kendra said.

Marie smiled. "Me and Zombie." Kendra inwardly shuddered as the giant snake wrapped around Marie's neck and arm.

"Now you girls get. I've had enough excitement for

one night. This is supposed to be a peaceful place."

****

Jared slipped in and out of consciousness as voices came and went, and images flickered through his mind. At one point he could have sworn he saw his mother, but she had kissed his cheek and faded away. He'd seen Angelique and the mulatto woman Taneen standing over him, their hands clasped, chanting words he couldn't comprehend. At times his pain was unbearable, then a floating sensation would come over him, and welcomed darkness would descend.

"Jared, I want you to open your eyes and come back to me," he heard a voice say. Was it Kendra? He felt as if he were swimming through thick brine he couldn't quite surface from. A cool hand brushed his hair from his forehead.

"Jared, can you hear me? It's Kendra, I want you to open your eyes."

Nausea roiled his stomach. He tried to do as she asked but couldn't find the strength.

"Please my love, you have to come back to us." He felt her soft lips on his and with everything he had moved his lips against hers.

"Oh, thank the Gods, Jared. That's it, sweetheart."

Slowly, ever so slowly, he forced his eyes open. He saw Kendra's beautiful face, her gray eyes bright with tears. He tried to speak, but his tongue felt thick and his throat raw.

"Oh, Jared." She kissed him again. "You're okay. I was so scared. No, don't try to talk. Would you like some water?"

He nodded.

"Here, you have to drink from this straw. The

325

healers don't want you moving."

The cool water tasted like champagne as it slid down his throat. "Thanks," he croaked feebly. "Where…?"

"You're at the Dupre. The healers thought you'd be more comfortable so they brought you home a couple of days ago. We've all been taking turns watching over you. Your father has been incredible. He set aside rooms for the healers and has been feeding everyone."

Jared frowned. "Days. How long…?"

"Counting today, six. You scared the hell out of us all. Adam hurt you pretty badly." Her eyes filled with tears and her voice broke. "I thought I was going to lose you."

"Come here." He managed to raise his arms, then winced. He noticed the sling she wore. "How bad are you hurt?"

"Just a sprain; I'll be fine."

Pain shot through his entire body as he held her tight. He brushed the hair from her face and kissed her trembling lips.

Kendra shuddered and buried her face against his neck. "Adam is dead. I've never seen anything so awful. I was so scared."

He ran his hand up and down her back. "It's over. You were incredibly brave. I couldn't have finished him off without your help. But you shouldn't have come."

She sat up. "I know you didn't want me there, and I didn't do much, but I had to try and help. I love you. I couldn't let you face him alone." She hesitated. "Did you see Angelique go after the spirit of Augustus?"

"Kind of. I kept blacking out."

"The curse is ended. The entire night freaked me out, and I never want to experience anything like that again."

He ran his finger along her tear-streaked cheek. "Adam's gone and you're safe. As soon as I can get out of this bed, we have a wedding to attend."

She smiled and lifted her left hand where her engagement ring sparkled. "I'll be waiting."

Epilogue

Three weeks later

Friends and family shouted and waved from the pier. Kendra and Jared stood on the deck of the cruise ship waving back. Kendra laughed and called, "Get ready, girls, here it comes." She tossed her bouquet of wildflowers over the railing toward the laughing ladies below.

"Oh, Jared, look. Deanne caught it." Kendra clapped delightedly.

"Now it's my turn," Jared said, kneeling down and running his hand up Kendra's leg past the lacy garter she wore.

"Jared, stop that." Kendra squealed to the applause of their fellow passengers and those shouting below.

Garter in hand, Jared stood and sent the piece of lace flying through the air.

Andre, standing with the other men, had his hands in his pockets, an expression of dismay filling his face.

"Well I'll be damned," Jared said shaking his head. "I purposely aimed it away from Andre and it still landed at his feet."

Kendra laughed and threw her arms around Jared's neck. "Like you always told me, you can't fight fate."

"No, love, you certainly can't." He held her close and kissed her welcoming lips. As their kiss deepened, igniting their passion, Jared murmured. "Perhaps we should go to our cabin and begin our honeymoon."

Kendra's voice was a little breathless. "We'll be sailing out into the Gulf in a little bit."

Jared nibbled her neck while he ran his hand up her back. "We might have to miss it. It'll still be there tomorrow."

"Oh, but I wanted to—" Her words were cut off by another kiss.

"Sweetheart, I plan on making love to you all the way to St. John's."

Kendra giggled. "That will take days."

Jared swept her into his arms. "I know. They can bring us food."

The long, mournful moan of the cruise ship's horn died away as the ship eased into the channel. On the quay below, Deanne and Loren raised their arms and a cloud of colorful balloons appeared floating above the ship as it headed down the Mississippi toward the Gulf of Mexico.

A word about the author...

Debby Grahl lives on Hilton Head Island, South Carolina, with her husband, David. Besides writing, she enjoys biking, walking on the beach, and a glass of wine at sunset. Her favorite places to visit are New Orleans, New York City, Captiva Island in Florida, the Cotswolds of England, and her home state of Michigan. She is a history buff who also enjoys reading murder mysteries, time travel, and, of course, romance. Visually impaired since childhood by Retinitis Pigmentosa (RP), she uses screen-reading software to research and write her books.

Her first published book, *The Silver Crescent*, won the Paranormal Romance Guild Reviewers' Choice award. Her second book, *Rue Toulouse*, a contemporary romance set in New Orleans, was a finalist in the National Excellence in Romantic Fiction Award and was selected as a May 2016 "local read" by *Hilton Head Monthly*.

Her third book, *Decorated to Death*, is a holiday mystery cozy. She also has stories in three anthologies, *The Haunted West*, *Never Fear / Christmas Terrors*, and *Ebb and Flow* from the local Island Writers' Network.

Debby was featured in the January 2016 *Hilton Head Monthly* article "Intriguing People of the Low Country." She is a member of Romance Writers of America, Florida Romance Writers, and First Coast Romance Writers.